Dear Readers,

Rake the leaves. Put up the storm windows. Get the sweaters out of mothballs. Start planning the Halloween costumes. But save lots of time for reading our four new Bouquet romances.

Pull the afghan up over your knees and settle down for a heart-stopping read with Marcia Evanick's **Somewhere In The Night.** Years ago, clairvoyant Bridget MacKenzie "saw" a harrowing crime in her dreams. Now, the nightmare is back, so she turns to Detective Chad Barnett to find a vicious killer . . . who is about to strike again. But solving the crime is only the beginning for Bridget and Chad. Next comes the fulfillment of an irresistible passion.

In Lynda Sue Cooper's **Unguarded Hearts,** a beautiful professional bodyguard is assigned to protect a threatened pro-basketball coach. Posing first as his "girlfriend," then as his "wife," Nina soon finds that keeping Mitch safe is only part of her job. Once his body is out of danger, it's time to guard his heart.

Everybody loves a cowboy, and Sarah Keller is no exception . . . even when her fantasy cowboy roars onto the ranch in a flashy sportscar. But city slicker Cole Jaegar quickly learns to savor life's simple pleasures in Connie Keenan's appealing Montana love story **And Then Came You.**

Who can resist a story about a wedding? Lynda Simmons's **Perfect Fit** will thrill readers with its charming heroine—wedding dress designer Rachel Banks—and its reluctant hero—international news cameraman Mark Robison. He's in town for his sister's wedding . . . or so he thinks until he meets Rachel . . . and begins to picture a wedding of his own.

Munch a bright red apple, carve a pumpkin, mull some cider, and leave the sugar and spice to us. We'll deliver it between the pages of these autumn Bouquets. Enjoy!

The Editors

SEDUCTION BY DESIGN

"I'm curious," he said. "What kind of wedding does a woman who makes wedding gowns imagine for herself?"

"Small," Rachel said immediately. "A ceremony at sunset, on the beach. Dinner afterward—beef Wellington, I think—and dancing until dawn." She laughed, embarrassed. "I've had a lot of time to think about it."

"I can tell."

She felt it, the sudden change in the air that this man could create with just a glance.

"What kind of dress will you wear?" he asked, his voice low and a little husky, like a whisper in the dark.

"That's the one thing I don't know," she said, her own voice a little shaky. "I've made so many, I guess I've confused myself along the way. All I know for sure is that it will be different from anything I've ever made. And something my husband will remember for years."

She held his gaze for a moment, watched his eyes lower to her mouth and linger before returning to her eyes. And she waited for him to touch her, to make good on the promise in his eyes.

Mark touched his lips to her forehead, her eyelids, not yet allowing himself the pleasure of her mouth as he breathed in the scent of her skin, her hair. She raised her head and he felt her breath on his lips, warm and sweet, as he finally gave himself over to the need that had been building for far too long. . . .

PERFECT FIT

LYNDA SIMMONS

Zebra Books
Kensington Publishing Corp.

http:www.zebrabooks.com

ZEBRA BOOKS are published by

Kensington Publishing Corp.
850 Third Avenue
New York, NY 10022

Zebra and the Z logo Reg. U.S. Pat. & TM Off.

First Printing: October, 1999
10 9 8 7 6 5 4 3 2 1

Printed in the United States of America

For Lindsay with love, always

ONE

He stood in the doorway, tall and broad, a silhouette framed in moonlight. Neither spoke and the moment stretched out, taut and breathless, until at last she slipped the robe from her shoulders and stood as he did, naked and vulnerable, and more alive than she'd imagined possible.

Close the door, she thought, and he did. As though he had heard. As though he had always heard.

The night clung like a second skin, warm and heavy with the tang of salt, yet she shivered as he came toward her; moving slowly but with purpose, and a grace she had not expected.

Suddenly shy and nervous, she stepped back toward the open window and a breeze that moved like a whisper across her breasts. He rounded the foot of the bed and she blushed, the heat spreading through her limbs, making her restless and lazy at the same time.

She still couldn't see his face, so deep were the shadows in the room. But she felt his eyes on her, hot and searching, and she raised her arms to cover herself.

He took her hands in his and returned them to her sides, accepting no such modesty. "Let me look at you," he said, his voice no more than a silvery Southern whisper inside her head.

"Close your eyes," he said, standing close enough now that she could feel the heat of his skin on hers. She did as he asked and he reached a hand around behind her head. She heard the snick of metal as he undid the clip and let her hair fall loose around her shoulders. Gently, tenderly, he traced with his fingertips the strong line of her jaw, the fullness of her lips and the softness of her throat, while every sense heightened, filled with the feel, the sound, the scent of him.

He cupped her breasts in his hands and she swayed against him, as he slowly turned her to liquid. He bent to her then, touching his lips to hers and smiling as her nipples grew tight and hard beneath his palms.

Never had she felt so overwhelmed, and in a moment of fear, her feet stepped back of their own accord, taking her to the window and the square of pale, watery moonlight.

"Stay," he murmured, following her, reaching for her, his touch tender and compelling. She took his hand, could not have done otherwise if she tried, for he was her intended, her husband, her love.

She drew him to her, bringing him into the moonlight, anxious now to see his face, to feel his hands on her, to hear that voice again saying—

"Helloooo, Madeira Beach. Are you ready to rock!"

Rachel sat up with a jerk, clutching the sheet to her breasts as she fumbled to turn on the light. It took a moment for the room to settle and her vision to clear.

Then the voice asked if she wanted to get down tonight, and she knew exactly where she was.

She was at home, in bed. She'd fallen asleep with the radio on, as usual, but had forgotten to set the timer. And at exactly one A.M., the romantic ballads of "The Midnight Hour" had given way to the driving beat of "Party All Night."

The room was air-conditioned cool, the window was closed, and no man stood in the moonlight. She searched the darkened corners as well, finding nothing. But he had seemed so real.

"A dream." She tugged at the camisole that had knotted itself around her neck, shoved her hair out of her face, and touched the switch on the radio.

The room was suddenly, eerily quiet, as if under a spell. "Dream," she repeated, louder this time, to make herself believe it. Then she lifted the corner of her pillow, pulled out a small round pillbox, and sighed deeply as it all came back to her.

The Bain-Miller Wedding: Scarlett O'Hara hoop skirts catching on the doors, the groom's brother dancing her out to the terrace, and Granny Miller cornering her by the dessert table.

Rachel set the box in the palm of her hand and smiled, remembering the way Granny had pulled her to one side and hushed her with a finger to her lips. "I'm only going to tell you this once," she'd whispered, her thick Scots' brogue giving weight to her words. "So listen well."

But it wasn't until they'd huddled behind a pillar near the rose-covered arch that Granny had finally opened her hand, revealing the little tin box. Green it was, with a hand-painted rose on the lid, and she'd checked over her shoulders before pressing it into Rachel's palm.

"In this tin is a piece of the wedding cake. Only a crumb, it's true, but more than enough on a night with a full moon." She closed Rachel's fingers around it and gave her a wink. "Put that under your pillow when you sleep tonight, and sure as you live, you'll dream of your one true love."

Rachel had opened her hand and stared at the box. "This is so cute. I mean, I've seen cameras, flower arrangements, even beer as keepsakes, but never anything like this." She'd smiled at Granny. "Do you need some help giving them out?"

Granny's mouth pinched. "It's no' a keepsake and I'll no' be giving any more away."

Rachel held out the box. "So this is just for me?"

Granny slapped her hand over it and nodded briskly.

Rachel stared into the old woman's earnest green eyes. She'd heard of the old custom, of course. It used to go hand in hand with catching the bouquet and having someone's Neanderthal cousin slip the garter on your leg, but she'd never known anyone to carry out any of them, until now.

Rachel moistened her lips. "Let me get this straight. There's a room full of single women here, but I'm the only one who gets the cake?"

Granny nodded again.

Rachel leaned closer. "Why?"

Granny patted Rachel's arm, her eyes grown soft and dreamy. "Because, dear. You look like a woman who believes."

Rachel sighed and set the tin on her nightstand. A woman who believes. In what? The magic of love? The power of cake? The power of chocolate maybe, but hazelnut torte? Even she knew better than that.

She tossed back the covers and threw her feet over the side of the bed. Then why had she done it? She glanced back at the box. Because Granny Miller had seemed so sincere and the groom's brother so perfect. They'd danced every dance, shared punch and croquembouche, and he'd given her his number when he left.

So she'd put her faith in a piece of wedding cake and what did she get? A dream that was still so vivid and real, she'd have sworn she could still hear that whisper inside her head, still feel those hands on her skin, but no matter how hard she tried, she just couldn't see a face.

Serves you right, she told herself, *for believing in old wives' tales and silly superstitions.* "Never again," she said to the cake, but even as she crossed the room, she found herself looking over her shoulder, checking the corners, unable to shake the lingering warmth of that dream.

Restless and edgy, she stood at the window, staring out at granny's full moon, the deserted beach, and the sea beyond. She'd lived in Florida all her life, in a house not far from the cottage she rented on Madeira Beach now. And in all that time, the ocean had never failed to fascinate her, to calm her.

Hoping to find some of that peace now, she cranked the window open, closed her eyes, and breathed deeply, forcing herself to relax, to concentrate on the roll of the waves and the heavy bass of the Rolling Stones.

Her eyes popped open. The Stones? She glanced back at the silent radio, then opened the window a little wider. "Brown Sugar" poured into her bedroom. But from where? she wondered, listening intently and trying to place the direction. It was far too late for the Washingtons on the right, and Mrs. Dempster on the left was away. Which left the condo a little farther along or the new club where Mr. Fleischer's house used to be. The club had been debating DJs versus live bands since the grand opening three weeks earlier.

DJ must have won, she decided, humming along with the chorus as she turned away from the window.

Too wide awake to sleep, she grabbed a clip from the dresser, piled her hair on top of her head, and headed out into the kitchen. Not bothering with lights, she padded across the tiles to the swinging door on the other side, the music following her through to the showroom at the front of the cottage.

The Bridery was dark and filled with shadows. The Carbone gowns—heavily beaded satin for the bride, moss crepe for six attendants—hung by the door, waiting to be bagged and boxed. Bolts of fabric for the Wilson wedding stood in the corner by the cutting table, and on the dressmaker's form, Julie Hetherington's gown was quickly taking shape.

Rachel wandered past the rack of fabrics, running her fingers over the satins, the silks, the crepe de chines; seeing the shape of a gown, the line of a skirt, and the faces of the women who would wear them.

The Bridery was her life, her joy, and the reason was simple. As Granny Miller had suspected, Rachel was a woman who believed—in soul mates, destiny, the whole idea of marriage and forever. But she'd always hoped it didn't show.

The music outside changed again, to something slower, bluesier, matching her mood. She opened the door and stepped out onto the porch, smiling as Eric Clapton got down on his knees for Layla. Then she froze, her eyes fixing on the house next door. Every light was on, and the driveway was jammed with cars. But no one was supposed to be in that house for a month; she was sure of it.

Heart pounding, Rachel raced back inside, flicked on a light, and flipped open the calendar on her desk. There it was in black and white: Mrs. Dempster's next guests would be the Gagnons from Shawinigan, the French family who came every summer for three weeks—two kids, a Pomeranian with a speech impediment, and never, ever any parties.

Rachel slammed the calendar closed and glanced back at the door. So who was in there now?

She dashed back into the bedroom, grabbed her shorts from the hook and a key from the dresser, trying to think whether there had been any sign of a party when she came home. A light, a car, but there was nothing she could remember at all.

She yanked on her shorts, then held perfectly still, listening, but hearing only the roll of the sea. No music, no laughter, nothing out of the ordinary. She stared at the window. Could she have imagined the party?

Then suddenly the Stones came rolling across the beach again, and Rachel raced for the door, casting a glance at Granny's cake as she passed, oddly relieved that at least one thing was real.

Mark Robison stood on the porch of the sprawling beach house, "Ruby Tuesday" in his head and one of Brodie's famous margaritas in his hands—two essentials for any good party. He glanced back as laughter drifted through an open window. And that was definitely a good party. He sighed and drained the last of the margarita. Too bad he wasn't in the mood anymore.

Setting the glass on a railing, he wandered down the stairs to the beach. The sand was cool beneath his feet, the breeze warm against his skin as he strolled down to the water's edge. He stood, watching the moonlight shimmer on the waves and wondering how long it had been since he'd walked a stretch of sand like this, or dropped a line off the end of a pier? Five years at least; probably longer.

It was odd how the years all blended together, marked only by the moments he'd missed, the stories he'd followed, and the choices he'd had to make. Christmas at his sister's or the war in Burundi? New Year's Eve with his fiancée or a hostage crisis in Belfast?

The decision had always been easy. Send a gift and grab the next flight out, hoping to God he was the first cameraman on the scene. He'd always been so sure there would be another Christmas, another New Year's, until a sniper opened fire on his news team in the Sudan, and nothing had been certain any more.

He shoved his hands into the pockets of his shorts and walked on, away from the noise and laughter of the party. With no destination in mind, but no way to sit still—just as it had been every day since the ambush.

If not for his sister's wedding, he'd still be rattling around his apartment in London, thinking too much and doing too little. Dwelling on the hole in his shoulder, the stories he was missing, and the decisions he'd have to make once this forced leave of absence was over.

He stopped and stared out at the water. But for now, all he had to worry about was what brand of sunscreen was best for four weeks of sun and sand. He planned to play best man at the wedding, grow a decent beard, and make a few vacation memories. He glanced back at the beach house, a wry smile curving his lips. The beard, at least, was going well.

He was heading back when a floodlight flicked on outside the little cottage to the left of the beach house. Mark shook his head. That had to be the prissiest little place he had ever seen. White shutters, ruffly curtains, and enough dried flower wreaths to decorate a small cemetery. The kind of place that could make a man hang antlers over the fireplace just to even things out.

He stopped when the door swung open and a woman stepped out onto the front porch. She dashed down the stairs and sprinted across the sand toward the beach house.

He stood absolutely still, just watching her.

She was tall, with real hips, a narrow waist, and full breasts—the kind of body that had been out of fashion for decades and mourned by men like himself the world over. Her blond hair was tied up on top of her head, but whatever was holding it there wasn't up to the job. Long tendrils had escaped to curl softly around her face and brush against her shoulders as she ran. Mark glanced over at her cottage as she drew closer, thinking there might be something to be said for prissy after all. And making a mental note to always invite the neighbors when he held a party.

She spotted him by the water and drew up short, panting slightly from the run. "Do you know what's going on here?" she called.

All he knew at that moment was that she could single-handedly turn jogging into a spectator sport, but he opted for the much safer, "Where?" instead.

"There." She pointed up at the beach house just as someone plugged Jerry Lee Lewis into the stereo. "Do you know anything about that party?"

As a field cameraman, Mark spent most of his days looking for trouble. But something in the tilt of her chin made him tread lightly this time. He walked toward her. "Why do you ask?"

"Because that house is in my care." She jerked her head around as fifty-three voices hollered, "Goodness, gracious . . ." Then she turned back, her eyes narrowed and fists clenched. "And whoever is in charge up there has a lot of explaining to do."

Mark nodded slowly, realizing an invitation to join him for a margarita on the porch was probably not in order at the moment. He might not know half those people in there, but it was still his party—a fact that was not going to go down well with this particular neighbor.

A glass of wine by the water, however, might just work out well. And he happened to know that the club down the beach was still open. But first, he had to get rid of his company.

"I couldn't agree more," he said and started toward her. There would be plenty of time for her to think badly of him tomorrow, but right now he was looking forward to playing the good guy for a change.

"I'm Mark Robison," he continued. "And I'm out here looking for some answers myself."

Rachel could only stare as he came toward her. He was tall and broad. A silhouette framed in moonlight.

He stopped and dipped his chin. "Are you all right?"

She gave her head a quick shake. "Fine, yes. Just pre-occupied. With the house."

She turned away and pulled in a long, calming breath. There was no question about it. That had definitely been an award-winning dream. Why else would she have thought, for even a moment, that he was the man she'd seen in her room?

An overactive imagination, she told herself.

But then he said, "Then why don't you tell me your name?" in a silvery Southern whisper that was all too real, and Rachel found herself moving closer for a better look.

A smile curved his lips as she drew up in front of him. "Am I that strange-looking?"

"No," she said, and almost laughed with relief. "Not at all."

Broad shoulders, slim hips, all of that was right, but this guy had a beard. Never would she have dreamed a beard. Neatly trimmed sideburns, even a dapper ponytail perhaps. But a beard? Definitely not.

She stuck out a hand. "I'm Rachel Banks," she said, and tilted her head to the side.

But he did have a rather nice smile. And eyes that were deep blue, heavy lidded, and fringed with long dark lashes. The kind of eyes that give a man a sensuous, soulful look and seemed to see—

"Did you want to sit down and talk strategy?" he asked. "There's an all-night club down the way—"

Rachel backed up a step and focused on the beard again, telling herself that there was no magic and there was no man. It had been a dream. Nothing more. And blue eyes hadn't even entered into it.

"Thank you," she said, shifting her attention back to the house. "But I have to take care of this right now."

She turned and headed up to the house, intent on getting some answers. And froze, when he touched her arm.

His fingers were strong yet gentle, just like—

Stop right there, she told herself, and turned around slowly.

"Let me take care of it," he whispered, and she just couldn't shake the feeling that she'd heard that voice before.

Rachel glanced up at the moon as he passed, but there were no answers in that smile. Not that she'd expected any. She'd put a piece of hazelnut torte under her pillow, for heaven's sake. And she hated hazelnut torte.

She watched him walk toward the stairs. There was grace in his stride. Grace combined with a power and strength that was undeniably sexy—

"And has absolutely no connection to anything," she muttered as she trotted after him. It was all just coincidence—and a very persuasive granny.

"Wait," she called, making a mental note to refuse all offers of cake, wedding or otherwise, for the foreseeable future. She motioned to the house when he turned. "This is really my responsibility."

"Just let me test the mood first." He waved her around to the side of the porch as he climbed the stairs. "You never know when these things might turn ugly."

Rachel looked up at the door. "I hadn't thought of that." She turned to leave. "But you're absolutely right. I'll call the police instead."

"No," Mark said quickly, then gave her a reassuring

smile when she looked back. "It may all be perfectly innocent."

She shook her head. "If you get hurt, I'll never forgive myself."

"It was my idea," he reminded her. "And believe me, I want those people out of that house as much as you do. Just stay out of sight until I get a feel for how this is going to go."

She ducked around the corner and he knocked on the door, knowing exactly how it would go even before Brodie appeared.

Brodie MacIntyre had a halo of dark curly hair, a sturdy build, and the kind of face that would look young even when he was old. They'd met in high school and traveled cross-country in a car, making the worst road movie on record, but forging the kind of friendship that didn't need constant attention to keep it strong.

Brodie had come back to Florida after college, trading in his camera for a pair of work boots and his father's construction firm. And his had been the first number Mark had dialed when his plane touched down in Tampa.

Brodie grinned and started to speak, but Mark shushed him with a small shake of his head.

"It's getting late," Mark said sternly. "The neighbors are wondering when you're going to turn that music down."

Rachel's voice drifted around the corner of the porch. "And we want to know who's in charge, and how they got in."

Mark gave Brodie a significant look, and Brodie touched a hand to his chest.

"I'm in charge?" He tried again, with feeling this time. "I'm in charge."

Mark fought a grin. Brodie always had been a ham.

"I rented the beach house from Mrs. Dempster," he

continued. "A thoroughly charming woman. Spending the summer in Northern Ontario, I believe. I have the rental agreement, if you'd like to see—"

"That won't be necessary," Mark cut in, hating it when Brodie started to improvise. "Just do something about the music."

"Right." Brodie hollered along the hall, and the music changed to a soft, romantic ballad. He turned back to Mark and made a show of checking his watch. "I hadn't realized the hour." He raised his voice and aimed it at the party. "We'll be packing it in now."

"The neighbors thank you," Mark said solemnly and headed down the stairs.

Rachel rounded the corner as he came down the stairs. "I want to thank you for stepping in for me the way you did."

He drew up in front of her and she smiled for the first time. Just a small, slightly shy curve of the lips, but it was enough to make him stop and take a step back. There was no art, no strategy in a smile like that. Only heart, and an honesty he didn't deserve.

"I appreciate it," she said, her eyes wide, her lips slightly parted, like every vacation fantasy he'd ever had, only softer, sweeter. And he knew damn well that he should leave her alone.

Problem was, she was looking at him like he really was some kind of hero, like he really had done something noble and wonderful. And it had been so long since anyone had looked at him that way that he couldn't bring himself to admit the truth just yet.

"Just doing what needed to be done," he muttered and took her hand, leading her down to the water, away from the house and the crowd. Knowing he should lead her away from himself.

They stopped by the water and he stood behind her,

not touching but close enough to discover the delicate
floral scent that surrounded her. Like roses on a summer
breeze—old-fashioned, romantic, and frankly feminine.

He backed up a step and motioned along the beach.
"The El Dorado is still open. We could have coffee." He
thought of the dried flower wreaths. "Or herbal tea."

"Sounds lovely," she said, her voice soft and musical
as she turned to face him.

"It's not far," he said.

"Only a few minutes' walk," she murmured, but neither
made a move to leave. She looked into his eyes, then
lifted a hand to his face, her smile turning shy as her
fingertips brushed across his beard.

"Do you like beards?" he asked, his voice suddenly
husky.

"I've just never imagined one," she whispered.

"Who are you, Rachel Banks?" he asked, slipping an
arm around her waist, forgetting about guests and wine,
everything but the woman in front of him.

"I was wondering the same thing about you," she murmured, and he pulled her close.

He heard the catch in her breath, felt the softening of
her spine, and then she came to him; slender arms circling
his neck, soft breasts brushing his chest, and wide brown
eyes telling him everything he didn't want to know.

A twinge of guilt, as unexpected as it was unwelcome,
made him hold back. Who was she seeing when she
looked at him that way? he wondered. And why was he
hesitating now? It wasn't as though he had anything to
live up to, or anything to lose.

Pushing the guilt aside, he bent to her, touching his
lips to hers, once, twice. She smiled at him. "It tickles,"
she said softly. And when her fingers curled in his hair,
urging him closer, demanding more, he heard himself

moan as he closed his eyes and gave, refusing to think, needing only to feel.

"Mark," someone called.

He lifted his head slowly, still lost in wide eyes and a kiss that had burned and soothed at the same time.

"Mark?" the voice called again, and they both turned as a tall man came down the stairs at the beach house. "Great party," the man hollered, and the woman beside him waved. "Call us when you have the next."

Three women started down the stairs behind them. The leggy brunette stopped at the bottom and blew him a kiss. "Nice to meet you, Mark. Call me."

"This is your party?" Rachel asked.

Mark sighed. Her voice had lost that lovely lilt. Meaning coffee or anything else, for that matter, was probably out of the question. He ran a hand over his mouth as he turned to her. "Technically, yes."

"Mark, honey."

He groaned and glanced over his shoulder as Brodie's sister, Anna, climbed into her car.

"Had a great time," she called and pulled the door closed behind her.

"I can explain," Mark said, turning back to see Rachel huffing across the sand to her cottage.

Brodie smacked a hand against his forehead as he came across the beach. "I am so sorry. I got them out too quick, didn't I?"

"Just a little," Mark agreed, still watching as she climbed the stairs.

"Maybe she'll forgive you," Brodie offered, then winced as she slammed the door. "Or maybe not."

Which was probably for the best, Mark figured. Whoever those wide brown eyes had been looking for out there on that beach, it definitely hadn't been him.

He shifted his gaze to the cars pulling out of his drive-

way. The brunette, on the other hand, hadn't been looking
for anyone *but* him all night. She leaned out the window
and sent him a two-handed kiss as she and her friends
bumped onto the road. Now *there* was a vacation memory. If only he could remember her name.

"Lucy," Brodie whispered, and grinned when Mark
turned around. "She's a friend of my sister's. Just passing
through on her way to the Keys. Left her number by the
phone. Big print. You can't miss it."

"Thanks," Mark said and clapped him on the shoulder.
"Come on. I'll buy you a drink."

"I almost forgot," Brodie said as they headed up to
the house, "someone named Chuck Bennet called while
you were out."

Mark grunted and kept walking. Chuck Bennet was a
friend at a rival agency. They'd shared tips and competed
for stories from the Gaza Strip to Beijing. The only reason
he'd call would be to let Mark know that something big
was breaking somewhere, and to rub it in that he was
missing out.

He glanced over at Brodie. "What did he want?"

"Wouldn't say. Just asked when you'd be in. Told me
he'd try again."

Mark had to smile. "I'll call him back. Let him gloat
and get it over with."

But as he climbed the stairs his gaze was drawn to the
cottage next door. Through the windows he could see
Rachel moving back and forth, pacing it looked like. Then
she stopped abruptly and looked out the window. He
smiled and waved.

She yanked the curtains closed and switched out the
light.

He grinned at Brodie and went back down to the walkway. "Maybe I should go over and apologize. It's only
neighborly."

Something hit the wall inside that little cottage, and he started up the stairs again. "Or I could wait until tomorrow."

"You want my advice?" Brodie opened the front door and glanced back over his shoulder. "Call Lucy."

Brodie went into the house, but Mark held back, still watching her window. Maybe Brodie was right. A ruffles-and-lace woman was always trouble. Too many expectations and not enough bad habits.

He sat down on the top step. On the other hand, he really did owe her an apology, an explanation at the very least.

"Great party," a voice Mark didn't recognize said, and he turned as the last of his guests filed through the front door. He rose to hear their good-byes, shake the hands that were offered, and was grateful when they slapped him on the good shoulder. But he couldn't quite give them his full attention.

When Brodie pulled away, Mark was still standing in the moonlight, waiting for the last light to go out in the cottage next door, and wondering what kind of apology she liked best.

TWO

Rachel tucked the hem into the plastic bag, tied the knot, and shoved the pink bridesmaid's gown along the rack. Two down, four to go. She slid the blue dress forward and glanced at the clock. Nine forty-five, and she'd promised delivery by eleven. She pulled another bag from the roll and gave it a sharp shake. Five minutes to bag and box each gown, plus twenty minutes to drive there, thirty if traffic on the causeway was heavy. It was Saturday, after all.

She lowered the bag over the next dress and knotted the top. Okay, she'd allow forty minutes to get there and twenty minutes to box. Close but do-able, if she kept moving.

She snatched up a coffee cup from the floor and took a quick slurp, burning her mouth and wishing again that she'd just finished the job last night. After all, it wasn't as though she'd been sleeping.

She'd tried everything after she came home—meditation, hot milk, a chapter from the tax accounting book she'd bought—but nothing worked. Every time she closed her eyes, Mark was there, that smile drawing her close while those blue eyes dared her to back away.

She cupped the mug in her hands and wandered over to the window. His jeep was gone from the driveway,

and there was no other sign of him anywhere. No towels
on the railing, no sandals on the porch, not a thing to
give him away. He might well have been a dream after
all, if not for that kiss.

Even now, she couldn't believe that she'd kissed him
right there, on the beach. A total stranger, and she'd
kissed him. Not just a peck on the cheek either. Oh,
no. That kiss had been a soul-stealing, bone-melting,
heart-pounding mistake. And so completely unlike her,
it still took her breath away.

She gave her head a shake and took another, smaller
sip of coffee. A cautious sip. Careful even. She slapped
the cup down on the desk. Now that was more like her.

Never rash, never impulsive, she could count the number of men she had kissed on the fingers of one hand.
She blushed and turned from the window. All right, so
now it was two hands. But either way, she hadn't been
herself. Not since Granny Miller's wedding cake.

She snapped around and looked at the clock. And she
still wasn't now. But with a little luck and a second cup
of coffee, she might just get back on track and make this
delivery on time.

Her shoulders slumped when someone knocked on the
door. "What is it?" she asked as she opened the door.

Amanda Goodman stood on the porch, roller blades
on her feet and a huge grin beneath her helmet. She was
the only woman Rachel knew who ever took how-to-
meet-men articles seriously. She'd studied woodworking,
hung around cigar shops, and could talk intelligently
about any vintage car that happened to come up in conversation. And Rachel could only assume that she hadn't
yet given up on sports as the guaranteed road to couple-
dom.

Amanda held out a bright red gift bag. "Ribbons on
Wheels, You Ring We Bring."

Rachel grabbed her arm and hauled her through the door. "Am I glad to see you." She waited until Amanda caught her balance, then pointed to the boxes lined up on the cutting table. "I need lids and bows, fast."

Amanda set her helmet on a chair and unsnapped the pouch at her waist. "Your trademark bows or mine?"

Rachel tossed her a roll of white satin ribbon. "Just tie."

Amanda chucked her elbow pads and wrist guards on the floor with the pouch. "Don't you want to see what I brought first?" She waved the gift bag like a red flag. "I guarantee you'll be impressed."

Rachel shot her a quick smile. "And this would be new?"

Amanda was not only the best supplier of beads and trim that Rachel had ever found, but was also the most tenacious woman she had ever met. Antique ribbons, French lace, tapestry-covered buttons—there was nothing Amanda couldn't find and no lengths to which she wouldn't go, including boxing gowns for a client who was more of a friend.

Rachel reached for a lid. "I'm guessing it's the sash for the Jane Austen wedding gown."

"And the matron of honor as well." Amanda drew two delicate watered-silk ribbons from the bag, one yellow and one blue. "Genuine reproductions, imported from Massachusetts." She held the sash against the wedding gown. "I believe Jane herself would be pleased." Her smile dimmed as she stepped back. "With the ribbons, at least." She blew out a long breath as she skated around the form. "I have to say, this is one ugly dress."

Rachel shot a quick glance at the dress while she wrapped ribbon around the box. As much as she liked Julie Hetherington, Amanda was right. The simple day dress the bride had originally described was still there somewhere, buried under all the trims and additions she had made in the last few months.

From bows and shirring to lace collars and shawls, there wasn't a detail Julie had missed, right down to flower-covered bonnets and sheer gloves. As the wedding drew closer, Rachel didn't even want to imagine what more Julie would come up with.

"It's part of her wedding theme." She turned back to the box and focused on tying the bow. "She's trying to capture an era."

"An era? She's got the whole century in there." Amanda draped the sashes over the form and rolled over to the table. "I hate to say it, but that dress is Jane Austen hell."

Rachel carried the box to the door. "It's her wedding."

"But your reputation. As the old saying goes, 'The customer is seldom right.' " Amanda looked over at the dress and shuddered. "And if you tell anyone I supplied anything at all for it, there will be no safe place for you to hide."

Rachel laughed. "Don't worry, the wedding is small. And once it's over, I promise we will never speak of this again." She measured out three feet of white ribbon and handed it to Amanda. "Bows, please."

Amanda grunted a reply, then snapped the ribbon around a box. "So ask me how my night was."

Rachel could tell by the smile exactly how it had been. "You're in love again?"

Amanda raised a brow. "Could be." With a deft flick of the wrist, she finished the bow and carried the box to the door. "I was skating out to the end of the pier when one of my wheels caught in the boards and I landed smack in the lap of a blond god. What are the odds of that happening?" She waved a hand as if to say "Don't answer that," and continued. "His name is Ethan, he's a stockbroker, and he loves alternative jazz." She sighed and came back for another box. "I really think he could be the one."

Rachel grabbed her purse and checked for car keys. "Just like the computer whiz you met kayaking? Or the dentist on the white-water rafting trip?"

Amanda snapped on her equipment and opened the door. "That was chance. But this . . ." She lowered her voice as she bent to pick up a box. "This is fate."

"Fate," Rachel repeated and stood at the door with a box in her hand. "Do you really believe that? I mean, do you think it's possible for two people to be destined for each other? Like soul mates." She shook her head. "Forget it. Let's go."

Amanda blocked the door. "Who did you meet?"

"No one, and I'm late."

Amanda planted her skates sideways. "You cannot do this. Not after I told you about the stockbroker."

Rachel looked through the fringe of Amanda's bangs into her frank brown eyes and wondered if she should take a chance. "Let me ask you this."

She moistened her lips and looked past Amanda's shoulder. The beach was like a thoroughfare now, with a steady stream of walkers, joggers, and shell-gatherers weaving around blankets and beach chairs.

Rachel lowered her voice and leaned closer. "Have you ever heard of dreaming on a piece of wedding cake?"

Amanda nodded. "It's an old custom, like walking to church because it's lucky and passing on a green wedding gown because it's not, although I've never seen it done."

Rachel tried a smile. "I have."

"Someone gave you cake to dream on?" She laughed and folded her arms. "So, did you do it?" When Rachel didn't answer, Amanda's mouth dropped open and her voice rose. "You did, didn't you?"

Rachel pulled her inside as heads on the beach started to turn. "Keep your voice down."

Amanda looked at her impatiently. "So, what happened? Did you have a dream?"

It was on the tip of Rachel's tongue to say no. To deny that anything out of the ordinary had occurred. But she found herself nodding instead, and watching Amanda's eyes grow even rounder.

"Did you see him? The man you're supposed to marry?"

Rachel took comfort in the fact that her friend had been sucked into the fantasy as easily as she had and nodded again.

Amanda moistened her lips and stepped closer. "Okay, this is important. Where exactly did they get this cake?"

"I have no idea." Rachel picked up the boxes, flipped her purse over her shoulder, and headed through the door. "But it doesn't matter anyway because the dream was a dud." She glanced back as she started down the stairs. "I didn't see his face."

Amanda clomped down the steps behind her. "But you must have some idea of what he looks like."

Rachel crossed the driveway to her car. "Tall, broad shoulders, narrow hips."

Amanda rolled up beside the car and pulled a pencil and pad from the pouch at her waist. "How tall are we talking?"

Rachel's gaze strayed to the beach house. "Over six feet."

Amanda jotted it down. "Body-builder shoulders or working man?"

"Working man," she said softly, because she couldn't picture him behind a desk.

Amanda made a note on the pad, then pointed the pencil at Rachel. "You know, I have always thought in terms of professionals myself, but there is definitely something intriguing about a man who works with his hands." She set pencil to pad again. "Okay, what kind of legs are we looking for?"

"Long. Very long." The sight of Mark's Jeep pulling into the driveway was like a shock of cold water. Rachel ducked her head and fumbled with the keys in the door. "Why are we doing this?"

Amanda stared at her. "So we can find him, of course." She blew out an exasperated breath, then glanced down at her notes. "Now, road crews and construction sites are the natural starting points. And if I remember correctly, there's a new condo going in down on Treasure Island." She tucked the pad into her pouch and zipped it up. "We'll check it out on Monday, but in the meantime—"

"There is no meantime," Rachel interrupted, "and there is no man. It was a dream." From the corner of her eye, she saw Mark take his front stairs two at a time and disappear inside the house. "A humiliating one at that." She stuffed the boxes into the back of the car, kicked her shoes off, and tossed them into the front seat with her purse. "And don't you dare mention this to anyone." She slammed the door and headed around to the front of the car. "There's a fine line between hope and desperation, and I'm not sure that I haven't just crossed it."

Amanda laughed and followed. "Don't be ridiculous. What you did was as natural as picking petals off a daisy or wishing on a star. But when the star answers, you pay attention. And for the record, I do believe in destiny, one true love, and soul mates. But like the saying goes, 'Nothing comes to those who wait.' "

Rachel opened the hood, propped it with the rod, and walked over to the shed at the side of the cottage. "Meaning?"

Amanda skated after her. "Meaning you can't just sit

around, waiting for this guy to come walking up your driveway. You have to go out and find him."

"And how do I do that? Hand out flyers? Wanted—tall, dark stranger—"

"You didn't tell me he was dark. Is he dark?"

Rachel rolled her eyes. "I am not doing this anymore."

Amanda touched her arm lightly. "Rachel, all I'm trying to say is that you have to get out more."

"I'm out all the time. In fact, I met a man at the wedding just last night. His name is Kevin, he designs Web pages, we danced all night, and his phone number is tacked to the board above my desk right now."

Amanda made appropriate approval noises. "Sounds promising."

"Except he's blond." Rachel dropped her head back and slapped a hand over her eyes. "I cannot believe I said that."

Amanda laughed. "Just do yourself a favor and call him. Chances are he's not Mr. Right after all, but what difference does it make? It's a start." Her lips curved in a truly wicked smile. "And I know for a fact that Mr. Totally Wrong can be a lot of fun."

Rachel closed her eyes against the memory of Mark and a kiss that should never have happened. But she couldn't deny the sharp, sweet tingle that stirred deep inside, and Amanda would never understand why she had to.

"Thanks for the tip." Grabbing a bottle of motor oil from a shelf, she closed the shed and headed back to the car. "But right now, the only thing I want to do is get to Tiffany Carbone's house on time."

"Just promise you'll call," Amanda hollered as she rolled down the driveway. "And if you remember anything else about the dream, let me know."

"I'll be sure and do that," Rachel muttered and dared a quick glance at the beach house. Mark was lounging on the top step, legs stretched out in front of him, portable phone pressed to his ear, completely unaware of her.

She took a step closer. Maybe Amanda was right. Maybe it was time to just have fun, with no thought of tomorrow or where it was all leading. He turned suddenly, as though he had felt her eyes on him, and she snapped around, heart pounding, face burning, and fairly certain that it wasn't time to just have fun after all.

She glanced up at the cottage. But it was quite possibly an ideal time to call Kevin. She checked her watch. With Amanda's help, she'd gained some extra time. Enough for one quick phone call. She slapped the bottle of oil down on the roof and dashed across the sand to her front stairs. And who better to call than the man of her dreams?

Mark frowned into the phone as Rachel raced through the front door. He took a quick look up and down the beach, trying to figure out what had sent her running like something was chasing her.

"You still there?"

Mark nodded. "Yeah, sorry, Chuck. But I missed that last bit. Could you repeat it?"

"I said you should be down here."

Mark tried to focus on what Chuck was saying, but his gaze kept returning to the little cottage next door, waiting for her to reappear.

He'd spent most of the night on the porch, watching the moonlight on the waves and her house. Seeing her lights flick on now and then. Resisting the temptation to knock on her door and ask if he could start over again, and not even sure why it mattered.

Last night, he'd known that she wasn't vacation memory material. He smiled as she came back through the door. Seeing her in the sunlight had only proved the point. She wore a white cotton dress with thin straps, no back, and a hem that brushed her ankles. Her feet were bare and her hair was tied up and falling down all at the same time again; making him long to take that clip out once and for all and let her hair spill into his hands and across her shoulders.

She went down to that old clunker of hers, a satisfied smile on her face as she grabbed the bottle of motor oil from the roof.

He pushed a hand through his hair as she bent over the engine and poured in the oil. The woman was sexy as hell yet seemed to have no idea of the image she created or the effect she had on him. He knew instinctively that he should leave her alone, but the longer he watched her wrestle with that damn car, the more the idea of being a real hero appealed to him.

"You listening to me or not?" Chuck asked. The connection was weak and filled with static, but his cocky tone came through loud and clear. "Man, between the drug lords and the terrorists, I'm going to have tape on the news every day for the next year. Too bad you can't get down here. How's that shoulder anyway?"

"Fine," Mark said, trying to remember the reason he'd called Chuck back. Something to do with penance, no doubt, and a weak moment. "Well, it sounds like you've found heaven, so I'll let you go—"

"Wait," Chuck said quickly. "I wanted to ask you a favor."

Mark shook his head. "No, I will not nominate you for *Time's* Man of the Year—"

"This is serious," Chuck cut in. "It's about my daughter."

Chuck had spoken so often about his daughter, Brittany, that Mark almost felt he knew the girl. Eight years old, long dark hair, apparently brilliant, and living in the States with her mother.

Mark turned away from Rachel so he could concentrate. "Nothing's wrong, I hope."

"No, she's fine. I just need you to videotape her school play for me."

Mark slowly got to his feet, all the anger and doubt he'd been pushing aside since leaving London suddenly right on the surface. "Sorry to disappoint you, Chuck, but I don't do tiny talent time, weddings, or conventions. I'm still a newsman, remember?"

"I know that, man," Chuck said quickly. "And I wouldn't ask if it wasn't important. Or if there was anyone else who could help me out." He hesitated; then Mark heard him sigh. "I'm desperate, Mark. I really need your help."

Mark crossed to the edge of the porch as Rachel dumped the empty bottle into the trash.

"She's got a lead in this play, some kind of singing thing." Chuck's voice took on a pleading tone that Mark had never heard. "I can't get there, man. I want to, but there's no way. You understand what I'm saying, don't you?"

Mark nodded. Of course he understood. If he'd been the one in Central America, he couldn't honestly say that he wouldn't have asked someone to make a tape of his sister's wedding and send it to him. Theirs was a competitive field. If you didn't get the film, someone else did. And Mark had always been at the top of the list.

"My ex won't send me anything," Chuck continued. "Not a program, snapshot, nothing." He stopped. "I know it's asking a lot, but we've been friends a long time. And I was hoping that, since you're in Florida anyway, maybe you could slip down to Miami and tape the performance for me. As a favor."

Chuck sounded tired all of a sudden, defeated. Like

he needed a friend. Mark searched for a pen. "Give me the details."

Rachel let the hood down with a thud. There had been no need to check the oil level. The old clunker always needed a bottle. And while it drove her crazy, every extra month she got out of it was a bonus.

She checked her watch as she dashed back to the shed for a rag. So far so good. She was still on time for the Carbones. And when she got back, maybe Kevin would have returned her call.

An elderly couple in matching shorts and hats paused on their way by. "How's the car running?" the old man called.

"Same as usual, Bill," she called as she hurried back to the car. "One of these days I'll break down and get a new one."

His wife, Margaret, drew up beside him. "I keep threatening him with the same thing."

Rachel laughed as Bill gaped in mock horror. She knew the Washingtons had been together on that beach for almost fifty years, and everyone figured they'd be there another fifty if they could. Theirs was a marriage to last a lifetime. Exactly the kind Rachel wished for every bride she met, and the kind she dreamed of for herself.

She didn't need kisses that made her legs weak or a touch that made her skin burn. All she needed was a man who would look at her the way Bill looked at his wife, every day for the rest of her life.

They waved and wandered back to their house. "Let us know if you need anything."

"I will." Rachel sat down behind the steering wheel, pushed the key into the ignition, and turned. The car clunked and banged but refused to fire. Rachel sat back.

The old clunker knew when she was being impatient. She consciously relaxed and tried again. Nothing. She spoke lovingly to it. Nothing. She bashed a fist on the dashboard. Nothing.

"Not now," she muttered and threw open the door.

Mark stood by the front bumper, smiling at her. "Need help?"

That beard still hid most of his face, but if it was possible, his eyes seemed even more blue than they had last night—and just as amused.

She grabbed a screwdriver and a small aerosol tin from beneath her seat, then pushed past him. "Isn't there a party you should be at somewhere?"

He laughed. "Not until noon." He followed her around to the front of the car. "Would it help if I apologize?"

"Probably not." She propped the hood, then turned slowly to look at him. "You're in my light."

"At least let me do that for you," he said as she twirled the wing nut on top of the carburetor. "As a neighborly gesture."

She kept her head bent over the engine. "We won't be neighbors that long."

"Better part of a month."

"Three weeks, four days." She glanced over at him. "Mrs. Dempster was very definite about the dates when I called her."

"Understandable." He pulled the cover off the carburetor and balanced it on the fender. "What else did she tell you?"

"That you're originally from the area, you're here on vacation, and came highly recommended. I suggested she check her sources a little more carefully next time."

"Did you suggest a ban on parties as well?" He reached for the air filter. "Let me get that for you."

"I can manage," she grunted, snatching it off before

he did. "And I didn't mention the party. As a neighborly gesture."

"You're a regular welcome wagon. And if it makes you feel any better, there was no damage to the house." He grinned at her. "You're welcome to come and have a look."

She gave him a tight little smile and pulled the cap off the tin. "I'll take your word for it."

"Why don't you give me that? I'm sure you can do it alone, but the job will go a lot faster with two." He gestured to the can. "Give me the screwdriver and the tin. I'll spray while you turn the key."

She ground her teeth. She didn't want his help, or anything else for that matter. But because it made sense and she was in a hurry, she slapped them into his hand. "Two, one-second bursts. No more."

He gave the tin a shake. "Just let me know when you're ready."

She shoved the air filter into his stomach and dashed around to the driver's side, refusing to be grateful. And when the month was up, she would hold a welcome-back party for the Gagnons from Shawinigan.

He positioned the screwdriver, held the tin in front of the carburetor, and waited, figuring she had a right to hold on to her anger a little longer.

"Hit it," she called.

He sprayed, she turned, and still the engine refused to cooperate. "Once more," she hollered. But there was no coaxing it to life.

"It's dead," Mark called, setting the air filter into place and fitting the cover back on.

"It just needs more time," Rachel insisted, then let her hand drop from the ignition. "Or a ring job," she muttered.

The mechanic had warned her that it was coming. She

climbed out and slammed the door behind her. But why
did it have to be now?

Mark lowered the hood. "Do you need a ride?"

She motioned to the house next door. "The Washingtons will take me."

Mark shaded his eyes against the sun. "Do they drive
an old Galaxy, light blue, mint condition?" She nodded
and he let his arm fall. "Then you're out of luck, because
they're pulling out now."

Rachel spun around to see the Washingtons treasured
Baby Blue backing down the driveway. She waved and
Margaret waved back, obviously assuming Mark was the
answer to all of Rachel's problems.

Mark stood beside her as the Galaxy drove off. "Where
are you heading?"

"Tampa," Rachel said and gestured to the boxes in the
backseat. "Those dresses have to be there in fifteen minutes."

"You're a dressmaker?"

She headed up the driveway. "Nothing gets by you,
does it?"

He was right beside her. "Let me take you."

She stopped when she reached her stairs. "Another
neighborly gesture?"

A half smile curved his lips. "What else?"

Rachel glanced over at the Jeep in his driveway, the
top off, ready to go. She thought about it. Thought about
sitting next to him, the wind in her hair and the sun on
her face. She turned back to him. "Thanks, but I'll take
a cab."

He looked at her curiously. "Which is it you don't like,
the jeep or me?"

"Both," she whispered and headed up to the porch.

In the showroom, she peered out the window as she
punched in the numbers for the cab company. He was

still out there, leaning back against the side of her car, eyes closed, face lifted to the sun, looking lazy and relaxed, and content to wait.

"Stubborn," she murmured but couldn't help smiling as the line was answered.

"You have reached the Diamond Cab Company. Your call is important to us . . ."

"I can tell," Rachel muttered, and turned from the window. She sank into the chair at her desk, wondering exactly how long she'd be in priority sequence while she pushed a few papers around. A bill for fabric, a reminder to pick up more seed pearls for the Wilson gown, and a contest entry form, filled in and waiting, needing only the registration fee to be complete.

"We appreciate your patience—"

She crammed the receiver between her ear and shoulder, picked up the entry form, and let the chair rock back. The New Designer Showcase in Miami was less than a month away. Buyers from all over the States and Europe would be there, searching for the next bright star. Registration closed at the end of next week. If her car needed that ring job after all, she could kiss the contest good-bye for another year.

"Please stay on the line and—Diamond Cabs, how can I help you?"

Rachel set the entry aside. "I'd like a taxi at the Bridery," she said, sneaking a glance out of the window and telling herself that she was glad Mark had left.

"I have nothing for an hour," the dispatcher said, winning her full attention again.

Rachel dared a glance at the clock. "But this is an emergency."

"It's also Seniors' Day at the mall, and I've got a waiting list a mile long. If anyone found out I let you jump ahead, my drivers could get mobbed."

"I won't tell a soul, I promise."

"Lady, we're talking my best customers here. Do you have any idea how long those people can hold a grudge?" Rachel hung up the phone. She paced the showroom. Now what? She could start calling friends and neighbors, see if anyone was around. She stopped at the window. Or she could simply knock on Mark's door and get those dresses delivered.

She headed for the door. Tiffany Carbone's peace of mind was more important than her pride.

She was halfway across her driveway, excuses prepared and gas money in hand, when she spotted Mark leaning against the side of his Jeep, keys in hand, her boxes already stacked in the back.

He smiled when he saw her there. "Seniors' Day," he called. "You'll never get a cab." He opened the passenger door. "It was on Mrs. Dempster's 'Tipsheet for Guests.' "

Rachel stood absolutely still and completely at a loss. What he'd done was either unforgivably arrogant or incredibly sweet. She only wished she could figure out which it was.

He raised a hand and let it fall, the universal gesture of the misunderstood male. "I know I should have asked first, but it seemed faster this way."

In spite of what she might have preferred, *sweet* was starting to win. And because time was running out, she picked up her sandals on the way and sprinted across the sand to the Jeep. "By the way," she said, smiling as she climbed up into the passenger seat, "remember last night when you asked if I liked beards?" She slammed the door. "Well, I don't."

THREE

They pulled up in front of the Carbone house, wind-blown, breathless, and late. The home was a sprawling ranch with a flagstone walk, a sprinkler on the front lawn, and six faces watching from the front window—not a smile among them.

Rachel smoothed a hand over her skirt, then lifted the boxes from the backseat. "You stay here," she said to Mark, balancing the boxes on the fender while she checked the window again. "No point in both of us being in the line of fire."

"Danger is my life," he said in a deep, solemn tone that made her smile. Then, before she could stop him, he wrapped his right arm around the boxes, sucked in a quick hissing breath as he switched them to his left, and started up the walkway to the house.

"What's wrong with your arm?" she called after him.

"Old war wound." He glanced back at her. "I'll tell you about it some day." He gestured with his chin. "You want to get the door?"

Rachel stood by the Jeep, watching the long, easy stride, the confident tilt of his head, and wondering about war wounds and danger, and what it was that he really did for a living.

The romantic in her put the Southern accent and long

legs together to come up with cowboy, or better yet rodeo rider; an injured champion, at that. The kind of man who'll put everything on the line, hold on tight, and not let go till the end.

Fortunately, the realist whispered, "Sequined shirts," and Rachel hurried up the walk, reminding herself that "the end" for his kind came in about eight and a half seconds.

"I'll take it from here," she said as they reached the end of the walkway. But Mrs. Carbone was already there, door swung open, arms folded across her ample chest and mouth set in a grim line. "You're late," she said, then gave Mark a quick once-over. "Who is this?"

He held out a hand. "Mark Robison, ma'am. I'm just helping Rachel out."

"My car wouldn't start—" Rachel began, but the mother of the bride held up a hand. "Tell it to Tiffany." She stepped back and jerked her head in the direction of the living room. "In there."

As Rachel entered, Mr. Carbone glanced over from the leather recliner where he sat watching the television. "You're late," he said, then turned back to the news.

But the six women by the window weren't so forgiving. They flanked the bride and advanced as a pack.

"Tiffany, I'm sorry—"

But all eyes shifted when Mark walked in behind her, holding the boxes aloft.

"For the lovely bride to be," he said, then turned up the heat on that slow, sexy smile and aimed it straight at Tiffany. "And that just has to be you."

Tiffany's face went from pinched to pretty as she dipped her chin. "How did you know?"

"Your eyes give you away," he said softly, then set the boxes down on the coffee table and stepped back.

The bride to be laughed and tugged at the ribbon, her anger dissolving in a sea of white pearls, satin, and lace.

While Tiffany and her friends pored over the gown, Rachel edged over to where Mark stood. She kept her eyes on the bride and her voice low. "You didn't have to do that." He looked at her quizzically and she angled her body toward him. "I didn't need you to run interference for me."

"Is that what I did?" He glanced back as Tiffany held the dress in front of her. "Funny, but I'd have sworn the only thing I did was smile at a woman and hand her a box." He leaned closer, his breath warm in her ear. "Lighten up, Rachel," he whispered, then touched his lips to her neck. "Life is short."

Heat, unexpected and unwelcome, spread from that single point of contact, warming her blood and making her shiver at the same time. Damn him, she thought, and snapped her shoulder up. "If one more person tells me to lighten—" she started, then managed a quick smile when she realized that the maid of honor had taken his place beside her. "Your dress is in the second box."

"I've seen it," she said, and gestured with her chin toward Mark. "New boyfriend?"

Rachel shook her head and rubbed at her neck. "Just a neighbor."

The maid of honor's eyes followed him across the room. "I didn't realize you lived in such an interesting neighborhood." She glanced back at Rachel. "Mind if I cruise?"

Rachel shrugged. "Go for it," she said, and tried to focus on the bride instead. "Well, Tiffany, what do you think?"

"It's wonderful," Tiffany said.

Rachel nodded, but from the corner of her eye, she could see the maid of honor sidling up to Mark. Chin down, eyes up, lips not quite pouting but so darn close it was like she was going to walk right up and—

"Rachel?"

She turned, and Tiffany smiled at her. "Anything special I should know before I try it on?"

Rachel raised a shoulder, let it fall. "Not a thing."

"Go now and try on the gowns before Rachel leaves," Mrs. Carbone said, shooing the bridal party upstairs. She frowned at the maid of honor. "Angela, you, too."

As the bride and her friends rushed up the stairs, Mrs. Carbone pointed to Rachel. "You come into the kitchen. And you"—she motioned Mark to the sofa—"you stay there."

Rachel followed her out and Mr. Carbone turned to Mark. "You like cannolis?"

Mark watched Rachel disappear into the kitchen as he crossed the room. "Sure."

"Then sit down. You won't be sorry."

While Mark sat, Mr. Carbone pointed the remote controller at the television. "News channel. I like to keep up."

Mark nodded, already caught in the images on the screen. The lead item. A bomb in a crowded shopping center. Ambulances. Blood. And a sniper picking off rescue workers. But what held Mark's attention was the voice, the one off-camera, asking questions of a witness.

The woman on the screen was disheveled, trembling, close to hysteria. But the voice behind the camera remained calm, soothing, helping her to relax, to think.

"Did you notice anyone in the area just before the blast?" the voice asked.

Mark sat closer, listened harder. He was almost positive . . .

"And can you describe the man?" the voice asked.

The cameraman was Chuck, and sure enough he'd

caught himself the lead story. Mark smiled as he leaned back. His own agency would be chewing nails right now.

The woman on the screen blinked into the camera and started to describe the man she'd seen running from the building, when suddenly a bullet whistled past, exploding somewhere behind them. The woman screamed and ducked, but the camera never wavered.

Mark's eyes narrowed as he sat forward again, a calm settling over him as every instinct snapped into place. Keep the red light on and the camera steady. Nothing else matters.

He looked up as Mrs. Carbone held a tray in front of him. "Cannoli?"

Mark's hand moved to take a pastry, but his focus was still on the television.

Mrs. Carbone shook her head as Rachel came in with a tray of glasses and a bottle of wine. "Can we turn the TV off? Who needs to see such things in the middle of the day?" She made a noise of disgust as the camera zoomed in on a man and woman huddled under what was left of a wall. "Why do they always have to show the worst?"

"This isn't the worst," Mark said, his own voice soft, distant. "The worst was cut in the editing because it might spoil someone's dinner." He gestured to the screen. "The cameraman is doing it exactly right. See how he's gone wide first, keeping a distance, drawing you in? Now he hits you with a little blood, a few bodies, and some attractive witnesses, if he's smart." He felt himself smile as the shot narrowed to a young woman shielding a group of schoolchildren. "And this guy is always smart. Guaranteed himself a spot on the six o'clock news, and wound up with the lead spot as well."

"You sound like a reporter," Mr. Carbone said.

Mark raised his head and realized that his heart was

pounding and his fists were clenched. He sat back, embarrassed. "Not a reporter, no. I'm a field cameraman." He drew in a long breath as he reached for his plate. "These look wonderful." He looked up at Mrs. Carbone. "Did you make them?"

"Of course." She waved a pastry at the television. "So you work for a TV station?"

Mark shook his head. "For a news agency in London."

"London," Rachel murmured, then gave him a quick, bright smile. "You're a long way from home."

He looked over at her, trying to understand what he saw in her eyes, but she turned away too soon, and Mrs. Carbone was asking more questions.

She gestured to the television. "This agency, they send you out to shoot things like this all the time?"

He shrugged. "They send me where there's news. A world chess match or a riot in Europe. Whatever sells." He turned back to the television. "Of course, nothing beats bullets."

He picked up the cannoli and bit into it, tasting nothing, but making all the right noises. "Very good," he said, and washed it down with a gulp of wine. Then he smiled at Mrs. Carbone and set the plate aside. "So when is the wedding?"

Rachel nibbled at the pastry and wondered which Mark was real—the one charming Mrs. Carbone and turning down cannolis, or the one who had made her skin prickle just a moment ago. The same one who'd looked haunted and dangerous, and undeniably sad.

She heard footsteps and a voice on the stairs, and told herself she didn't need to know. She needed to pay him for the ride and that was it. He was a neighbor, nothing more—and he'd be gone in a matter of weeks. Back to London and a life she couldn't begin to imagine.

"Mom, Dad, come and see," Tiffany called.

Rachel followed the Carbones into the hall and stood back while Tiffany made her entrance.

The bride glided down the stairs, the beaded train dragging six steps behind as she rounded the curve. With huge puff sleeves, layers of lace, and over one hundred hours of beadwork, the gown was truly one of the most spectacular Rachel had ever made.

"Bella," Mrs. Carbone whispered.

Mr. Carbone looped an arm around her waist. *"Molto bella."*

"It is beautiful," Mark said as he drew up beside her.

"Yes," Rachel agreed.

He looked down at her. "But?"

She shrugged. "But nothing. It's lovely."

He leaned close and whispered, "You ask me, she looks like she's drowning in a sea of meringue."

She nodded but didn't look up at him. "And there's not a damn thing I can do about it."

Pushing aside the familiar sting of disappointment, Rachel took a step forward and touched Mrs. Carbone's arm lightly. "We'll be going now."

The Carbones thanked her and Mark, shaking their hands, pulling Rachel into a warm hug, and finally escorting them to the door.

Tiffany rustled behind them. "Rachel, wait."

They turned, and Rachel watched as the bride made her way along the hall, struggling with the train and tugging at the bodice as she came. But her eyes shone and her smile looked like it was quite possibly permanent, and Rachel couldn't help but smile back.

"Since you can't make it to the wedding," Tiffany said, "I want you to have this." She held out a small white box with silver lettering across the top.

Rachel recoiled. "It's not wedding cake, is it?"

Tiffany looked puzzled. "Almonds. For luck."

"Almonds," Rachel said on a wave of sweet relief and opened her hand.

"Not a fan of wedding cake, I take it," Mark said as they walked to the door.

Rachel smiled. "It keeps me awake."

"Thanks for the ride," Rachel said when they reached his driveway. She held out a folded bill. "This is for the gas."

Mark shook his head. "It was my pleasure. After all, what are neighbors for?"

She tucked the bill under the visor and opened the door. "Not a free ride, I'm sure."

He climbed out and stood at the front of the Jeep. "Are you going back to work?"

She slammed the door and swung her purse over her shoulder. "What else?"

"Maybe a little fun." He captured her hand as she passed. "Why not take the afternoon off? Come out with me."

He brushed his thumb across hers and she gave a rueful smile, feeling the draw even as she pulled away. "You're the only one on holiday."

He shrugged and ambled off to the beach house. "Suit yourself. It's just a shame to waste a day like this."

She watched him walk away, suddenly aware of the sun on her face, the breeze at her back, and the scent of the sea all around her. Summer—hot, sticky, and the busiest time of the year. June brides alone accounted for one-third of her year's business. And she had at least ten more hours of beadwork to finish on the Scott-Wilson dress.

She couldn't remember the last time she'd taken an afternoon off. She sighed and looked out at the gulf, torn between seed pearls and sunshine. Then a gull reeled and turned, laughing at her as he passed overhead, and there didn't seem to be a good reason to go inside just yet.

She ran a few steps. "What are you going to do?" she called, and pulled up short when he turned.

He squinted into the sun. "Rent a boat and go catch some fish."

She laughed. "You may have been local once, but you're strictly tourist now."

"You have a better idea?"

She felt the hum along her spine, a tingle on her skin as he came toward her. An afternoon with a neighbor, she told herself. Where's the harm in that?

"It depends," she said, folding her arms while she looked at him thoughtfully. "You ever hear of Bunce's Pass?"

Rachel leapt out of the Jeep and pulled on her sneakers. "We've hit the tide just right. Redfish will be there for the taking."

Mark lifted out his rod and the backpack he'd filled with sandwiches and beer at the deli. "I've never eaten redfish."

"And you won't today either." She swung her tackle box up from the backseat and grabbed her rod. "When I'm the guide, it's strictly catch and release. And the hooks are barbless." She tugged a baseball cap on her head and grinned at him. "If you want to eat seafood, try Charley C's. The grouper is to die for."

Still adjusting to the fact that there would be no fish on the barbecue that night, Mark followed her across the parking area to the mangroves and grass flats of the east beach.

About eight miles south of Madeira Beach, Bunce's Pass was tucked into a quiet corner on the island of Mullet Key. They'd crossed three bridges to get to the spot Rachel swore was the best shore fishing on the Gulf Coast.

Her step was light and quick, her skin and hair golden in the sun. She'd donned shorts and a tank top with an oversize shirt. Her hips swayed naturally as she made her way to the water's edge, making it hard for him to concentrate on anything else. But when she stripped off that shirt, leaving only the clingy tank top between her and his imagination, Mark knew this would be anything but a relaxing afternoon.

Sandpipers darted away as she waded into the water, her eyes scanning the surface, her attention focused solely on the search for fish. Mark set his gear down next to hers and followed, vaguely irritated by the notion that he had ceased to exist.

The maid of honor who had tucked her number into his pocket earlier wouldn't be so easily distracted, he was sure of it. She'd already offered to show him the sights, take him to all the high points. So why hadn't he called her instead?

"See those shadows?" Rachel called and pointed about fifteen feet out. "That's where they are, lying on the bottom, just scratching and eating." She smiled as she walked past him to the beach. "They always did love this spot."

He pulled the card out of his pocket. Why didn't he just go to the Jeep right now, pick up his cell phone, and dial the number? Set up something for tonight? Dinner, a movie, breakfast.

Rachel crouched down and popped open her tackle box. "I'd start with a soft-tailed jig," she called. "If they don't like that, we can move on to something else. There's lots of bait around for the taking." She looked over at him. "Are you fishing or not?"

Her smile was warm and friendly—the smile of a neighbor, nothing more. Yet he'd felt the tug earlier, subtle yet definite. And no matter how hard he tried, he just couldn't think of that kiss as neighborly.

"I'm just giving you a head start," he called.

"You are on my turf, Robison," she said. "You don't stand a chance."

She laughed then, a wonderful, musical sound that made him smile in spite of himself. He crumpled the card in his hand as he trudged back through the water, and felt only a small pang of regret for the breakfast he wouldn't have.

He crouched beside her as she opened her tackle box. "I gather you're a regular here."

"I used to be. I grew up just outside Largo, and my dad taught all six kids to fish on this beach. My mother wasn't much of a fisherman, but she'd sit up there on the grass with the little ones and watch."

"Not much choice with a family that size."

"Too true," Rachel said with a laugh. "But all my brothers and sisters loved to fish. Rivers, piers—if there was water, we'd toss in a line and see what happened. Of course we didn't have the luxury of catch and release back then. What we caught, we ate." She sent him a quick grin and held out a soft-tailed jig. "To this day, I have secret cravings for catfish."

"I'll have to remember that," he said, laughing as he tied the jig to his line. "Does your family still live in Largo?"

She shook her head. "I'm the only one who stayed in Florida. The rest are in New York, California, all over the place."

"What kept you here?"

"It's home," she said, as though the answer was so simple, so elementary. And for her, he supposed it was.

"Which is why they all make it back at Christmas." She bent over the tackle box again. "Needless to say, it's bedlam for three days."

Her smile told him she wouldn't miss a minute of it. "Your parents must enjoy having everyone back."

"They used to." She glanced over at him. "My parents were killed in an ice-fishing accident in Minnesota three years ago."

"Rachel, I'm sorry—"

"Me, too," she said softly, and turned back to the box. "How about you? Where did you learn to fish?"

His gaze drifted out over the flats. "On an eighteen-foot high-performance boat with a one-hundred-fifty-horsepower Mercury engine, high-power sonar fish finders, and a guide who would bite your head off if you made a mistake."

She pursed her lips. "Not looking for catfish, I assume."

Mark leaned close and lowered his voice. "My father would have been appalled."

She raised her chin and sniffed. "The man doesn't know what he's missing."

Mark nodded. "He never did."

She looked at him curiously for a moment, then closed up the tackle box and flipped up the locks. "Did you have any brothers or sisters out there on the boat with you?"

"One sister." He looked over at her. "To this day, the sight of a kingfish can make her break out in hives."

Rachel laughed and got to her feet. "So, what kind of fish do you catch these days? I imagine it's all different in England."

"I wouldn't know," he said as he rose. "I'm never there long enough to find out."

Rachel watched him wade out into the shallow flats.

He'd changed before her eyes, his smile dimming and his expression darkening the same way they had when he'd seen the newscast that afternoon, when he'd side-stepped the subject just as nimbly.

Telling herself that she didn't need to know more, that it was none of her business, Rachel gathered up her rod and headed down to the water. Leaving him to prowl the shallows alone, she moved on, casting into a spot where the surface was coppery red, knowing that was where the fish were.

Her form was rusty and her timing off, but the jig landed close to where she'd aimed, and she had a taker—a huge redfish that had no intention of going quietly.

With a whoop of delight, she played the fish out—skills she'd thought long forgotten coming back in a rush. She reeled it in at last, grabbed hold to pull out the hook, and for an instant felt the struggle, the panic, the very wildness in its soul just before she let it go.

She straightened and saw Mark standing only a few feet back, preparing to cast into an unlikely looking spot. "I'd forgotten how much fun this can be," she called.

He drew his left arm back, and she knew there was pain by the set of his jaw, the tension in his shoulders. But her curiosity about the old war wound gave way to something more elemental as she watched the muscles across his back tense and release, moving like liquid beneath his shirt.

He snapped the line, sending it out over the water. Then he turned and smiled, and caught her completely off guard. "Am I forgiven then, for last night?"

She turned away and focused on her form. "I suppose so."

Silence fell between them, awkward at first, but growing more comfortable as they lost themselves in the game of catch and release. But as the tide changed and slowly crept back in, they made their way up to the clearing by the parking lot, sand squishing in their sneakers, water glistening on their skin, and the tension left far behind with the fish.

Rachel dropped her gear and shoes into the Jeep, pulled on her shirt, and strolled over to the tree, where Mark was already opening the backpack.

"Ham on rye was all the deli had left," he said, handing her a beer and a sandwich.

"Right now, anything is good." She set the bottle and the sandwich on the grass, then stretched her arms up, knowing exactly where she was going to feel the fishing tomorrow. But as she unscrewed the cap and raised the frosty bottle to her lips, she couldn't bring herself to regret a moment.

She let the cold beer quench a thirst she hadn't realized was so strong, then set the bottle aside and tore open the wrapper on the sandwich. She took a bite, savored a moment, then leaned back against the tree with a sigh. "Bees, beer, and a sandwich. Life doesn't get much better."

Mark took a long pull on his beer, then sank down on the grass by her feet. "You know, you surprise me. I would never have pegged you as a woman who'd get out in the water and wrestle with fish."

"And I would never have pegged you as a man with insight." He raised a brow and she grinned. "When you walked into the Carbones' living room, how *did* you know that Tiffany was the bride?"

He took a bite of his sandwich and washed it down with the beer. "There was a picture of her on the hutch."

Rachel laughed and tossed her sandwich wrapper into the backpack. "You're very observant."

"Sometimes," he said, and she could feel those blue eyes on her as she sat back.

"Tell me something," he said at last. "If you didn't like the dress, why didn't you suggest something else?"

She sighed, the peace of the moment slipping slowly through her fingers. "Because it's not up to me. Tiffany came in with a picture. She knew exactly what she wanted." Rachel shrugged and ran a hand up and down the length of the bottle. "I pointed out that she's only five feet tall and the model in the picture is close to six, but she couldn't see my point. And since the customer is always right, I shut my mouth and I made the dress."

He nodded with entirely too much understanding. "Whatever sells."

She caught and held his gaze. "Like bullets."

"Exactly," he said, then raised the bottle in salute. "To sales," he said, and drained what was left of the beer.

Rachel set her own aside, her taste for it suddenly gone. "When you said earlier that danger is your life, I thought you were kidding. Then, when I heard you talk about the cameraman, I realized you were serious."

"I usually am," he said and shoved the empty into the backpack. Then he leaned back on his elbows and closed his eyes, putting an end to the conversation.

But Rachel wasn't ready to let it go so easily this time. She stretched out her legs and crossed her feet at the ankles, equally relaxed, equally comfortable. Equally determined. "Do you like your work?"

"As a rule," he said, an edge in his voice that hadn't been there before. "But that's how most people feel about their jobs, isn't it?" He opened his eyes and looked directly at her. "Even you."

She met his gaze squarely. "Tell me what you like."

His mouth curved slowly in a smile that was more wry than amused. "It's the joy that comes from knowing that I have brought a full-color record of someone else's misery into living rooms all across the country."

She kept her expression neutral, resisting the reaction he was obviously looking for. "Are you being serious now?"

"Absolutely." He paused, his eyes still holding hers. "Because without pictures, how will anyone know what really happened?" He ran a fingertip along the side of her left foot. "So where is this Charley C's you like so much?"

"Reddington," she said, pulling her foot away, annoyed by a glib answer that told her nothing while allowing him to neatly step into another conversation. "You'll need a reservation," she continued, and tried another route. "So you feel you're bringing truth to the news, is that it?"

Mark would have laughed if he hadn't once believed it. He'd swallowed the whole journalistic line about being a public service, of keeping governments honest and people informed. Not only had he believed, he'd gone into the worst hellholes imaginable to prove it. Somalia, Bosnia.

Sudan.

The smell of those places was still with him, as well as the memory of what he'd done, what he'd become while he was there. He didn't know what he believed anymore, but when his leave of absence was over he'd go back, because it was what he knew, what he was. And the idea of filming grade-school plays for the rest of his life scared the hell out of him.

He lifted both her feet into his lap. "Sounds very noble when you say it."

"Only because that's how you made it seem." She leaned forward. "But is it?"

"Sure," he said, not wanting to think any more. "I have a phone in the Jeep," he said, and pressed his thumbs gently into the arch of her foot, making slow circles up the length of her instep. "We could call Charley's now and be there in under an hour. What else do they serve besides grouper?"

"Everything, but I can't have dinner with you tonight."

"Can't? Or won't?"

"Both," she said, and tried to pull her foot away, too aware of the warmth his touch could bring. "So, when did it become just a job?"

He tightened his grip fractionally, holding her there. The air was instantly charged, alive with possibilities, or warnings, she couldn't tell which. She moistened her lips and asked again. "When?"

A shadow passed across his face as he put her feet back on the ground. "When one of the news teams was ambushed."

She shook her head, not understanding. "Ambushed?"

"Not everyone likes to see their face on the news. They sent one of their best, though; I'll give them that. Crack shot. Knew exactly where they'd be and when." He squared his shoulders and got to his feet. "It was over quickly."

She drew back, shaken. "You say that as though it happens all the time."

His voice was flat, his expression neutral. "It does. An occupational hazard, so to speak." He bent to pick up the backpack. "I'll take you home now. Dinner probably wasn't a good idea anyway."

Rachel watched him lift the pack, saw him wince and switch it to his left hand. And the full horror slowly sank in. She rose and laid a hand on his arm. "Mark, what happened to your shoulder?"

"Me?" He glanced down at her hand, then turned and headed for the Jeep. "I was the one that got away."

FOUR

"Rachel? It's Kevin Grant."

The voice was slightly nasal, the tone flat. She set the bag of groceries on the desk and turned up the volume on the answering machine.

"Looks like we're playing telephone tag," he continued. "I always hate that."

"Me, too," she said, trying to remember whether he'd sounded that way at the wedding.

"I've got allergies," he said, and she stared at the phone. It was as though he'd known what she was thinking.

"I'm in Cleveland," he went on. "Maybe we can have dinner when I get back. Call me at the hotel."

"Slow down," she muttered, scrambling for a pen while he rhymed off a number.

" 'Bye."

"A man of few words," she said, and tacked the message to the board above the desk. Right beside the list of construction sites that Amanda had dropped off that morning.

Rachel had to smile. Every site within a ten-mile radius was there, sorted by distance, with ratings included for her convenience. A condominium on Gulf Boulevard had been ranked as a four-star must-see, while an office tower on Fifth had only rated one-star and a beer belly warning.

Across the bottom, Amanda had scrawled a note. "The Dream Lives! Your car or mine?"

"Neither," Rachel said aloud, and punched the number Kevin had given her into the phone.

Kevin was a great dancer, considerate in a buffet line, and, more importantly, he was a local. In short, he was perfect. But she couldn't explain her sense of relief when he wasn't in his room.

"Me again," she said when prompted to leave a message. "Sorry I missed your call. I'd love to do dinner. 'Bye."

"The dream lives," she murmured, pinning the number to her board again. But her gaze was drawn to the window by her cutting table—the one with the best view of the beach house next door. From there, she could see the patio in the back, the garden that needed watering at the side, and of course Mark, holding court on the front porch.

She wandered closer. In the last three days, she'd seen him on the beach early every morning, sometimes walking, sometimes running, but more often than not, just sitting alone at the water's edge, as though he was waiting for something or someone.

But when he was on the porch, there was always a pitcher of something frosty, a tray of glasses, and a steady stream of people coming and going. Shell gatherers stopping to chat, invited guests bearing bottles of wine, and more bikinis than Rachel could ever remember seeing. It seemed that sooner or later every stray on the beach wound up at Mark's.

Mrs. Dempster's, she corrected herself, trying to picture the family from Shawinigan on that porch but seeing only the redhead in a purple bikini top and sarong perched on the arm of Mark's chair. She was laughing, talking, and every once in a while, she'd reach out and touch his arm, letting her hand linger just a little too long.

"Could she get any more obvious?" Rachel muttered, but in her heart she knew the redhead was only doing what Amanda and every other woman in the world seemed capable of—enjoying a man with no thought of his being The One. Mark was attractive and available, the ultimate summer fantasy right next door, yet she couldn't make herself go over and take what she wanted. She was a coward, pure and simple.

She watched him rise, refill the glasses, then carry the empty pitcher inside. The redhead waited a heartbeat, then slipped through the door behind him. Rachel felt her face burn, as though she'd witnessed some intimate act, and turned quickly from the window.

Could she do that? Just stroll over there right now, smile casually, and apologize for asking questions that were none of her business? Say she'd love to take him up on that offer of dinner, or anything else he might have in mind, knowing it was only short term, a good time? Would he even be interested, now that the redhead had staked her claim?

Rachel made herself turn back to the scene framed in her window, made herself watch the drama play out. And she couldn't help but smile when the redhead returned, a full pitcher in her hands and a scowl on her face.

Who knew? Maybe she and Mark could have coffee after all. Get to know each other, go back to his place, sit on the porch in the moonlight, then just slip inside and let the summer night unfold.

She shook her head in disgust. Who was she trying to kid? She grabbed the grocery bag and pushed through the swinging door into the kitchen, hoping Kevin called soon.

* * *

Brodie poked his head into the living room. "You coming outside?"

Mark looked up from the television. "I just wanted to catch the end of this report."

Brodie walked in and sat down on the arm of the sofa. "More of Chuck's stuff?"

"Not this time." He pressed a button on the remote and the screen went black. "Just the usual."

Brodie nodded. "Any luck with his ex-wife?"

Mark shook his head. "She won't even take my calls. If she doesn't talk to me soon, I don't know what I'm going to tell Chuck."

Brodie got to his feet. "You tell him to get his butt up here so he can see his kid's play."

Mark picked up a notebook and a pen as he rose. "If it was that easy, he'd do it."

"No, he wouldn't." Brodie followed him to the kitchen and leaned a shoulder against the doorframe. "You and Chuck, you're like peas in a pod. You can't stand to be out of the loop, away from the action. The only reason you're here is that hole in your shoulder."

"I'm here for the wedding—"

Brodie shook his head. "Save it for someone who'll believe it. You know you're lucky to even be alive, yet you'd be gone in a flash if the agency called. I've always respected your dedication, but you lose all sense of proportion where your job is concerned. Like you can't figure out what really matters in this life."

He made a sweeping gesture with his hand. "That's why Chuck is off God knows where, missing one of the most important days in his little girl's life. And he can't even see that he's wrong." He wandered over and opened the fridge. "You can use more beer in the cooler out there."

They'd had one version or another of this conversation ever since Mark arrived, going round and round the whys and wherefores of Mark's future, and never arriving on common ground. But this time Mark let it go, discovering that he wasn't in the mood to defend either himself or Chuck, and not sure why.

"Help yourself," he said, then tossed the pen and paper onto the table and pulled out a chair. "I'm going to make a few more phone calls. See if I can find anyone in Chuck's family to help me out. Maybe talk to his ex."

"Don't hold your breath." Brodie hooked three beers in each hand and closed the door with his hip. He turned and spotted Lucy's phone number still scrawled on the wall. He leaned closer and rubbed at it with his thumb. "I didn't realize this would be so hard to get off. I've got some of the paint left over from when I did the kitchen. If this doesn't come clean, let me know."

He turned back to Mark. "She's still in town, by the way."

Mark glanced up. "Who?"

Brodie jerked his thumb at the wall. "Lucy. I know she'd love to hear from you. I'd bet she'd even bring the spray cleaner. You never know what can happen when you work up a good sweat."

Mark scribbled a note on the page. "I'll take care of it myself."

Brodie plunked the bottles down on the table and straddled a chair next to him. Mark looked up and Brodie nodded. "You apologized, didn't you?"

"I don't know what you're talking about."

"The blonde next door? Fabulous legs, body to die for—"

"That's enough."

Brodie slapped the back of the chair. "I knew it. So how much of a disaster was it?"

Mark considered. "I'd say full scale." He put the pen down and sat back. "She hates Jeeps, beards, and me. But she does have a hell of a casting arm."

"You took her fishing?" Brodie shook his head. "It's a good thing you're back in the States. You are sadly out of touch with women."

Mark only laughed. "There are a few in London who would argue that point. Besides, she took me."

"A woman with her own tackle." Brodie's expression turned thoughtful. "Interesting."

Mark shook his head. "I'd say she's more confusing than anything. Grew up not twenty miles from here and makes wedding gowns for a living. I can't imagine a life that simple."

"It works for some of us."

Mark knew he'd hit a nerve. "That's different. You went away and came back. She never left." He looked over at him. "You still glad you did it?"

"I wouldn't be here if I wasn't. I like having a business, small as it is. And I like coming home at a decent hour, having free time, a regular life." He got to his feet and picked up the bottles. "It's pretty pedestrian compared to what you're used to, but there's a lot to be said for a simple life. Including the women who are looking for exactly that."

Mark thought of Rachel, with her picket fence and her ruffled curtains. And a kiss that was anything but simple.

He pushed it aside and focused on his notes. "I'll remember that when I'm ready to retire. Until then—"

"Yeah, I know," Brodie cut in. "A good time, not a long time." He crossed to the phone and tapped a finger on the wall. "Then you really should give Lucy a call, and forget about fishing."

Mark stared at the number by the phone while the front door closed. Lucy was exactly what he needed right now; a woman who was passing through, same as himself. Not someone with roots so deep she couldn't ever get free. Lucy wouldn't ask awkward questions, or make him wonder who she was seeing when she looked at him.

They'd be a distraction for each other, nothing more. And somehow he couldn't see Rachel ever being content with an arrangement like that.

He'd already proven he was no good at a long-term relationship, but since then, he'd become a master at casual encounters. No rings, no promises, no keys exchanged. And when it was over, no one was ever surprised.

He rose and crossed to the phone. There was no question about it: Lucy was the one to call. He moistened a fingertip, rubbed at the numbers, and walked over to the sink, wondering how long it would take to get them off the wall.

With ten minutes to spare, Rachel fastened the last buttons on her blouse with one hand and plucked a sprig of forget-me-nots from a pot with the other. She tucked the flowers in beside the daisies and roses already in the vase, then stood back, going over the setting with a critical eye. Taking tea at the last fitting was not only a tradition at the Bridery, but Rachel's favorite moment with the bride, and she liked everything to be perfect. Which was why the pastries were homemade, the linens freshly pressed, and the table set with hand-painted china cups—and in case anybody took it all too seriously, a cabbage-shaped teapot that sang "Ave Maria" while she poured.

It was corny, she knew, but it never failed to take the edge off the formality and make a nervous bride smile,

which was always the goal: to create a little oasis of calm
for the bride and her party, if only for an hour.

Rachel laid a hand on the covered basket. The scones
were warm, the butter soft, and the cream whipped and
sweet. A three-tiered tray held dainty finger sandwiches,
fresh strawberries, and lemon squares, but no cake. The
kettle had already boiled and Earl Gray was in the pot.
Everything was ready, including the dresses. Which was
really too bad.

Rachel sighed as her gaze fell on the two gowns hanging on the rack. Jane Austen hell was putting it lightly,
but if the bride loved them, that was all that mattered.
And Rachel could only be glad that the wedding was
going to be small. The fewer people who knew the
Bridery was involved, the better.

A bell tinkled as the front door opened. "Air conditioning that works," Julie groaned. "There is a Goddess."

"And she loves a pregnant woman," Rachel called.

Hoping Julie hadn't arrived with cameos or reticules
or anything else to add to the horror, she wheeled the
dresses around behind the screen and hurried out to greet
the bride. "Did you bring the shoes?"

Julie stood in the open doorway, her eyes wide and
haunted and fixed on the tea table in the corner. She tried
to smile as she held up a bag. "Right here, as promised.
All ready for the big day." But the smile wouldn't stick.
One hand absently moved to her very round belly as she
shook her head. "Oh, Rachel," she whispered, "I don't
think I can do this."

Julie Hetherington was a struggling actress by choice,
eight months pregnant by accident, and the most reluctant
bride Rachel had ever met. She'd changed the date three
times already and confessed at the last fitting that she
still hadn't opened any wedding gifts, just in case. In fact,
the only things Julie seemed sure about were that she

loved Harry, the baby, and those horrible gowns. So Rachel used all three to keep her moving through the door and on course to the church.

"Of course you can," she said, taking Julie's hand to lead her into the showroom. "Harry's a great guy, the baby is rooting for both of you, and those dresses turned out just the way you imagined."

Julie looked at her for the first time. "They're finished?"

Rachel feigned horror. "You doubted me?"

"Let's just say that she'll be picking up the tab tonight at Verdi's," a male voice said.

Rachel smiled as she turned. "Thanks, Harry, it's nice to know someone believes—" but the rest of her greeting died on her lips when she saw the man standing at her door.

Harry Desrosiers was sweet, slope-shouldered, and balding. A psychiatrist who just couldn't figure this particular woman out, and wanted to spend the rest of his life trying. But the man at the door was tall with high, pronounced cheekbones, a set to his jaw that was anything but obliging, and an aura of sexuality that said his bedside manner would be anything but soothing.

Yet there was something familiar about his smile. The way it came slowly, tilting his mouth on one side, as though he found the whole world amusing and just a little unbelievable. And those blue eyes—

Rachel groaned. What was he doing here? And why did he have to shave?

Julie lifted her hair from the back of her neck and fanned her face with a hand. "This is my brother, Mark. Harry had an emergency at the hospital, so I asked him to come along. You don't mind, do you?"

Rachel moistened her lips as he stepped into the room. "The more the merrier."

Julie blew her bangs out of her face. "I told him you'd say that. But it's only the three of us anyway because my mother missed her flight and I have no idea where the matron-of-honor is." She pulled the neck of her dress away from her chest. "Can we close the door? It's already heating up in here."

Rachel nodded as Mark closed the door and came toward her, invading more than her shop. She told herself to move, to see to the bride. But he drew up in front of her and she had the strongest urge to cup his face in her hands, to feel his skin beneath her palms, brush her fingertips across those tender lips—

He rubbed a hand over his chin. "What do you think?"

"An improvement," she said and turned away, telling herself that he'd shaved for the wedding. Because it made sense, and because anything else was just too hard to think about.

"I wasn't surprised when Mark told me you'd already met." Julie waved a hand. "Knowing Mark, he'll be friends with everybody on the beach before the month is out." She lifted her nose and sniffed the air. "You really did bake."

"Scones and lemon squares," Rachel said. "Plus there's chocolate and strawberries for dipping. Help yourself." She turned to Mark as Julie edged past her. "I'm the one who owes an apology this time. I had no right to pry into your life."

He shook his head. "It's already forgotten. And I still haven't been to Charley C's."

His smile was easy, genuine. He was the Mark she had met that first night on the beach, the one who loved a good time, and Rachel found no reason to doubt that he really had put it behind him. But it didn't mean that anything else could change. A man who dodged bullets for a living was not someone she'd ever imagined for herself. She'd always pictured herself with a man whose farthest destinations could be reached by commuter train or a domestic flight. Like Cleveland.

Besides, Mark would be gone in a matter of weeks, and a summer fantasy wasn't anything she'd ever wanted either.

"Charley C's has a great Tuesday night special," she said, then pulled a coupon from the corkboard and handed it to him. "You'll get two for one with this. Take a friend."

He studied her for a moment, as though he knew there was more, but then his gaze moved past her and his smile was gone.

"Julie, what's wrong?"

Rachel turned to see Julie by the table, holding on to the screen.

She gave them a crooked little smile. "Baby's kicking. I'm fine, really." But Rachel saw the effort to breathe, the slight sway when she tried to straighten. And the unmistakable concern in Mark's eyes as he crossed the room.

"Sit down," he said, not ungently, but it was enough to make Julie raise a brow. He laid a hand on her arm, his tone softening. "You have to take it easy."

She rolled her eyes. "Honestly, you'd think I was going to break." But when he pulled out a chair, she sank into it, and the sigh Rachel heard could only be described as grateful.

And Rachel honestly tried not to be touched when he plucked a strawberry from the plate, dipped it in chocolate, and handed it to her. "For the baby."

Julie took the berry, her scowl slowly dissolving into a smile. "And when she grows up, I'll tell her to blame her sweet tooth on Uncle Mark." She nodded at the seat beside her. "Pull up a chair," she said, then turned to Rachel. "You're joining us, aren't you?"

"As soon as I get the tea." She watched Mark eye

the wrought-iron chair next to Julie. It was narrow and dainty, and exactly like all the others at the equally dainty table.

He glanced around, obviously looking for something like the chair he'd offered Julie, then finally raised a brow at Rachel.

She smiled as she breezed by. "Make yourself comfortable," she said, but couldn't resist pausing at the swinging door. And she didn't even try to conceal her laughter as he folded up his legs and tried to settle into the little chair.

"Welcome to high tea at the Bridery, Mr. Robison," she crooned, then turned the air conditioning up a notch, plugged a Mozart concerto into the CD, and went in search of ice. With luck, by the end of the fitting, Julie would finally be convinced that she was doing the right thing, and Mark would be so tired of chewing his knees, he'd never knock on her door again.

Mark waited until she disappeared through the door, then wiped his damp palms on his jeans and straightened his shoulders. This was ridiculous. He'd dodged land mines, hand grenades, and only one bullet got lucky so far. How difficult could high tea at the Bridery be?

Julie licked chocolate from her fingertips and reached for a scone. "I hear these are heaven," she said, and set one on a plate for him. She passed a doily-covered tray with flowered jam pots and dinky little silver spoons. "Try one."

He followed Julie's lead, slitting the scone, spreading it first with jam, and finally heaping on cream. Then he took a bite and sat back, stretching out his legs under that poky little table and deciding that high tea might just be a civilized practice after all.

He smiled when Rachel returned with ice, lemon, and the ugliest teapot he had ever seen. And he didn't move

an inch when her leg brushed against his as she sat down;
just toasted her with his scone and watched the blush
slowly warm her face as she swung her legs around to
the other side of the chair, jostling the table and sending
berries tumbling onto the cloth.

She scrambled to keep them from rolling off the edge,
set them back on the plate, then cleared her throat as she
reached for the ice tongs. "Would you like to see the
dresses now, or wait until the maid of honor arrives?"
She filled the glass with ice and smiled. "Lemon?"

"And sugar." Julie glanced at her watch. "I'll wait a
while," she said, then looked back at the door. "But I
can't imagine what's keeping her." She started to get to
her feet. "I should call—"

"Let me," Mark offered, and rose without knocking
over a thing. He flipped his napkin with a flourish and
leaned close to Rachel as he laid it on the table. "Save
my spot," he whispered, enjoying the way her chin lifted
even as she fumbled with the glasses.

"The phone's on the desk," she said, adopting that
slightly haughty tone she used every time her cheeks
turned pink. But her smile for Julie was pure warmth.
"Laurie's probably just stuck on the bridge." She reached
for the cabbage teapot. "So just sit back and relax, and
tell me you've finally decided where you're going on your
honeymoon."

"It's still up in the air," Julie said as Rachel tipped the
pot over her glass. "Montreal's beautiful this time of year
but—" She froze as the teapot suddenly broke into
song—a chipmunk voice singing the chorus of "Ave Maria," tinny, far too fast, and over and over again. She
stared a moment, then suddenly smiled. "I wish Harry
was here. He would love that."

Rachel peered at her over the handle, a smile slowly

curving her lips. "Want to borrow it for the rehearsal dinner?"

Julie's eyes widened, and then she laughed, really laughed, for the first time since Mark had arrived. "His mother will be horrified." She grinned at Mark. "Come to think of it, so will ours." She snagged another lemon square and sat back, the tension around her mouth suddenly gone. "I cannot wait for the rehearsal party."

Mark smiled. Her face was animated, her eyes bright. She was Julie again. And all because of Rachel Banks and an ugly singing teapot.

Mark headed for the desk, feeling the strain of the past few days drain away as he dialed the matron of honor's phone number. If things kept going as smoothly, this wedding might just happen after all.

"Did I tell you about the lace you ordered?" Rachel's voice drifted across the room, low and husky, a voice made for secrets and whispers in the dark. A voice that had been floating on the edges of his mind for days, but always out of reach.

He turned to watch her while the line rang and rang. Her cheeks were flushed, her eyes carefully averted, but every once in a while she would glance over, as though she couldn't help herself. And he'd smile, because he definitely couldn't help himself.

"It was the strangest thing," she said to Julie, and pointedly turned her back on Mark.

He laughed, shifted the receiver to his other hand, and took a long look around the showroom. Fluffy, yes, but not as bad as he'd expected. Tall mirrors near the wooden fitting screen reflected the windows and the sea beyond, making the room seem larger, brighter.

While she hadn't turned on the overhead fluorescents, rows of spotlights on the functional side of the showroom provided plenty of light over the cutting table and sewing machines. The walls had been washed with muted shades of green and pink that blended with the airy chintz curtains and seat covers in the showroom.

The whole effect was soft and feminine, yet practical—a reflection of the woman who had filled it. He closed his eyes and inhaled deeply, letting the scents of home baking and fresh flowers fill his head. The very air smelled like her.

On the twelfth ring, Mark glanced out the window, then checked his watch. The agency would be calling the beach house any minute, as they did every day at this time; keeping him up to date on the latest stories and the gossip, asking how his recovery was coming along. A matter of minutes and he'd be on top of it all—the world's newest hot spot and late-breaking developments that even the networks weren't following yet; things that would have kept him on the edge of his seat if he was back in London. And still did, if he was honest.

Then there would be Chuck, wondering if he'd spoken to his ex-wife, if he'd set up the taping, and if he'd seen his little girl. Mark sighed and hung up the phone. Until he had some better news, he was in no hurry to talk to Chuck.

"No answer?" Julie called.

Mark shook his head, and she tossed her napkin on the table.

"Then bring on the dresses. I can't wait any longer."

Mark watched the two women cross to the rack by the fitting room, leaving the scones behind.

He shot one last glance at the empty beach house, then strolled back to the table. He could find out about the world tomorrow, but who knew when he'd ever taste one of Rachel's scones again?

"Oh, my gawd." Julie gasped.

Mark's hand froze above the plate when Rachel rolled Julie's wedding gown into the showroom.

"I don't believe it," Julie went on.

"Amen to that," Mark muttered.

"I shall wear a bonnet," Julie quoted, her English accent plummy and rich. "And bring one of my little baskets hanging on my arm." She grinned at Rachel. "Miss Austen would be pleased," she said, then grabbed Rachel's hand and dragged her around the screen. "You have to help me get it on."

Mark shook his head as the two disappeared around the screen. He knew Julie's tastes sometimes ran to extremes and could only be glad that she hadn't picked a Thousand-and-One Arabian Nights as the wedding theme. But how did Rachel feel about the gowns? He watched her face as she came back for the bonnet. Nothing but a grin as broad as Julie's. He turned his attention to the scone. The customer was always right, as usual.

He stood beside the table, weighing the merits of strawberry preserves over peach, while the chatter behind the screen washed over him. Julie proposed a cameo. Rachel said nothing. Julie wondered about a mussie-tussie. Again, Rachel said nothing. Mark opted for peach and wandered closer, intrigued by the idea that anything could seriously be called a mussie-tussie, and found the table oddly empty without Rachel beside him.

Julie was discussing flowers now and the ice sculpture, and finally the Cornish hens that would be served at the reception. Mark strolled on, relieved that Julie was finally talking about the wedding again. Poor Harry just couldn't take another cancellation.

Left to fend for himself, Mark did what came naturally, what he always did—he explored. Curiosity, after all, was the newsman's stock in trade. Journalists could rant and beat their chests and say it was the search for truth, the need for justice that drove them. But in the end, it all came down to curiosity, and the need to see beyond the obvious.

Within minutes he discovered that the leg on the cutting table wobbled, the sewing machines were new, and the scissors horribly sharp. Interesting, but not unexpected. He continued on, following the bolts of fabric along the wall, deciding he preferred silk to crepe, and white to ivory. Before he had to make a decision on beads versus pearls, he was saved by the discovery of a door that swung both ways.

Having learned years ago that opportunity never knocks twice, he ignored the sign that said EMPLOYEES ONLY, gave the door a push, and took a peek at the other half of Rachel's life, the part that didn't show.

Her kitchen lay directly ahead of him, a narrow galley in a common room of white, sun-washed walls, and sparkling windows. To the right was a small bathroom and a bedroom, with a huge brass bed and more pillows than he could count.

He stared at the bed, wondering what side she slept on, what she wore, imagining a nightgown with long sleeves and a high neck. The kind that left everything to the imagination and looked better on the floor.

Quickly reining in that thought, he turned his head and spotted a studio on the other side of the kitchen, with a couch, a chair, and a drafting table piled with sketches.

He glanced back at the screen where his sister and Rachel were still working. "Be honest," Julie was saying. "Do you think the fichu is too much?"

"God, I hope so," he muttered, and stepped into her kitchen.

FIVE

"Honestly?" Rachel pursed her lips and told herself to count to ten before she answered. She made it to five. "Yes," she said, then waited a beat and gave the dress a thoughtful look. "I'd have to say the fichu is a bit much."

She hoped her sigh wasn't audible as Julie unfastened the clip, removed the collar, and said, "You're right. The shawl is probably enough."

Rachel took the fichu, folded it carefully, and chalked up a point for sanity. But while the dress itself was overdone, she had to admit that the demure styling worked well with Julie's delicate features and rounded belly, making her appear vulnerable and earthy at the same time. Now, if she could just do something about the bows on the sleeves . . .

Rachel carried the fichu out to the showroom. "Mark, your sister looks—" She set the collar on a chair and glanced around. "Lovely."

"He's probably gone home." Julie called over the screen. "His agency phones every afternoon around this time to give him his daily news fix."

Rachel stood by the table, remembering the brush of his thigh against hers and a smile as secret and intimate as a fingertip across her skin, and realizing again how little she knew about him. Which was fine. Perfect, in fact.

She didn't want him too near. Not with his touch still on her skin and the dream inside her head. She was weak where he was concerned—rash and reckless. And she knew she'd regret every minute when he'd gone. As long as he looked after Mrs. Dempster's house, she didn't need to know anything more than she did. She glanced back at the screen. Of course, if Julie wanted to talk about him . . .

She gave the fichu a brisk shake and folded it on the cutting table. "He told me a little about his work," she said, then paused for effect, wanting to convey nothing more than a passing interest. "Sounded like a dangerous job."

"Only because he makes it that way," Julie called. "He could go for the safer assignments, but he never does. Wherever bullets are flying or bombs going off, that's where he'll be. Standing smack in the middle of it with forty pounds of equipment on his shoulder." She paused. "Do you think I should lose a few of these bows?"

"If you like," Rachel said, her gaze drawn to the window and the beach house next door. The porch was deserted, the windows dark, as though the house was empty. She heard again his distant tone when he'd described the newscast, saw the bitter smile as he'd turned away from her on the beach. And she wondered where he sat when he got his fix.

With a sigh, she turned and picked up a pair of scissors. "We'll start with the bows on the sleeves," she said as she rounded the screen. "And go from there."

Standing next to Julie, she carefully clipped the threads on the bow at her wrist; then she watched Julie's face as she lifted it up and off. Julie nodded and touched the next one up. "This one, too, I think."

Biting the inside of her cheeks to keep from smiling, Rachel separated bow from cloth and asked the question that was still on her mind. "If his work is so dangerous, why does he do it?"

Julie shrugged and held up one side of the bow at her elbow, making it easier for Rachel. "He thrives on it; always has. He was ten when my mother found him hanging upside down from the overpass on the highway with a camera. He was trying to get a picture of a raccoon who'd made a nest in the catwalk. He thought he could save the babies if people knew it was there."

"Just doing what needed to be done," Rachel murmured, and started on the other sleeve. "You must be glad to have him home for a while."

Julie nodded as she took the bow from Rachel. "Despite the way it sounds, he's always careful. He doesn't take stupid chances. But sometimes the situations get out of control. And after what happened in the Sudan, I wish he wouldn't go back at all."

An ambush and an old war wound in the Sudan. Rachel piled the bows on a chair and told herself that she wouldn't pry. That it was none of her business. But she wondered all the same.

"He doesn't talk much about it, but it only figures that if you get shot, you must think about it now and then, right?"

"Right," Rachel echoed, thinking of what he'd said. About being the one that got away.

"Anyway, it doesn't matter, because I know he'll go back," Julie said. "He can't see himself doing anything else." She laid a hand on her belly. "Which means that this little one will have to travel halfway around the world just to see her cousins."

Rachel kept her eyes on the bow at Julie's shoulder. "Mark has children on the other side of the world?"

Julie laughed. "God, no. I meant that if he ever does settle down, it won't be here." Her face softened as she looked into the mirror. "This dress is almost enough to make me believe this whole marriage thing can work."

Rachel held her gaze in the glass. "Are you saying you don't believe that it will?"

"I want to, but I'm afraid. Harry and I have been happy for six years. We didn't need rings or a license or anything else to keep us together. Now, with the baby coming, suddenly Harry wants tradition."

Julie sighed and laid a hand on her belly, instinctively soothing the baby within. "I wasn't very good as a wife the first time I tried it, and I've never seen myself as a mother. I'm scared to death that once we say those vows, he'll expect to wake up with someone different, someone responsible who'll do car pools and bake cookies. And that he'll turn himself into the Perfect Husband or something equally horrible."

She tried to smile, laugh it off, but the shine in her eyes gave her away. "As much as I tell myself it's ridiculous, I can't help thinking that if we get married, everything we have will be gone." Her eyes sought Rachel's again. "Does that make any sense at all?"

Rachel put the scissors down slowly. On the day she'd opened the Bridery, she'd made only two rules: deliver on time and don't get involved. She kept her head down while couples fought, pretended not to see when they kissed as though they'd never see each other again, and said nothing when the topic of mothers-in-law came up.

But how could she look into Julie's eyes and follow the rules when she knew exactly what she meant? Especially when Julie was picking up those damn bows again.

"It makes perfect sense," she said at last. "You're taking a risk, putting everything you know, everything you are, on the line for something uncertain, something you're not even sure you want. But sometimes you have to take a chance, just plunge in, because if you don't, you'll always wonder."

"You're right about that." Julie smiled at the bows, then laid them on the chair again. "Thanks."

"Like they say, nothing comes to those who wait," Rachel continued, and when she couldn't stand it any longer, turned her back on the hypocrite in the mirror and hoped Julie didn't notice the flame in her cheeks. "Okay, let's get you out of that dress."

Mark stood in the doorway of her studio, a room of sunlight, white wicker furniture, and shells. But instead of clutter, the feeling was restful, serene—a perfect place to work, he mused, judging by the number of sketch books lining the shelves beside the drafting table.

He moved closer. On the desk was a sketch of a bridal gown, but it was nothing like the dress Rachel had made for Julie. The skirt was long and breezy, full and feminine, and topped off by a severe jacket. Mark propped up the sketch and stood back. Restrained sensuality—a fascinating and beautiful contradiction, much like the woman who had designed it.

More curious now, he took one of the sketch books from the shelves and turned back the cover. A gown sculpted of pale pink silk, simple and ethereal, demanding attention but never overpowering the bride.

He flipped through the pages, finding designs for bridesmaids, flower girls, mothers of the bride—every one distinct and different and signed by Rachel Banks. Feeling as though he'd discovered a buried treasure, he propped the sketch of the pink gown on top of the shelf and kept going; flipping open sketch books, finding a favorite, and setting it where it could be seen.

There were at least twenty books and he filled the

room, propping the drawings on the couch, the table, the windowsill. Surrounding himself with her work, her essence, her very soul, and finally finding the one that took his breath.

A floating, airy skirt and a top that was sleeveless, backless, slightly tailored. There was nothing more. No jewelry, no gloves, nothing to take away from the design and Rachel, for hers was the face in the picture—no other could do the gown justice.

"We thought you'd gone." Her face was pale, her voice cold. "And what exactly are you doing back here?"

"I know I had no business—"

"You're right about that." She let the door swing shut behind her and lowered her voice so Julie wouldn't hear. "Did you not grasp the meaning of Employees Only when you read the sign?"

Mark had no glib reply, nothing but the truth. "I was curious—"

"And that makes it all right?" She snatched the sketch book from his hand. "How dare you come in here! This is my home, for godsake." She took another step into the room and glanced around. "And this . . ."

She struggled for words as her eyes moved from one drawing to the next. Never had she seen her work displayed so openly, so wantonly, without any reserve whatsoever.

There was a disturbing sensuality to the sketches that was almost palpable when set out in such a fashion. She'd never noticed it in her work before, had always thought of herself as conservative, simple, and it embarrassed her to be exposed in such a manner. "Why, this is—"

"Innovative?" he suggested. "Fresh?"

"Mine," she cut in and jammed the book back into the case. "Your sister is waiting in the showroom. For her sake, I suggest you go there now."

He came toward her instead. "Tell me this first. Why are you wasting your time here on the beach?"

"I have no idea what you're talking about." She gathered up two more sketch books, closed them quickly, and stacked them neatly on the shelves again. "I run a successful business doing what I love. What can possibly be wrong with that?"

"Nothing, unless you want something else."

"Well, I don't." She grabbed two more books and flipped the covers down; making order out of the chaos he'd created and bringing truth to her words. But she couldn't bring herself to look at him.

"Your drawings tell me something else."

She turned on him then, wishing he'd leave, just go back and sit at the table so she could pretend that none of this had happened. "What would you know about it? You're not a designer, you're a cameraman."

"With a news agency who also covers fashion shows. I've covered enough to know when I'm seeing real talent." He grabbed a sketch book from her hand and opened it at random. "And I'm seeing it right here."

Rachel stared at the drawing—feathery ice blue skirt, tailored white top. She read the date on the bottom—eight months ago. She hadn't looked at it since then, but the details were still clear in her mind.

She'd roughed it out at the kitchen table when Jenny Miller's Scarlett O'Hara gown was in the planning stages—a response to the impractical hoop skirts and pantaloons the bride insisted she needed. Jenny might have envisioned herself on a gracious plantation, but reality was a legion hall with a narrow staircase down to the bathroom. But who was Rachel to shatter a fantasy?

So she'd made the dress Jenny wanted and sketched what she'd really have liked to see her wear. A waste of time and effort when you got right down to it.

"It's not that simple," she said and reached out to take the book back.

But Mark stood it up on the windowsill instead, right between a black bridesmaid gown and the fiery red wedding gown that still made her blush.

"Rachel, these sketches are so alive, they almost breathe. Surely you can feel it yourself." He pushed a hand through his hair as he prowled the room. "This kind of work deserves to be seen, to be worn." He snatched the drawing of Julie's Jane Austen hell from the corkboard. "And you deserve more than this."

His words stung. "I have what I need," she said, snatching the page from his hand and stabbing it back on the board. "I do the work I love, where I want and how I want. And I answer to no one, much like yourself."

His tone softened. "You can only kid yourself for so long."

She almost laughed. "That's the one thing I am not doing." She spread out her arms. "Take a look around. Do you see diplomas on the wall? Certificates from some famous school of design? No, because I don't have any. I'm a seamstress, a dressmaker, nothing more.

"Women come here with a picture and a budget." She picked up a file and threw it at him. Snapshots, pages torn from magazines and rough-hand drawings fluttered to the floor. "This is what they want. Other people's designs. They don't want my suggestions, don't want to see any of this. And it's their day, not mine. So I keep my sketch books closed and give them what they want."

"But what about what you want?"

"You don't understand. This is what I want." Anger spent, she bent to pick up the pictures, tucking them carefully into the folder again. "A wedding is about hope and joy, and just plain optimism. I love being part of that. I don't need anything else."

He took hold of her shoulders and turned her to face him, feeling the tension in her body and seeing the lie in her eyes. "Rachel, what are you so afraid of?"

Of success, of failure. Of finding out that she really was nothing more than a seamstress on the beach. But more than anything she was afraid of him.

"Nothing." She met and held that clear blue gaze. "Nothing at all."

"Liar."

The word hit harder than she would have believed. Was she so transparent, so easy to read? She shook him off, not wanting him near, not wanting to feel the things he made her feel, or want the things she couldn't have. "You have no right to judge me." She stepped out of the studio, making way for him to pass. "Get out."

"Soon," he said, and curved a hand around the back of her head, slipping his fingers into her hair and drawing her back into the studio. Her eyes grew wide and she moistened her lips, unconsciously he was sure, when he pressed her back against the wall and dropped his gaze to her mouth. Yet she didn't pull away, didn't make any move to stop him, and he felt his blood warm and his heart pound as he laid his hand on the small of her back, urging her nearer.

Slowly he bent to her, but not to kiss her mouth. Instead he touched his lips to her forehead, her cheek, the fine line of her jaw. Her eyes closed and he tilted her back, kissing a gentle path across her throat to the tender tip of her ear, while that subtle floral scent filled his head.

Her hands rose then, and his breath caught and held until her fingers rested and curled on his chest, not yet ready to take but not pushing away either.

Desire pooled and burned, but he held back, taking his time, enjoying the way she leaned her head into his hand, trusting him to hold her, to keep her safe as her arms lifted to circle his neck.

Her lips parted as he sought her mouth at last, barely touching his lips to hers, letting their breaths blend, fanning the need until she moaned low in her throat and rose up on her toes, claiming his mouth at last.

There was no triumph, no victory, just his own answering groan as he held her fast and surrendered to the sweet, velvet touch of her tongue.

Never had she wanted in this way, and it frightened as much as it thrilled. But even the shock of his hand on her breast, so bold and skillful as he teased her nipple to hardness, could not have made her pull away. She heard herself sigh, felt herself push against the palm of his hand, and knew she should be ashamed.

This was not her. This was some other woman. One who could take what she wanted from a man and simply enjoy, with no thought to tomorrow or where it would lead. What was it about him? she wondered, and thought briefly to stop him, to stop herself. But he ran his hands down the length of her body, and all she could do was feel.

She drew him closer, deepening the kiss and letting herself be drawn up into the spell, while he traced the curve of her waist, the flare of her hips, the softness of her thighs. And it was only the sound of someone crying that brought her down hard.

Julie. Her client. What in God's name had she been thinking about? Nothing, she realized. Nothing at all.

Shaken, she shoved him away and tugged at her skirt, only now aware of just how high it rode on her thighs. She pushed a hand through her hair as she straightened, feeling disoriented, breathless, and utterly bewildered. She looked into his face. His eyes were still dark with passion, but his mouth was tight and grim.

He stepped back, touching the side of his hand to his mouth as his gaze raked her lips, her throat, her breasts. He wanted her, she could see that. But he clearly didn't want to.

"Rachel," he said, his voice low and husky, still tinged with sex. "I never meant for that to happen."

Shame and humiliation came at once, but she forced herself to raise her chin, to meet his eyes. "It was nothing," she said, tossing him a quick, brilliant smile as she turned. "I was just lightening up."

But her smile faltered as she smoothed a hand over her dress and pushed back her hair, trying hard to imagine what she must look like.

"Rachel?" Julie came through the swinging door, clutching bows and fichu to her chest. She swiped at her eyes and sniffed. "The wedding is off."

Rachel moved toward her, the spell slowly breaking as she returned to herself. "Start at the beginning."

"I phoned Laurie's house one more time," Julie started, but her reply froze when she spotted Mark in the studio. "What are you doing here?"

"Mark?" Rachel took her arm to lead her out to the showroom, but Julie was immovable. "He's, uh . . . He's—"

"Getting something for the cutting table," he answered for her.

She couldn't stop herself from looking at him.

"It wobbles," he told Julie, but his eyes were on Rachel. "I was just hoping I could fix things."

"You've done enough already," Rachel said, and turned back to Julie. "So you called Laurie?"

Julie nodded miserably. "She didn't make it to the fitting because she had an accident."

Rachel's hand went to her chest. "A car accident?"

"Even worse. It was a freak accident." Julie bent her

head and toyed with the bows. "She was jogging this morning and a dog came out of nowhere. Of course, Laurie hates dogs, so she ran faster, didn't look before she crossed a road, and ran smack into a guy on a bike. They both went flying, she broke a leg, and the doctor says she won't be able to travel to the wedding."

Rachel shook her head. "So why do you have to cancel?"

Julie looked from Rachel to Mark and back again. "Don't you see? It's an omen. This wedding was never meant to be."

"What about Harry?" Mark asked. "What are you going to tell him?"

"The truth," Julie said. "He'll understand."

"Not this time he won't."

All heads turned. Harry stood in the kitchen doorway, his eyes on Julie. "You know I love you," he said to her, "but if you cancel this time, I won't ask you again."

"Harry?" Julie called as the door swung closed behind him.

"I'll talk to him," Mark said as he dashed past.

Julie looked helplessly at Rachel, her eyes brimming again. "Now what do I do?"

Rachel saw Mark through the window, running to catch up with Harry on the beach, but his scent was still on her skin and in her head. "Do you love him?" she asked softly.

"That has never been an issue."

Rachel watched until he disappeared, then turned to Julie. "Then there's only one thing you can do. You take a deep breath, and you jump."

"Just like that?"

Rachel nodded. "Just like that."

"But I need a maid of honor," Julie said. "Someone

to stand beside me, and hold the bouquet, and make sure I don't lose the stupid ring."

"You must have other friends, someone you can call on—"

"Not at the last minute," Julie said with a groan. "I put enough noses out of joint when I asked Laurie. Harry's sister, my cousins, you name it, they were all mad. To ask one of them now would be like saying, 'Oh, you weren't good enough before, but now I'm desperate, so be a dear and sub-in, will you?' " She stared at the wall while she shook her head. "And even if I did ask one, the others would be mad all over again." She looked down at her hands, then held out the bows. "Can you put these back on? And the fichu, too? I really think I need the fichu."

"Now don't be rash." Rachel set aside bows and fichu and followed her to the showroom. "There must be a way to work this out."

"Not unless I can find someone to wear that dress." Julie sank down at the table. "It's an omen, I know it." She turned her head slowly, her face brightening. "Unless . . ."

Rachel sat down beside her. "Unless what?"

Julie reached out and grabbed hold of Rachel's hand. "Unless you'd do it." Her grip was surprisingly strong. "Don't say no right away; just think about it. You're close to Laurie's size, you're not related, and we've known each other, how long?"

Rachel gave her hand a tug. No luck. "Six months."

"And never a cross word in all that time." She sat back, taking Rachel's hand with her. "Why, we're practically sisters, only better because no one knows you, so their noses won't go out of joint again."

Rachel eyed the yellow horror beneath the plastic. "I couldn't possibly—"

"It would mean everything to me. And to Harry."

Rachel looked into her eyes, so blue, just like Mark's, and now filling with tears again. She sighed and laid her other hand on Julie's, reminding herself to put her own rules on a poster and tack them above the sewing machine. Deliver on time and don't get involved. "Fine. I'll be the maid of honor."

Julie tried to leap to her feet just as Mark came back through the door.

"Sit down," he called when he saw her stagger, then hurried across the room to help her back into the chair. "And tell me you're not going to cancel this wedding."

She beamed up at him. "I'm not going to cancel the wedding—thanks to Rachel."

Mark's eyes narrowed. "Rachel?"

Rachel busied herself with clearing dishes, refusing to look at him, while Julie went on.

"She convinced me to take a deep breath and leap."

Rachel could feel his eyes on her as surely as she could feel the blush rising to her face.

"Sounds like good advice," he said.

Julie's smile was warm. "How could I doubt my maid of honor?"

Julie missed the look that passed between Mark and Rachel as she got to her feet. Which probably explained the smile she hit them both with as she made her way to the door. "It will be nice for you too, Mark, having someone you know to stand with in the receiving line."

Rachel blinked. "Receiving line?"

Julie laughed. "Of course. The best man always stands beside the maid of honor in the receiving line."

"Mark is the best man," Rachel muttered. "How nice."

"The rehearsal party is tonight, eight o'clock," Julie said as she looped an arm through Mark's. "Since Mark is right next door, maybe you two could drive in together."

"No," Rachel cut in, then smiled weakly. "What I mean is that with the wedding only two days away, I'll need every minute to work on that dress."

"Then come over early on Saturday," Julie said. "I'll show you around the garden and walk you through the ceremony." She pointed to the cardholder on the desk. "And give me some business cards while I'm here. That way I can put them on the tables so people know where the dresses were made."

"Crass personal promotion on your wedding day?" Rachel shook her head as she slid the cardholder out of reach. "Why, I wouldn't dream of it."

Julie looked truly touched, but Mark only laughed, not fooled at all.

Julie picked up the teapot as they headed for the door. "Thanks again for the loan of this." She paused as Mark opened the door and smiled over her shoulder. "And don't forget the fichu."

SIX

"So I said to him, what's the big deal? Just go to the movie and read the reviews later. Let it be a surprise. What's wrong with that?"

"Nothing." Rachel scratched her chin on her shoulder, blew a strand of hair from her eyes, and readjusted the maid-of-honor dress on the sewing machine. "Can you hand me the scissors on your way by?"

Amanda picked up the shears as she wandered past the cutting table again. "I told him I never like to know what I'm going to see. That I love to just get in a line and find out what's at the end." She pointed the scissors at Rachel. "Do you know what he said?"

Rachel shrugged but kept her head well back. "Forget it?"

"And he hasn't called since." Amanda tapped the shears against her palm as she paced back to the window. "So much for my big summer fling."

Rachel sighed and bit the thread. "It's still early in the season," she said through her teeth, then picked up the dress as she rose. "You'll have someone else by the first of June."

"Don't bet on it." Amanda handed her the scissors, then hoisted herself up on the cutting table. "I really thought this was the one."

Rachel put the scissors in a drawer. "You only met him a week ago."

Her shoulders slumped. "Feels like forever."

Rachel laughed and carried the gown around behind the screen and shucked off her shorts and well-worn T-shirt. "What are you going to do now?"

"The only thing I can do: go over there and talk some sense into him."

"And if that doesn't work?"

She shrugged. "What's the worst that can happen? I cry for a few days, eat too much ice cream, and go on. But at least I know I took the chance."

Rachel frowned as she drew back behind the screen. It all seemed so simple when Amanda said it, and so logical when Julie had asked. Take a breath and jump. And damn the rocks below.

She saw herself again as she'd been yesterday, her back pressed against the wall, her fingers in his hair as she arched into his touch. Filling herself with the feel, the scent, the taste of him, only to be left high and dry on the rocks, with no way back. But what else had she expected?

She never leapt into anything. She liked to know exactly where she was going to land, and what she should pack for the trip. She always knew where the emergency candles were, kept a first-aid kit in every room, and a blanket in the trunk of her car. Even in summer. In Florida. She was careful, thoughtful, pathetic perhaps, but at least she'd always known who she was. Until Mark.

She shoved her arms into the dress, her fingers searching desperately for a way through the full, cumbersome sleeves. After today, she would steer clear of him. She would sit inside, bolt the door if necessary, but she would never again have him in her house. Sweat glistened on her upper lip by the time she finally worked the dress up to her shoulders.

Amanda leaned a shoulder against the screen. "Aren't you supposed to have an annabelle to help you get into those things?"

"An abigail," Rachel said as she fumbled with the sash.

Amanda curtsied smartly and adopted the worst English accent Rachel had ever heard. "Let me 'elp you then, miss." She tied the sash into a jaunty bow, then took a step back. "Beggin' your pardon, miss, but yellow ain't really your color."

"Tell me something I don't know." Rachel shoved at the sleeves, primped the collar, adjusted the shawl, tugged at the sash, but there was no way to improve what she saw in the mirror.

Her shoulders slumped. "I look like a huge, frumpy banana."

The real Amanda tipped her head to the side. "Not huge, just . . . womanly." She ignored Rachel's groan and reached for the bonnet. "Maybe this will help."

Rachel fit the straw bonnet on her head, tied yet another jaunty bow, and flicked the dangling rosebuds out of her eyes. "Well?"

"Maybe you won't have to wear it for the pictures," Amanda said, a grin threatening to break through at any moment.

Rachel tossed the hat on a chair. "Go ahead, laugh. I might as well get used to it. My only consolation is that there's going to be a wedding at all. A blessedly small one at that."

Which meant she wouldn't have to stand beside Mark for long.

She unclasped the collar, untied the sash, undid the buttons, and finally let the dress fall from her shoulders. She gathered up shawl, dress, and hat, and handed it all to Amanda. "Can you hang that up? I don't want to see it again until the wedding."

Amanda laughed as she carried the dress to the rack. "You've done a good deed. There has to be a reward for that." She moved closer to the window while she arranged the dress on a hanger. "And I think I see it pulling in next door."

Rachel tugged on her shorts and shirt. "What are you talking about?"

"I'm talking about six feet, maybe taller. Dark hair, nice shoulders—" She snapped around. "It's the guy from the dream, and he's driving a Jeep."

Rachel refused to acknowledge the jump in her pulse as she crossed to the window. "There is no guy, remember? And if there was, that wouldn't be him." But she couldn't resist one look.

His shirt was open over a pair of worn denim shorts, revealing just a hint of golden muscles and dark curly hair, and giving her overactive imagination even more to work with. He pulled a video camera from the back of the Jeep, headed up the front stairs, and disappeared into the house.

"He didn't even look over," she murmured.

Amanda looked at her curiously. "You know him?"

Not well enough, Rachel mused, then yanked the cord and dropped the blind with a thud. "He's a neighbor. Just like all the others out there."

Amanda hooked the hanger over the rod, then parted the blinds and smiled. "Maybe, but he's the only one heading this way."

Rachel shoved in beside her and peered through the crack. He was halfway across the small stretch of sand that separated the two houses. She straightened and ran damp palms over her shorts. "What does he want now?"

Amanda studied her a moment, then gathered up her

purse and headed for the door. "Whatever it is, you don't
need me in the way."

"You won't be." Rachel turned her head when she
heard footsteps on the stairs. But she wasn't aware that
she moistened her lips.

Amanda laughed. "I should have such a neighbor."

He knocked and she stood absolutely still, wavering
between curiosity and self-preservation.

Too late she realized that Amanda had made the choice
for her.

Amanda yanked open the door and smiled. "I'm just
leaving," she said as she slipped past him. But she
stopped long enough to give Rachel a thumbs up behind
his back.

"We'll talk later," Rachel warned, but Amanda only
laughed as she went down the stairs. Deciding she would
enroll in assertiveness training in the fall, Rachel planted
her feet and shifted her attention to Mark. "What do you
want?"

"Well, I ran out of coffee and had to ask myself who
I could borrow some from." He leaned a hand on the
doorframe, his smile warm and slow, like a caress. "And
I thought of you."

"Wait here." She grabbed a tin from the kitchen,
handed it to him, and closed the door.

He knocked again. "Sugar?"

She emptied her bowl into a yogurt container and
jammed it into his chest when he came a step closer. "I
won't need that back," she said and closed the door.

She kept her hand on the knob and pulled it open as
he was raising his hand. He looked startled for a moment;
then he grinned. "All the spoons are in the dishwasher . . ."

She rolled her eyes. "Why don't I just make it for you,
too?"

"Why, thanks," he said and strolled past her. "That really is neighborly of you."

She had to smile. The man was quick. Or maybe she was just too slow.

She grabbed the tin and the sugar from his hand. "One coffee," she said, and propped the door open. "To go."

He laughed as if to say "Your point," and started to follow her across the showroom. She stopped at the swinging door, barring the way. "Don't get too comfortable." She placed a hand on his chest and gave him a push. "I'll only be a minute," she added, and discovered just how nimble he could be as the door swung back.

She waited, not certain that he'd really stay there; then she blew out a breath and looked around the kitchen. "Coffee," she murmured, and felt herself smile. Without sugar.

His voice through the door was smooth and soft. "Rachel, about yesterday—"

She felt her stomach slide. "Look, you kissed me, I kissed you back, no big deal. And no more apologies, please."

"I wasn't going to. How could I, when I want nothing more than to kiss you again right now?"

She looked over at the door. "That's not going to happen."

She heard the smile in his voice. "Maybe not, but it doesn't stop me from wanting to open this door and start all over again."

She stared at the door. And if he did?

She pulled the pot from the coffeemaker and ran the water hard. Then she'd keep her head down and her defenses up, and hope it was enough. She filled the pot halfway, dumped the water into the reservoir, and opened the tin of coffee. "If you didn't come to apologize, then why are you here?"

She heard him turn and lean back against the frame. "I wanted to thank you for giving Julie the push she needed. If she'd canceled again, it would have been the end of the relationship. And that would have been a shame."

Rachel measured coffee into the basket and pushed the button. "They certainly seem good together."

"Best I've ever seen, but Julie's always been leery of marriage."

"Why is that?" Rachel asked, and pulled two mugs from the cupboard and a tin of cookies. With a shake of her head, she put the tin and cups back. What was she thinking? They weren't having coffee, or anything else for that matter. She pulled out a plastic travel mug, unsnapped the lid, and set it down by the pot.

"The usual," he continued. "Our parents divorced, and it wasn't even remotely civilized. Custody battles, ruined holidays, the works."

His tone was too offhand, too casual, and Rachel found herself walking to the door. "Is Julie afraid the same thing will happen to her and Harry?"

"It's hard not to be, especially when her first marriage only lasted a year. She was eighteen and searching for a family. His was big and close. I think she just wanted to be part of it. Unfortunately, her husband was part of the package. She left, went into acting, and figured marriage just wasn't something the Robisons are very good at."

She stood at the door, tempted to open it, yet afraid something would be lost if she did. "And do you feel the same way?"

He didn't answer right away and she strained toward him, not even sure what she wanted to hear.

His voice had grown soft, distant. "It only came up once. I met a woman in London, asked her to marry me.

Gave her a ring and let my little one-room flat go. Rented a huge townhouse to show her how serious I was, that it really could work."

Rachel laid a hand on the door, as if to touch him, to hold him there. "What happened?"

She heard him turn, face the door. "I was supposed to meet her family on New Year's Eve in Stourbridge, about two hours outside of London. She was already there, waiting, when my pager went off. Unrest in East Africa again."

Rachel pressed her cheek to the wood, her own voice no more than a whisper. "Did you go?"

He sighed, but she couldn't tell if it was with regret or resignation. Or perhaps both. "I left a message with her mother and took a cab to the airport. When I got back, she'd moved out. Left me a note that said I was not to call, or write, or in any way contact her. Her exact words were, 'You're better as a memory than reality.' "

She closed her eyes. "And do you believe it?"

"I've no reason not to."

She heard him walk away and almost called out to him, tried to draw him back, to restore the intimacy, but it was too late. His tone was brisk again, casual. He was already gone.

"I almost forgot," he called. "Your teapot was a hit at the rehearsal dinner last night. You missed a good party."

She backed away, letting chatter fill the space, take them back to where they'd been, where they would stay.

She turned to the coffeepot and made herself smile. "And who better to judge?"

"True enough," he said and laughed, but for the first time it sounded hollow to Rachel. "Coffee smells good."

Mark roamed the showroom, missing the scones, listening while she poured coffee he didn't want, and wondering why the hell he'd told her about Joanna.

All of that had happened years ago. He rarely thought about it anymore, and spoke of it even less. Yet he couldn't deny that while he wasn't in love with Joanna anymore, her words still rang true. And trust Rachel to dredge all of it up in a matter of minutes.

He paused at the cutting table, studying the coaster under one of the legs and still not sure why he'd come. Julie and Harry were going to stop by later with the pot and a thank-you.

He moved on to the wrought-iron table and smoothed a hand across the cloth. It was different this time, less formal than when she'd served tea, with a strawberry pattern and a ruffle around the bottom. He pulled out a chair and sat down. Nothing had changed. His legs still didn't fit, the chair was too damn small, and the cloth was all caught up on his knees.

So why was he there?

"How much sugar?" she called from the kitchen, and he smiled.

That was why, he admitted. To hear her voice, to see her smile. And to make sure he hadn't imagined that kiss.

He wasn't a romantic by nature, had never been caught up in the idea of a perfect fit. But when he'd held her, she'd molded to every contour of his body, filling him up and entering all the places that had been empty for so very long.

And when she moved, they'd found a rhythm that was ageless and sure, as though they knew each other well and had loved before, would love again. So he'd walked the beach at dawn, trying to understand, to make sense of it. Past her house again and again, watching her windows, wondering if she was awake, and calling himself every kind of fool. There was nothing of destiny here, no past and no future. Only coincidence and a woman who was slowly driving him mad.

She wasn't his type, and he certainly wasn't hers, but the attraction was real and he didn't know how to stop it.

So he'd jumped in the Jeep and driven across the causeway, needing to put some miles between himself and the lace-edged cottage. But had found himself heading back too soon, with nowhere else to go.

The walk to her door had been short and humbling. But then he'd seen her face, and he'd known he hadn't imagined a thing. Whatever was happening, she was feeling it, too, and didn't want to any more than he did.

"One," he called, feeling relaxed for the first time that day. He leaned back, wanting nothing more than to eat scones, hear her laugh, and carry her to that huge brass bed with too many pillows that he knew was right around the corner.

"Not going to happen," he said, repeating her words while he pushed aside the image of long, golden arms reaching around his neck and pulling him down—and knowing it was for the best.

Restless again, he tapped his hands on the table, toppling the spool of white thread on the other side of it. It rolled, tumbled over the edge and into the wastebasket.

He reached for it and spotted an entry form in the bottom. The New Designer Showcase in Miami—billing itself as one of the biggest forums for undiscovered talent in North America. She'd filled it in, then thrown it away, but why?

Without stopping to think, he reached in and pulled the page out, returning to the table as she came into the showroom.

"Coffee to go," she said, and carried the travel mug past him to the front door. "I won't need the cup back either." Her eyes narrowed as he came toward her. "Where did you get that?"

"Wastebasket. The newsman's most reliable source." He took the cup and popped off the lid. "You filled out the form, so why aren't you entering?"

She folded her arms across her chest. "That's none of your business."

"True," he conceded, and she honestly believed he was going to let it go. Until he set the lid on the desk and sipped.

"But you could win with that ice-blue wedding dress."

"Not that again." She snapped the form out of his fingers. "I'm not going to play this game. I have too much work to do." She turned and walked to her desk. "Close the door on your way out."

He made no move to leave, and she promised herself that she wouldn't look back. He could stand there all day if he wanted to; it made no difference to her. The contest was out for another year, and nothing could change that. Not now.

She raised her head. Pegged to the board above her desk was an estimate from the garage. The car needed more than a ring job; it needed a new engine. The cost was just about what she'd have to pay for fabric and trim for the ice-blue wedding gown, or any wedding gown for that matter.

Without the car, she wouldn't be able to make deliveries, pick up fabrics, or shop for the best bargains in trim. She'd be taking taxis, buses, or worse, relying on relatives and friends. And for what? A one-in-a-million shot at a dream.

She glanced over at the calendar. If the contest was a month from now, she'd have completed two more gowns and would have the money. But as it stood . . .

She crumpled the entry this time and stuffed it deep inside the basket. As it stood, it was all a matter of practicality. And if she was honest, there was a small part of her that was relieved.

The warmth of his breath on the back of her neck made her jump. "Is it the winning," he whispered, "or the losing that bothers you most?"

She swiveled her head around to look at him. "Neither," she said and stepped away, not willing to think about that side just yet.

"The contest was a whim," she continued. "A fancy. But I'm too busy right now." She crossed to the cutting table and gathered up needles, thread, her favorite shears—things familiar and safe that gave shape to her life. A life that was simple and ordinary, and usually enough. She dropped everything into a drawer and slammed it shut. "Besides, I have nothing to prove to anyone."

"Except yourself." He took hold of her shoulders and turned her to face him. "I don't believe you're just a seamstress on the beach. And I don't think you do either."

She couldn't look into his eyes and lie. So she dipped her head and pulled away—and was vaguely disappointed that he let her go so easily. "Why should it matter to you, anyway?"

He almost smiled. It mattered because she did. Because when she'd found him in her studio yesterday, surrounded by her drawings, he'd seen the flash of pride, the shock of pleasure when she'd recognized her own talent—and the look of resignation as she'd buried it all on the shelves again. But he couldn't for the life of him understand why.

He thought of the yellow dress she was going to put on tomorrow, and the one his sister would wear down the aisle. She needed someone to snatch those drawings out and hold them high while there was still time. While she still sketched and dreamed, and kept the spark alive inside her. Because once it died, there was no way to get it back. God knows, Mark had tried.

Her eyes were still on him, tense and wary. She was right when she said it was none of his business. He wasn't a lover, not even a friend. Just a neighbor with too much time on his hands, and a sudden, desperate appreciation for beauty.

He walked toward her. "It's important because you're talented."

She shrugged, as though his answer didn't matter, and sighed because it did. "Your coffee's getting cold, and I have work to do."

He reached out and drew her to him. "The coffee's fine, and the work will always be there."

But you won't, she thought. She'd left him an opening, but as he cupped her face in his hands, she was the one in danger of falling through. With a touch of regret, she leaned into his touch for a moment, savoring the warmth, the tenderness, then pulled away while she still could.

She crossed to the door, picked up the travel mug, and held it out to him. "Thirty seconds in the microwave should be enough."

He smiled and took the cup from her hands. "Shall we car pool to the wedding tomorrow? It only makes sense when you think about it."

What made sense was calling a cab or renting a car. That way she wouldn't have to spend any more time with him than necessary. And she was free to leave the reception as soon as dinner was over. A car pool only complicated everything. "Sorry, but I promised Julie I'd go over early in the morning."

"I'll be picking Harry up at seven-thirty," he said. "Is that early enough for you?" She nodded, and his smile broadened. "Then a car pool is only reasonable."

As much as she hated to admit it, he was right. At

least for the drive over. And she could always call a cab home.

"Fine," she said. "We'll car pool. But only if you keep the top up."

His grin broadened. "Of course. We wouldn't want anything to happen to that lovely yellow dress."

She started to close the door. "Good-bye, Mark."

He reached a hand around the back of her neck, leaned in close, and kissed her—slowly, deeply, thoroughly.

He set her back, holding on while she gained her balance; then he saluted her with the mug and headed down the stairs. "Seven o'clock. Top up."

She could only nod as she closed the door, knowing she'd be in real trouble if he came back for cream.

SEVEN

As dying arts went, it was one of the best. Hot towels, straight razors, and a leather strop to keep things smooth and sharp. Wedged between an Internet café and a center for yogic flyers, Frank's Barber Shop was an anomaly in a neighborhood the tourist magazines called "sleek and urban." The salon across the road was trendier, the one a block over busier, but as the red-and-white pole outside quietly proclaimed, Frank's was the last bastion of pure male indulgence.

No chrome-and-glass salon could compete with the soul-deep comfort of a heavy antique chair that tipped all the way back, giving a weary customer no choice but to put up his feet and rest a while. And while any sane man would think twice about letting a goateed stylist named Raoul anywhere near his throat with a straight razor, a white-coated barber was a figure of trust.

Frank's had passed, virtually unchanged, from father to son for three generations, and Frank Jr. had stayed true to the old ways when he took over. Computers and modems aside, the overriding feeling at Frank's was 1915. And a shave was still a thirty-minute luxury.

Which was why Mark, Harry, and Brodie were at the door as the sun was coming up. The shop wouldn't officially open for another two hours. But Brodie was a regular, and any friend of Brodie's was a friend of Frank's. And for a groom, he would even open early.

While Frank tied a cape over Harry, Mark and Brodie lay back in the chairs on either side. Brodie had picked up a magazine, but Mark closed his eyes, intending to put his mind on hold, his senses on high, and just enjoy.

He'd lost most of the night to research, sitting on the porch with his laptop, pulling up articles and searching news databases, but not for anything that would help Chuck. Instead, he'd spent the night looking for anything he could find on the Designer Showcase in Miami, and discovering that the contest was indeed everything it claimed to be and more.

After tracking the careers of the winners for the last five years, he'd come to the conclusion that Rachel had to be in that contest. She wanted to enter; that much was clear. But she was holding back, and he couldn't for the life of him figure out why.

A more enlightened, sensitive man would have let it go right there. Just reminded himself that it was her life, her decision, and moved on to issues that concerned him—like when they were going to eat breakfast, and just how sharp was that razor anyway?

But Mark had never been accused of being either enlightened or sensitive. He smiled to himself and folded his hands on his chest. All that remained now was to convince her that he was right.

"What changed your mind about the beard?" Brodie asked.

"The usual," Mark said. "Upkeep, personal hygiene—"

"Tan lines," Harry put in.

Mark nodded. "Always a concern."

The barber laid a steaming towel over Harry's face. "It was a woman."

"That's what I said," Harry mumbled around the cloth. "But he won't admit it."

"He doesn't have to." Brodie set the magazine down and sat up. "Statistics prove that the majority of men who shave off their beards do so because of a woman." He pointed at Mark. "And there sits the proof."

Mark opened one eye and looked at him. "What proof?"

"First, there's Lucy."

"Ah, yes, Lucy." It had taken him three days and a trip to the hardware store to get those seven digits off the wall. "How is she?"

Brodie shot him a considering glance. "Wondering why you never called."

He'd thought about it. Each time he went at the stain with a new cleaner, he thought about it. But where was the point, when it was Rachel who'd left her mark in his mind?

He shrugged. "I've been busy."

"You're on vacation," Harry muttered. "How busy can you be?"

"Exactly," Brodie said, unmistakably triumphant as he sat back and let the barber wrap a towel around his face. "Trust me. There is a woman at the bottom of that baby-soft chin. And if I was a betting man, I'd say she's the girl next door."

Harry's head swiveled. "Rachel Banks."

"Brodie has a great imagination," Mark said. "Ignore him."

Brodie merely laughed. "If she's the one you're after, then you're the one with the imagination."

Harry pulled back a corner of the towel and peered over at Mark. "Julie mentioned that you seemed well acquainted at the fitting." He drummed his fingers on the armrest. "She's a nice woman. Quiet, trusting. From what

I gather, she's not into casual relationships either. I'd hate to see her get hurt."

Mark had seen Harry's protective side plenty of times with Julie. He was by nature a gentleman, and it didn't surprise Mark in the least that he should act the big brother for Rachel.

"We're just neighbors," Mark assured him, then carefully redirected the conversation. "But she certainly has a way with a wedding dress. The ones for yours are truly . . . unique."

"They're ugly," Harry said, while the barber filled a mug with warm, snowy lather. "But I hope I get to see Julie in it just the same."

The barber swirled a brush in the mug. "Wouldn't be the first time I've heard of a groom getting left at the altar."

"Nobody's getting left anywhere," Mark said, sorry now that he hadn't let the conversation take its own course. He sat up and faced Harry. "What's going on?"

"I wish I knew," he said on a weary sigh. "Julie was up half the night, prowling around the garden, checking the tent again and again, as though she was afraid it wouldn't be there in the morning."

"That's just Julie," Mark assured him. "You know how she fusses over a scene."

"I suppose," Harry said, his fingers gripping the arm of his chair as the barber drew the razor down his cheek. "But she slept in a separate room last night, the first time in all the years we've been together. And to make matters worse, she wouldn't come out before I left. She said something about it being bad luck to see the bride before the wedding." His fingers relaxed, but he stared ahead, his expression blank. "I just hope she's still there when I get back."

"Everything will be fine," Mark said. "Rachel's with her."

Brodie sat bolt upright. "How do you know that?"

"I dropped her off when I picked up Harry."

Harry's eyes swiveled to look at him. "I thought she'd come on her own."

Brodie smiled as he lay back down. "I told Lucy it was the blonde."

Mark dropped his head back and watched the fan go round and round, endlessly. "We're neighbors," he said evenly. "We car pooled. And Harry, relax. You don't have a thing to worry about. Julie will be there when the wedding starts. Rachel will make sure."

Mark didn't stop to wonder at his faith in her; it was simply there. As surely as the need to deny everything else that he felt for her.

Harry nodded, but the worry was still there, stealing the joy from his eyes. Mark pulled out his cell phone and laid it on Harry's chest. "Give Julie a call and you'll find out I'm right. But if you say anything to her about Rachel and me, you may be the one who doesn't make it to the wedding."

High noon.

Rachel had always thought it strange that Julie had chosen that hour for her wedding. But as she stood in front of the mirror in Julie's guest room, adjusting her bonnet for the third time in as many minutes, she sensed that the timing was completely appropriate. With the crowd gathering outside, she definitely felt like a lamb to the slaughter.

"A frumpy banana," she muttered, and stalked over to the window.

Julie and Harry's home was a traditional two-storey

with a Georgian influence. But it wasn't the house that
had prompted them to buy; it was the property.

One and a half acres with a walled garden, fruit trees,
live oaks, and roses everywhere. There was a definite
English feel to the grounds, and that was what had in-
spired Julie's theme.

A striped tent for the reception occupied most of the
lawn, but the wedding itself would take place near the
walled garden. Rows of chairs separated by a red carpet
sat in the shade of two live oaks. A string quartet played
softly and the minister already stood behind a lectern on
a raised dias at the front. An archway of roses sat at the
end of the aisle, and there was another in front of the
minister.

Rachel counted the rows of chairs one more time, just
to be sure. Ten rows down, ten across. One hundred seats,
and every one of them filled.

"A small wedding," she said and snorted in a most
unladylike fashion, knowing Jane Austen would not be
pleased and taking some comfort in that, at least.

"It's time." Julie stood in the doorway, looking scared
and overdressed. But she glowed, too, like every bride
Rachel had ever known, and when she smiled, Rachel
knew a moment of longing, and a faint tug around her
heart. But it was gone as quickly as it had come, replaced
by a need to get Julie out the door and down the aisle.
The sooner this was over, the sooner she could get out
of that dress.

"Let's do it," Rachel said, taking her arm and leading
her to the stairs. White-gloved waiters bustled about, the
caterer shouted orders in the kitchen, and Rachel kept
Julie on course.

At the bottom of the stairs, Julie's mother waited. She
had the same hair coloring and the same delicate features
as Julie but was dressed in a classic oyster silk suit with

matching pumps and a leather clutch. She stared as they came closer, then put on a smile Rachel could only call valiant and hugged her daughter.

"Good luck, darlin' " she said, then stepped back and gave Rachel a quick once-over, her smile straining. "So you're the one who made the gowns."

Julie put an arm around Rachel's shoulder. "She's too modest to talk about it."

The woman sniffed. "I'm sure she is."

Rachel adjusted her basket. "So, how did you find out?"

"My son told me." She plucked a card from her purse. "He gave me this as well."

"My card?" Rachel felt her stomach slide. When had he taken those? And how many?

Julie's mother tucked the card into Rachel's basket. "Don't worry, dear, I won't spread it around." She turned and hurried to the door. "I'll tell them to start the music," she called, then paused with her hand on the knob and pulled a tissue from her purse. "Just one question, dear. Did you know your father was bringing that, that . . . woman with him?"

"She's his wife," Julie said evenly.

"I should have known he'd find a way to spoil my day." She tucked the little clutch purse under her arm again. "By the way, did you want Mark to come and give you away?"

"No one gives me away," Julie said through clenched teeth, and her mother wisely stepped out into the sunshine.

"Her day," Julie muttered, then stiffened as the violins struck the familiar first chord. "Oh, God."

One hundred people rose and turned.

She grabbed Rachel's wrist. "I can't do this."

"Of course you can." She pried Julie's fingers loose,

then linked her arm through hers, not trusting Julie to follow on her own.

Julie's feet didn't budge. "What if this really is a mistake?"

"It's not a mistake," Rachel said softly. "Do you remember what you said when you ordered the dresses?"

She looked over at her and Rachel drew her along a few steps.

"A ramble in the roses, that's what you said you wanted your wedding to be."

Julie nodded. An usher opened the door.

Rachel tightened her grip and kept going. "Look out there and tell me what you see."

Julie's eyes misted. "Harry," she whispered. "Under the roses."

Rachel smiled up at her. "Let's ramble."

Julie laughed and pulled her forward. Rachel felt that silly tug again as they crossed the lawn. And even the audible gasp of horror when they stepped onto the aisle couldn't shake her foolish grin.

"Wasn't that a beautiful wedding? And you are?"

"Rachel Banks," she said, smiling and nodding as she shook the first hand that came through the receiving line. After the ceremony, the wedding party and families had arranged themselves at the end of the red carpet, to the right of the arch of roses.

Rachel looked into the face of aunt somebody from somewhere, blew her wilted bangs out of her eyes, and tried to remember the name Julie had given her as she passed the woman along. Mary? Mazy? She gave up and took the aunt's hand. Names weren't important anyway. Speed was what mattered at this point.

"It was charming, yes," Rachel said and tried to urge the woman along. "May I introduce Harry's—"

"Brother-in-law," Mark said as he wedged himself into the receiving line beside her. "And you must be Harry's Aunt May. It's so nice to meet you."

Rachel bristled. It had been bad enough standing beside him at the altar, feeling his smile through the brim of the bonnet, and hearing the laughter beneath the whisper while they signed the register. "You're a vision," he'd said, and wisely held on to her hand while the photographer snapped the pictures.

She shot him a quick glance as she tried to inch away. He still sported the redingote that Julie had ordered from the costume shop, a cravat, vest, and high-collared shirt. But instead of ridiculous he looked, well . . . dashing and romantic. Like a figure out of Jane Austen. Which figured.

She tried to edge farther away, then turned quickly to Harry's mother on her left. "I'm sorry, did I step on your foot?"

Harry's mother stared at her along the considerable length of her nose, then slowly turned her head again. "I guess so," Rachel muttered and inched back, resigned.

"I almost forgot." Mark pulled her bonnet out from behind his back. "You left this on a chair." He plopped it on her head and smiled. "I was sure you'd be missing it," he said, and turned his attention back to Aunt May. "Did you know that Rachel made the dresses?"

Rachel groaned and yanked off the hat in time to see the aunt's smile falter.

"They certainly are . . . different."

"One of a kind," he said, and held out a card. "Take one of these—"

Rachel snapped up the card before Aunt May's fingers could close on it, then smiled. "You have to forgive Mark.

He doesn't understand that this is neither the time nor the place for this sort of thing."

Like a magician, he flipped up another card. "She's just too modest."

Rachel grabbed that one as well. "And he just never knows when to quit." She smiled too broadly at the next guest. "Who have we here?"

Uncle Herbie scowled at her over his glasses, and she quickly turned him over to Mark.

"Herbie," he said, shaking the man's hand. "Good to see you again. Did you meet the lady responsible for the dresses—"

"And this is Carol," Rachel sang as she propelled a smiling redhead forward. "She's with him."

"Carol," Mark cooed. "Let me give you a card."

Rachel made a grab, but Carol was quick, and Rachel could only watch in horror as her card strolled on, out of reach.

Julie caught her eye behind Mark's back, her smile warm and relaxed. "I never want this day to end."

"Oh, God, please," Rachel whispered as Julie drifted back around, but forgot her plea as she studied the bride more closely. Julie looked different somehow. Better. The hat was gone, she realized. As were the gloves. And where was the basket?

Rachel tugged her gloves off and dropped them by the bonnet.

"What's good for the bride," she muttered, and was just doffing the fichu when she noticed a lull in the line.

She dropped the lace into the bonnet and bent forward, catching only bits and pieces of a tearful reunion with a long lost cousin at the front of the line. Hoping it lasted a while, she hooked an arm through Mark's and dragged him back a few steps. "We need to talk."

He held up a hand. "No, no. Don't thank me yet. Wait until after you hear the speech."

Her mouth dropped open. "You wouldn't."

He tapped a pocket. "Page two, line five." He leaned closer and lowered his voice. "But I'll forget all about it if you enter that contest."

She could only stare at him. "You can't be serious."

His grin broadened. "Don't count on it."

"Get back in line," Harry's mother snapped, and the two stepped quickly into place.

"But it's none of your business," she whispered.

"True," he said. "But I've learned not to let things like that bother me."

Her reply was cut short as another guest approached.

"Lovely ceremony," she said, holding on to her smile even when the woman shot her and her business card a look of disdain.

Mark sighed dramatically as the woman moved on. "It's not like I'm enjoying this, you know."

Rachel angled her body toward him and adopted a suitably haughty stance. "Then why bother? Nobody will remember tomorrow anyway."

"Hey there, little darlin'."

Rachel jumped as a hand slapped her on the butt. She whirled around and found herself looking down into the round, grinning face of a man old enough to be her grandfather. "Gord Jeffries," he bellowed and pulled a cigar from his pocket. "And I am mighty pleased to meet you."

EIGHT

Rachel didn't manage a reply before a woman twice the height of the old man sidled up and rubbed against his arm. She had bright red hair, long white fingernails, and a rock on her left hand that would keep her nicely weighed down in a windstorm.

"Gordy," she purred as one fingertip circled a button on his shirt, "are you trying to make me jealous by talking to this young woman all alone?"

He wiped at a bead of perspiration on his upper lip, then laughed and put an arm around her. "Why no, Tammy darlin', this here's the lady who made the dresses."

"I really can't take all the credit," Rachel stammered. "Julie had the idea; I just made the dress—"

"Which is exactly why I want you." Tammy's pout faded as she stepped out of Gord's embrace. "Honey," she said, and backed Rachel out of the line. "I think you and me can do some serious business."

Mark perked right up and followed. "You need a wedding gown?"

Tammy nodded. "And I know exactly what I want." Her gaze fixed on Rachel. "All I need is for you to make it."

Gord mopped a handkerchief across his brow as he

drew up beside them. "I do love a woman who knows what she likes."

Mark smiled. "So does Rachel. Makes her job that much easier."

She shot him a look that should have frozen him to the spot, but he just cocked a brow and laughed.

"Gordy and I met in Las Vegas," Tammy was saying. "And I want a dress that will always remind us of that night."

"Tight and sparkly," Gord sputtered. "But white, of course, right, darlin'?"

"Of course white," she snapped, then smiled at Rachel. "This gown is going to be a killer."

"I can picture it already." Mark leaned across and flipped her a card. "Tammy, you have definitely come to the right place."

Tammy tucked the card into Gord's jacket pocket, then threaded an arm through his as they walked away. "I'll call you next week," she called back to Rachel. Then she turned her head and smiled. "And hon—money is no object."

Rachel was dimly aware of the receiving line breaking up, of people drifting past and a waiter standing beside her with a tray of champagne.

"Another wonderful gown." Mark took two glasses from the tray and handed her one. "You must be so pleased."

She turned on him. "Go ahead and laugh. But as far as I'm concerned, a paying customer beats an expensive contest any day."

She hoisted the flute. "To the customer," she said, then downed the champagne and slapped the empty down on a passing waiter's tray. "May she always be right."

Mark grabbed her wrist, holding her back when she

would have left. "Are you telling me you can't afford to enter the contest?"

Her eyes went cold, her voice flat. "You are the quick one."

Guilt pricked him when he thought of Tammy and Gord, and all the cards he'd handed out. He'd been so sure the answer went deeper that he'd missed the obvious.

She tried to pull away, but he held on, unable to let it go until he was sure. "Is that the only reason? The money?"

"Do I need another?"

"Then I'll place an order for the ice-blue gown."

She stared at him, uncomprehending. "You want to buy a dress?"

"And I'll need it in two weeks."

She jerked her hand free and headed for the tent. "Don't patronize me."

He resisted the urge to follow. "Then it's not just the money, after all, is it?"

She stopped and turned around slowly. "Let me make this simple for you. I don't take charity."

"I wouldn't expect you to." He took a step toward her, needing her to hear him out, to understand. "I'm no different from any of your other customers. I know what I want and who I want to make it."

"I see." She folded her arms. "And when was the last time you ordered a dress?"

"Singapore, 1995. Julie was playing Tiger Lily and wanted authenticity." He gave his head an impatient shake. "Look, this isn't charity, it's an investment. I've seen what you can do on paper, and I'm willing to bet that it will be even better in reality. When you make it big one day, I'll have an original Rachel Banks hanging in my closet. I'll make a fortune. Still sound like charity?"

She shook her head.

"Then what's the problem?"

He stood directly in front of her, waiting for an answer, forcing her to think—about the offer, the question, about what she really wanted.

His voice softened. "It's easier, isn't it, when you don't have a choice."

She looked into his eyes, expecting to see triumph, a challenge, anything but compassion, and a tenderness that was too real to deny. She turned away, torn between finally finding out if she had what it takes to be a big name and never wanting to know.

She looked back at him. "It will be expensive."

"Hon, money is no object."

She felt herself relax, slowly warming to the project. "The timing is tight, so I can't guarantee delivery."

"That's understandable."

She hesitated, wavering between fantasy and fear.

Then she smiled, and for the first time in her life, she jumped.

"You've got a deal."

"And a hell of an investment," Mark said, reaching for her, but she whirled away, heading across the lawn to the tent and the rest of the wedding. Cornish hens, a few toasts, and she'd be on her way home, alone.

Somehow, though, she wasn't surprised when he fell into step beside her.

"I'll need measurements as soon as possible," she said, slowing her pace only when she spotted Julie's shawl draped over a bush. Casting one curious glance at the tent, she picked up the shawl and carried on. "And you'll have to approve the fabric samples right away so I can place the order."

"I'll trust your judgment on the fabric, and you make the dress to fit yourself."

Rachel shook her head. "It has to fit the model who'll wear it at the show." She sidestepped a bit of lace that looked suspiciously like Julie's collar.

Mark bent to pick it up. "My sister is shedding," he said and held it out to Rachel.

She had to smile. "So it seems," she said and carefully folded the collar over her arm, knowing Julie was truly happy at last. She lifted her head and carried on, her pace as brisk as her voice. "I'll give you the names of the women I've used in fashion shows. Maybe one of them will be available."

She stood at the entrance of the tent for a moment, her eyes moving slowly, taking in the ice sculpture, the flowers, and Julie and Harry moving from group to group, getting the party rolling.

"Jane Austen never had it so good," Rachel said as Julie turned and pointed at them.

"Hey you two," she called. "Wait right there."

Mark stood back, not quite believing it was the same bride. She was smiling, laughing, pausing to kiss a cheek or shake a hand, looking confident and relaxed. Looking like Julie again, he realized.

He ran a hand over his chin as she drew up in front of them. The dress looked different somehow, too. Better, without all the extras. In fact, as she drew closer, he saw now what she had meant when she'd told him that her wedding would be about romance and old lace. And he was glad Rachel had agreed to the deal when she had.

"We're going to cut the cake soon," Julie said. "And we'd like the two of you to be in the picture."

Rachel shook her head. "I really couldn't—"

But Julie was already floating away. "Don't go away."

Rachel hoped her smile was suitably chipper. "Wouldn't dream of it."

Mark reached out and took her hand. "Be honest. Does wedding cake really keep you awake?"

He stroked his thumb lazily across the back of her hand, and she sighed. "You'd be surprised," she said as she pulled away. "I know I was."

She watched Julie stop to chat some more and knew it would be a while before there were any pictures. She saw the head table, her place waiting and ready, but found she wasn't ready to sit down after all. She needed to walk, to think, to plan the dress. And avoid the wedding cake pictures if at all possible.

So she set Julie's accessories on a chair and strolled on, with no destination in mind, Mark still at her side.

"We could call a modeling agency in Miami," she suggested.

Mark shook his head. "But it was your face in the drawing."

She groaned. "Put it down to professional vanity. A pro would be a much better choice for the contest."

"Well, I can't imagine anyone else in that dress. And as you said yourself, the customer is always right."

"Caught by my own rule," she said, surprised to find herself warming to the idea. They reached the entrance to the English garden and Rachel slowed, the gown forgotten for the moment.

On the other side of the gate was a small private world of neatly trimmed box hedges, stone paths, and a pond with a splashing fountain. It was empty except for the odd bird darting between the trees.

"I honestly believe this garden is the whole reason they bought this house," Mark said. "It's Julie's favorite spot."

"I'm not surprised," Rachel said, stepping gingerly through the gate, as though she was trespassing. "She should have held the wedding here. It would have been perfect with the outfits."

Mark squared his shoulders, quite the gentleman all of a sudden, and offered his arm. "Miss Banks, may I escort you to the fountain?"

Seeing what he was about, she dipped her chin most coyly. "Mr. Robison, you put me in an extraordinary position. Is it not improper for us to be alone in such a secluded place?" She lifted a hand and laid it lightly upon his arm. "Twice around, shall we?"

"Julie had planned to have the ceremony in here," Mark said as they strolled. "But the guest list got out of hand."

Rachel nodded. "That explains why she said it would be small." She paused by the pond, watching the goldfish swim in lazy circles. "But the baby can rest assured that mom and dad are happy, and that's what matters."

"Do you ever think about having children?" Mark asked.

She looked up at him. "I know that I want them. But I'd need a husband first."

"How very traditional, Miss Banks."

She laughed and sank down on the grass. "I hear it's coming back into style."

"I'm curious," he said and sat down beside her, close but not touching. "What kind of wedding does a woman who makes wedding gowns imagine for herself?"

"Small," she said immediately. "Only family and close friends. A ceremony at sunset, on the beach. Dinner afterward—beef wellington I think—and dancing until dawn." She laughed, embarrassed, and smiled at him over her shoulder. "I've had a lot of time to think about it."

"I can tell."

She held his gaze for a moment, watched his eyes lower to her mouth and linger before returning to her eyes. She'd felt it, the sudden change in the air that this man could create with just a glance. And she waited for him to touch her, to make good on the promise in his eyes. But he didn't, and she turned away, knowing she should be relieved yet feeling only a growing tension, a tightening deep inside.

"What kind of dress will you wear?" he asked, his voice low and a little husky, like a whisper in the dark.

"That's the one thing I don't know," she said, her own voice a little shaky, uncertain. She leaned over the pool, dipping her hand into the water, needing a distraction. "I've made so many, I guess I've confused myself along the way." She ruffled the surface of the water and watched the ripples spread in ever-widening circles. "All I know for sure is that it will be different from anything I've ever made. And something my husband will remember for years."

Jealousy. It washed over him so suddenly that he had no time to think about what it meant. Knowing only that it brought back the memory of that first night on the beach and the way she had looked at him—those brown eyes soft and trusting, and seeing someone else.

Which was just as well. He was leaving in a matter of weeks anyway. Going back to a flat in London where minimalist didn't begin to describe the decor, and food was a four-letter word for take-out.

He could already picture himself there, watching the news and checking the stringers. Waiting for the next big story to break, and missing her so much it made him ache just to look at her now.

She lifted her hand from the water, the drops glistening on her skin. "We should return to the wedding, Mr. Robison."

"Miss Banks," he said, touching a hand to her arm when she would have left.

"You are impertinent, sir," she said, turning slowly, playing the game still.

But her smile faded when he moved closer, taking his hand from her arm only so he could seek out the tender nape of her neck and bring her to him.

Her fingers closed on his wrist as if to stop him, and his heart pounded harder when he realized that she meant no such thing. That she was simply holding on, waiting.

He touched his lips to her forehead, her eyelids, not yet allowing himself the pleasure of her mouth as he breathed in the scent of her skin, her hair. She raised her head and he felt her breath on his lips, warm and sweet, as he finally gave himself over to the need that had been building for far too long.

"Rachel," he whispered, but his words were cut short by the sound of running feet at the gate.

They turned as a waiter rushed toward them.

"Are you Mark Robison?" the man called.

Mark was already on his feet. "What is it?"

"It's your sister, the bride." The waiter stopped and looked anxiously from Rachel to Mark. "We've already called an ambulance."

NINE

The doors slid open before them, silent and efficient. The corridor was crowded, the waiting room full. Saturday afternoons were always busy in the emergency room at St. Michael's Hospital.

A small boy with a barking cough lay in his mother's arms, while across from them a young man sat with his bandage-wrapped hand in his lap, his eyes closed, his lips moving silently. Was he praying or giving someone hell? It was difficult to tell.

Mark and Rachel headed for the desk. A few heads turned as they passed, faces impassive, quickly assessing the rank of the newest additions. Were they in worse shape? Better? Would it affect their place on the list?

Mark cursed under his breath and quickened his pace, hating the idea that his sister was anywhere in this place. "Julie Hetherington," he said to the nurse at the desk, then turned to Rachel, suddenly at a loss. "Or is it Desrosiers now?"

Rachel took his hand and held on tight. "It's Hetherington," she told the nurse. "She came in a few minutes ago."

The nurse gave them both a quick once-over. "Nice costumes. You in a play or something?"

He thought of the rose garden, her skin heated, her

perfume warmed by the sun. And he wished he had kissed her when he had the chance.

"A wedding," Mark muttered, wishing he'd left more than the waistcoat and cravat behind.

"Not your own, I hope." The nurse pursed her lips as she reached for a clipboard. "Because this is a heck of a place to spend your wedding day."

"My sister's. Julie Hetherington." Mark rubbed at a knot of tension in the back of his neck. "Is her name on the list?"

A phone rang and the nurse held up a finger. "Hang on a moment," she said, then turned her back to answer the call.

"Great," Mark muttered and turned to Rachel, watching her drum impatient fingers on the counter. Her eyes moved from nurse to clock to nurse again.

"Enough of this," she muttered, then shot a hand over the edge, spun the clipboard around, and brought it up to eye level. "They took her straight to maternity," she said, then dropped the board back on the desk and scanned the hall. "Elevators are over there." She pulled him forward. "There's bound to be a floor directory nearby."

Mark smiled as she led him along the hall. She might still be dressed in the style of another era, but there was nothing demure in the set to her jaw or the length of her stride. And when she jabbed a finger on the directory board and said, "Third floor—come on," he wondered if she realized who was running interference now.

A knot of people waited by the elevators—a man with a bouquet of daisies in a pink ceramic bootie and a broad, secret grin, two middle-aged women in golf skirts and visors, faces drawn, drained of color, and a few feet away a teenager holding up the wall and trying not to look worried.

Mark stood back, watching the numbers above the door, saying nothing, but still holding tight to Rachel's hand, glad to think of nothing beyond the warmth of that touch and the need for both Julie and the baby to be fine.

The elevator opened on the third floor. Paddington Bear waved from his spot on the wall, the man with the flowers smiled an apology as he squeezed past, and the women and the teenager hung back, their stop yet to come.

While Rachel asked questions at the nurses' station, Mark's eye was drawn farther along the hall, to where the man with the flowers had paused at the nursery. He saw the tenderness in the man's face as he leaned close, his thick fingers barely touching the glass while the nurse lifted up the child that was his.

Mark knew nothing of babies beyond what he had captured on tape over the years. A birth in the middle of mortar fire in Bosnia. A mother, still a child herself, hunched over a bundle in an alley in South America. A firefighter in Ireland, tears staining his cheeks as he placed an oxygen mask over a baby's face and shouted a prayer to any God that was listening.

He'd been witness to all of those moments, but not part of any of them. When the red recording light clicked on, a detachment took over, turning everything on the other side of the camera into just another scene, another news story. But there was no camera to separate him now, nothing to hide behind. And he stood, unable to move, watching the man and thinking of Julie, and caught between wonder and fear.

"Rachel, Mark," Harry called.

Mark turned to see Harry coming toward them, his shoulders more stooped than usual and his face drained of color. There were no questions in his eyes this time, no curiosity about them being there together. Only Julie and the baby mattered now.

"Thanks for coming," Harry said, his voice ragged and soft.

Mark hugged him hard. "We wouldn't be anywhere else." He glanced around. "Are my parents here?"

Harry shook his head. "They fought in the lobby over who would come up first. My parents ended up driving them back to their hotels. Separate cars, of course."

Mark nodded, resigned.

"Where is Julie now?" Rachel asked softly, still standing back, as though she was somehow intruding. Mark reached for her hand and drew her forward, needing her to be part of the circle.

"She's with the doctors," Harry said. "But they won't let me in." He gave a short, strangled laugh as he stepped back. "I guess frantic husbands aren't much use at a time like this."

"What have they told you?" Mark asked, and Rachel started to move apart. But he looped an arm around her waist, his fingers resting lightly on her hip, holding her there beside him.

She glanced up, questions in her eyes, but he stayed focused on Harry, simply tightening his grip a little, letting her know he wanted her to stay.

"Only that her blood pressure is far too high. They're trying to stop the labor, to give them both more time, but there's no way of telling which way it will go right now." He broke off and closed his eyes. "I never should have pushed for the wedding. I knew she was scared, but I kept at her, needing her to see that we could make it, that we were different." He opened his eyes and took a few useless steps toward her door. "If anything happens to her or the baby—"

"They'll be fine," Mark cut in, refusing to show his own fear. "She's too stubborn for anything else."

A shadow of a smile touched Harry's lips. "You're right there."

"Mr. Desrosiers."

They turned as one and a nurse beckoned from a doorway. "The baby is definitely coming. Your wife needs you now." She held up a hand as the three moved forward. "Just you. Your friends will have to wait in the lounge."

Harry shot them an apologetic look. "If you want to leave, I'll understand."

"We'll be right here," Mark told him, and was rewarded with a slap on the wrong shoulder and a smile.

The lounge was no more than a sunny nook with a leather couch, a line of wooden chairs, and a low table stacked with old magazines and new picture books. A pair of proud grandparents stood by the window, passing snapshots to a circle of smiling relatives, while a young woman sat with her baby on the sofa, rocking slowly back and forth, just watching the baby's hand curl and uncurl around her finger, letting the world pass by.

"I think that's what I like most about babies," Rachel whispered beside him. "You just can't hurry them."

"And you can't slow them down either." He crossed to the table and flipped through magazines, seeing nothing, but needing to move, to do something. Too restless to stand still, he dropped the stack on the table again and paced the length of the room.

The proud grandparents had made Rachel part of their entourage now, regaling her with stories and handing her snapshots one at a time so she wouldn't miss a thing. Their first grandson. Nearly ten pounds. Full head of hair. Too bad he has his father's ears.

It was all just noise to Mark, but Rachel seemed genuinely interested. There was nothing forced in her laughter, nothing patronizing in her questions. She was simply enjoying their happiness, just as she did with the women who came to her shop.

Yet every once in a while she'd turn, seeking his eyes, and then she'd smile; making him believe that everything was going to be fine.

Impatient for answers, he squeezed past the grandparents. "I'll be back," he said to her and stepped through the door.

The hall was mercifully quiet compared to the lounge, but there was no one at the nurses' station. He banged a fist on the counter, then scrubbed a hand roughly over his face.

"You're close to her, aren't you?"

He felt her voice as much as heard it, like the brush of silk across his skin.

He shrugged, and she fell into step beside him as he walked to the end of the hall. "When you grow up in a house where the adults are children, the kids learn to look out for each other."

He stopped at the window and stared out at the gravel roof, seeing himself and Julie on another roof, on another summer afternoon, listening to the shouts and accusations in their parents' room. All the while waiting for someone to miss them, to notice they were gone.

He turned his back on the window. "But if the kids are lucky, they also get to make their parents' lives hell along the way."

"You mean like hanging from a catwalk under a bridge to take pictures of a raccoon." He looked over at her and she shrugged. "Julie opened up a little yesterday." He raised a brow, and she laughed. "Okay, she's opened up a lot. But it was the first time she ever talked about you."

Mark wasn't sure if he was insulted or relieved. "She

always did like the raccoon story. Probably because the whole thing was her idea."

"And here I thought you were being a hero."

"I was determined to save them, sure. But dragging my mother into it, that was pure Julie." He smiled slowly, remembering. "She was very good at staging even then. My mother pulled into the parking lot under the bridge just as I let go and was in full swing. The scream that woman let out is still legend in parts of Key West."

He grinned, and Rachel saw the boy he had been, cocky and swaggering, full of the bravado that comes with being nine and knowing he'd won, and Rachel couldn't help smiling back. "And the raccoons?"

"The shots I took ended up on the local television station that night and a rescue team was out there the next day." His voice took on the deep, solemn tones of a network anchorman. "Never underestimate the power of a camera."

"Is that when you were hooked?"

"Both of us were. I was going to be a filmmaker. Not movies, mind you, but film. Gritty documentaries, life-altering shorts, and shocking, independent, full-length features. Julie would be the star, of course."

She laughed, and he felt the warmth of that sound seeping into him, lighting up corners that had been dark for so long, he'd forgotten all about them.

"So, did you ever make any life-altering shorts?" she asked, bringing him back.

He shook his head, then leaned his back against the wall and reached for her, expecting the hesitation, the doubt; but he was unprepared for the sudden flash of need when she slipped her arms around his waist and laid her head against his chest.

"But you and Julie were such a good team," she said. "What happened?"

"We grew up," he said, and she tipped her head back, watching the boy disappear, leaving behind a man whose eyes were shadowed with worry, and a sadness she'd seen before.

Without thinking, she raised a hand and cupped his face in her palm, wanting to bring him back, to know more, to understand. But a nurse poked her head around the corner and they drew apart, the moment lost.

"Mr. Desrosier asked me to come and tell you that it won't be long," the nurse said, her tone as brisk as her manner.

"How's Julie?" Mark asked as they followed her along the hall.

"She's doing fine. The baby, too." She stopped at the station and gestured to the lounge. "We'll keep you posted."

Harry's parents arrived, both of them talking at once, demanding answers from the nurse at the desk.

Rachel winced. "Looks like Julie's going to get more family than she bargained for."

Several hours and coffee runs later, Harry's mother finally admitted that the wedding dresses weren't so bad after all, and Mark was trying to explain digital cameras to Harry's bewildered dad. But all four turned as one when Harry appeared in the doorway, his eyes still moist, his legs unsteady.

"It's a girl," he whispered, then cleared his throat. "We have a little girl."

The baby was held in the nursery under observation for the next little while. But the nurse pointed her out to the crowd at the window, and it was generally agreed that she was the most beautiful baby ever born.

The nurse was less accommodating about the number of visitors in Julie's room. "Two," she said, holding up two fingers. "And five minutes max. She needs to rest."

It was agreed that Rachel and Mark would go first, only because Mark quietly threatened revenge if anyone went in before him. But Rachel forgave him, owing to the hour.

Harry was plumping a pillow behind Julie's head when Rachel and Mark stepped into the room. The only other bed in the room was still all crisp corners and tight blankets, waiting for the next new arrival.

Julie looked small and pale against the stark white sheets, and an intravenous line snaked across the blankets to the hands folded on her somewhat flatter belly. But her smile was bright and quick, and Rachel saw some of the tension in Mark's face ease.

"Did you see her?" Julie asked. "Did you see how perfect she is? I can't believe she's really here. She's really ours." Her smile froze. "But I ruined lunch, didn't I? All those people, all those Cornish hens." She groaned. "The caterer must have had a fit."

"Forget the caterer," Mark said, brushing the hair back from her forehead. "How're you feeling?"

"Good. Sore." Rachel pursed her lips as she took a glass of water from Harry. "Tired."

Harry was already closing the blinds. "I'll tell my mom and dad to go get something to eat. They can come back later."

Julie shook her head. "Don't do that. They've waited all this time. I want to see them."

He kissed her lightly and let his hand rest on hers. Then he slapped Mark on the arm. "Help me explain to my mother that five minutes really means five minutes."

Mark shot Rachel a quick glance, then followed Harry out the door, almost colliding with a nurse and a vase of yellow daisies. She swung the vase up and out of the way, then stepped back, laughing. "That was close," she quipped, and shot Julie a wide grin. "And these are for you."

She set the vase on Julie's tray, then pointed a finger at Rachel. "One more minute."

"Yes, ma'am," Rachel said, turning back as Julie opened the card. "Who are they from?"

"Harry, of course." She buried her nose in the trembling blossoms and inhaled deeply. "He knows I love daisies," she murmured, then sighed as she rubbed the yellow from the tip of her nose. "I just wish he didn't feel so guilty."

"He blames himself for the fact that you're in here early," Rachel explained. "He wishes he'd never pushed the wedding."

"That's ridiculous," Julie said. "The only reason I'm in here is because it's hot and I wouldn't sit down enough. The baby told me, everybody told me, but I was having such a wonderful time." She glanced over at the window. "Would you put the flowers over there, where I won't knock into them?"

She closed her eyes as Rachel set the vase on the ledge. "I really am happy that he wanted to get married, that he wouldn't settle for less. Of course, he doesn't believe me; but then, who would?"

Rachel smiled, remembering the lost fichu, the shawl draped over the bush, and feeling that silly tug around her heart every time she looked at her. Shedding as a sign of contentment. She smiled. They could do worse. "I believe you, and so will Harry."

Julie opened one eye. "I didn't get a chance to thank you for helping me out this morning. If you hadn't been there, I probably would have raced out the front door and blown it for good."

"No, you wouldn't." Rachel laid a hand over hers. "If I'd thought for a moment that you didn't really want to walk down that aisle, I'd have driven the getaway car myself. You just needed someone to confirm what you already knew, and there were plenty of folks who would have been only too happy to oblige. Your brother would probably have been at the front of the line."

"You're right," Julie said and settled deeper into the pillow. "He just wouldn't have been as subtle. The direct approach was always more his style." She stretched, winced, and lay still again. "I've always admired that about Mark. He wants something, he gets it. No waffling, no doubts, just action."

"That's for sure," Rachel murmured, the memory of that slow, sweet seduction in the garden humming through her, quick and hot. And making her wonder what would have happened if the baby had waited a while longer.

Julie studied her for a moment, then closed her eyes again. "I meant to ask: Did you two get on okay at the wedding?"

"Just fine," Rachel said lightly. "He's very friendly." She paused, listening to her friend's contented sigh. "I'm curious," she whispered. "When exactly did you know that you were doing the right thing?"

"When I saw him."

"Saw him?"

"At the altar." A tiny smile played on her lips. "All this time I've been so afraid that I was making another mistake, that I was going to end up in the same situation as last time. Then you told me to take a look outside, and there he was, standing at the altar with my brother, just waiting. And even though he was wearing a waistcoat and a cravat and a hat, he was still Harry. My Harry. The one who gets up first every day to make tea. The one who knows my moods almost before I do. The one who has never once asked me to be anything but what

I am. And he was standing there in front of all those people, waiting for me and our baby."

She opened her eyes and looked to Rachel, clearly still astounded. "And neither one of us could think of a single reason to run."

"So you saw it was Harry, and that was enough?"

They turned at the sound of Harry's voice in the hall, explaining to the nurses in that calm manner of his that his wife liked to have certain things around her. Like fresh flowers, and beeswax candles and Mozart concertos.

Julie looked over at her, speaking quickly now. "I know it sounds crazy"—she lowered her voice as the two men entered the room—"but all of a sudden I realized I didn't have to be afraid anymore."

"So you jumped," Rachel murmured.

"Jumped?"

Rachel waved a hand. "Just thinking out loud," she said as Harry approached the bed with his gifts.

She glanced over at Mark. He was leaning against the door, exhausted. But he smiled, slow and warm, and only for her. Her pulse quickened, the response as immediate as it was uncontrollable. And she only wished that she could take that jump herself. But some things she just couldn't change.

TEN

The beach was deserted, the air still, and the moon no more than a Cheshire cat grin riding far out over the gulf when Mark pulled his Jeep into his driveway. They hadn't spoken more than a few words since leaving the hospital, and every one had been about the baby—Such a beautiful little girl. What do you think they'll call her? Thank God, it's over.

But as much as Rachel would have liked to deny it, whatever had been humming between them earlier was there still, refusing to be dulled by exhaustion or the hour—or even common sense.

She glanced over at him as she swung the car door open. He was staring out at the ocean, his eyes smudged with circles and his hair ruffled from running his hands through it so many times. But still there was a restlessness, an energy about him that was almost tangible.

It was part of the appeal, she realized, the wildness that was always there, just below the surface. It was what made him prowl the beach at night and chase terrorists with a camera. And it drew her in a way she had never dreamed possible.

He turned, catching her watching, but there was nothing knowing or triumphant in his eyes as he reached for her. Just a need that was so stark, so honest, it humbled her.

He brushed a strand of hair from her face, his fingertips barely grazing her skin, but she was instantly awake— every nerve, every cell straining toward him. And wished she could be as honest.

But as she pulled away, the only thing Rachel would admit to wanting was a good night's sleep, alone. He wasn't her love or her intended, he wasn't even the man of her dream. Just a guy on vacation, with a home and a life on the other side of the world. The only thing they had in common was a contest and a wedding gown that neither of them needed. And she hoped her heart would keep that in mind next time he touched her.

She swung her legs around and stepped out of the Jeep. "Thanks for the ride," she said, plucking her bonnet and gloves from the backseat. "And if you're serious about that contest, I'll need a quick decision on the fabrics." She kept her head bent as she stuffed the gloves into the bonnet. "If you're free in the morning—"

"Why not right now?"

"It's too late." She swung the bonnet up under her arm and headed across the driveway. "How's ten o'clock sound?"

"Too early." He slammed his door and walked beside her. "Look, I don't know about you, but I couldn't sleep anyway." They stopped at her gate and he flicked open the latch. "Besides, I promised to be guided by your advice, so how long can it take?" His eyes narrowed as she passed. "You do have some suggestions, don't you?"

She smiled as she climbed the stairs. "A few."

The truth was that Rachel knew every detail of that dress, right down to the covering on the buttons, just as she did with every sketch in her studio. Before she even lifted a pencil, those gowns were already real in her mind. She saw the set of the sleeve, the curve of the skirt, and knew precisely the color, the feel, even the sound of the fabrics she would use, if given the chance.

The gown Mark had chosen had a list penciled on the back—fabrics, yardage, trim, notions. If he meant what he said about following her advice, they'd be finished in minutes, and she could sleep in tomorrow. She looked back at him as she unlocked her door. The only problem would be having him in her house while the moon was on the water and his face was cast in shadow.

She reached around the corner and flicked on a row of overhead fluorescents. She hadn't used them in so long, she'd forgotten that the harsh glare also came with a handy incessant buzz, a mood killer if ever there was one—and exactly what she needed. She'd keep the room overly bright, ignore the moon, and show him the door once the order was placed.

"Fine," she said, and waved him into the showroom. "I'll show you what I have in mind." She dropped her bonnet on the table, pulled the chain on the little banker's lamp, and frowned at the puddle of amber light beneath it. Shaking her head in disgust, she walked over to the sewing machines and flicked on all the lights above. She blinked at the brightness, then smiled as he closed the door. "If you don't like it, we can look at alternatives in the morning."

"That won't be necessary," he said softly and switched off the flourescent lights. "I'm sure we'll decide where we're going tonight."

His meaning wasn't lost on her. So she crossed to the swinging door and gave it a push. "You have to be very sure of what you want in matters like this." She smacked her palm against a switch on the other side, bringing the overheads to life again. "Otherwise everyone is disappointed."

He smiled and turned down the pot lights. "I don't think that will be a problem."

Awareness shivered across her skin as he came toward her, but she brushed it off with a lift of her chin and a new purpose in her step. "I always find it better not to anticipate too much." She turned on the gooseneck lamp on the desk and the track lights behind the fitting screen. "I'll get the drawing," she said, then paused at the swinging door and glanced back over her shoulder. "You wait there."

The door swung shut behind her and she stood for a moment, eyes closed, conscious of every footstep on the other side. Satisfied that he wasn't going to follow, she made her way to the studio and pulled the sketchbook from the shelf. She flipped it open to the ice-blue wedding gown, grabbed a pad and pencil, and headed back into the showroom.

She hit the overhead light switch before she went through the door and was surprised to find herself in darkness on the other side.

He smiled at her from the little table where he sat with a chair pulled way back and his legs stretched out underneath. "I always find it's better not to anticipate too much."

"That wasn't anticipating." She snaked her arm around the door and smiled when the flourescent lights started to buzz. "That was hedging my bets."

He nodded as she approached. "A subtle yet important distinction."

"Precisely," she whispered, staying just out of reach as she dropped the sketch book on the table. "The list of materials is on the back of the drawing. I'll show you the samples and we'll take it from there."

"Whatever you decide is fine with me." He set the

drawing down and got to his feet. "I trust your judgment."

It's nice one of us does, she thought, but she couldn't help watching as he came toward her, neither slow nor fast, just steadily, inevitably, crossing the space between them. She felt the tug deep inside, faint but familiar; as fundamental as breath itself. And she knew it had nothing to do with the moon or a dream or anything else. He was a beautiful man. Not in a pretty or traditional sense, but in a completely masculine way that unnerved as much as it fascinated. And she'd been a fool to think that bright lights could help her.

She turned, suddenly awkward and graceless as she grabbed two fabric sample books from the rack and walked briskly to the cutting table. "I think you'll like the selections in these," she said and slapped them down on the table, needing noise and chatter and the safety of things known and understood.

She flipped through the layers of shimmering silks and satins, focusing on the textures and colors, and the dress she would make for the contest.

"I see layers of washed silk organza for the skirt," she continued, knowing he was close and forcing herself to concentrate. "To give the dress a floating, gossamer feel."

"Gossamer," he whispered and slipped his fingers in her hair, seeking out pins and gently removing them one by one; taking her resolve with them. "What else?" he asked, and laid his hands on her shoulders when she would have pulled away. "Tell me what else you see."

"The color," she whispered, and closed her eyes against a rush of pleasure when his lips skimmed the side of her throat.

"What color?" he asked, his voice tickling inside her ear.

"Like ice," she breathed. "White. Blue. It's hard to tell because it changes with the light."

"Go on," he said, his fingers gripping her shoulders and pulling her back; cradling her against his shoulder as he kissed a moist, tender trail along the side of her neck.

"Satin," she said and tilted her head to the side. "The bodice is silk and satin, pure white, with a single satin rose on each shoulder."

"It's beautiful," he said. "And all the more so because you'll be wearing it."

She opened her eyes, remembering. The contest, the runway, the only thing they had in common.

"Only if we get this ordered," she said, and twisted away.

"Rachel—"

"Don't," she said, stacking the sample books on top of each other and sliding them farther down the table. Refusing to look at him, to feel anything more. "The prices are here," she continued, and flipped to the back page. "They're steep; I won't try and tell you otherwise. The organza alone is going to set you back a lot of money."

"I don't care about the money," he said and reached for her.

She flinched and walked away, not stopping until she had put the width of the table between them. "What do you care about then? The fabrics? The colors?" She shoved the books across the table. "Show me which ones you want. Do you even remember?"

"Ice blue organza for the skirt. Silk satin, pure white for the bodice." His voice was low, his tone neutral enough to make her skin prickle, but he made no move to follow her around the table. "One rose on the shoulder. How am I doing?"

"Just fine," she said, and crossed to her desk on legs

that were still shaky. She pulled an order form from the tray, scribbled down the names and colors of the fabrics, yardage, and trim, and carried it back to him. "Since everything is to your liking, sign here." She slapped it down on the table in front of him. "Press hard. You're making four copies."

He pushed the form aside. "What is this about?"

"The contest, the dress. Getting the entry in on time and the fabric ordered. What did you think it was about?"

He took hold of her hand. "I thought it was about us."

"There is no 'us,' " she said, and started to pull away.

He placed his other hand over hers, keeping her there. Not with force or strength, but with a tenderness she found much harder to fight.

"You can't deny that something's happening here." He raised her hand, his eyes never leaving hers as he kissed her fingertips, her palm, the racing pulse at her wrist. How could she have known that a touch so sweet, so chaste, could make her burn this way?

He laid her hand against his chest, his heart. The beat was strong and fast, an echo of her own, impossible to resist. His arms were around her now, pulling her close. "I don't want to be your neighbor," he whispered, his fingers finding their way into her hair, tilting her back. "Or your friend."

She saw the intent in his eyes, and with it the promise of passion, of endless nights and hot, shimmering days. All she had to do was take it. And God help her, she wanted to. But she couldn't move, could barely breathe, until his hand moved to her breast, and she could no longer be still.

She pressed against his palm and raised her mouth to his, her hands cupping his face, drawing him down. He spoke her name and kissed her softly, softly, while he stroked her, caressed her, drove her slowly mad with frustration and need.

She dipped her tongue into his mouth, felt him tense and then relax, deepening the kiss as he searched out the buttons on the back of her dress.

Her own fingers shook as she touched the buttons on the front of his shirt, wanting to see him, to touch him, and finding herself too shy, awkward. He helped her then, his eyes on her mouth, her breasts as the shirt slid to the floor, leaving him naked to the waist before her.

She splayed her fingers on his chest, allowing them to curl in the soft dark hair and explore the well-defined muscles. He drew in a long breath when she circled a nipple with her fingernail. She looked up, puzzled, when he took her hand. But she understood when he bent to her, nipping her earlobe as he whispered, "I want to take you to bed." He straightened and smiled. "But it's your house."

Rachel hardly recognized herself as she led him past the mirror by the fitting screen. But she kept going, past the desk and the table to the swinging door. He stopped to turn off the lights and she looked back, seeing, before the lights died, the scar on his back, the old war wound, and remembering all too clearly exactly who she was. And why she couldn't go through that door.

She drew her hand away and switched on the lights again. "I'm sorry. This is a mistake."

She watched his shoulders slump, saw him push a hand through his hair. And when he looked at her with understanding, with tenderness, Rachel felt her heart begin to break.

"It's okay," he said, reaching for her again. "We can take it as slow as you want."

The touch of his hands on her skin was almost enough to change her mind. But she knew in that instant that she could fall in love with this man. Grow accustomed to his touch, his smile, his voice in the dark. And when she did, she wouldn't be able to stop herself from thinking about marriage and children—all the things that meant love to her. And nothing to him.

"You don't get it, do you?" she said, anger making her tone sharp, her voice cold. "We aren't going to take it slow, fast, or anything else. Because I don't want what you have to offer."

Irritation crept into his voice. "What are you saying?"

"You said you don't want to be my friend or my neighbor. So what do you want to be, Mark? My lover? My summer fling?" She crossed to the cutting table and picked up his shirt off the floor. "Go ahead, pick one."

"You can't put it like that—"

She whirled and pointed a finger. "Crush du jour, how's that sound?" She tipped her head back, as if considering. "Slightly exotic, yet completely ridiculous. Much like ourselves."

"Rachel, stop—"

"No, you stop." She tore his copy from the bottom of the order form and held it out with the shirt. "I'll have the supplier send the confirmation to you. Payment is due on delivery."

He threw the shirt over his shoulder, tucked the bill in his pocket. "Will you sit down a minute? Talk to me at least?"

"You're leaving in a few weeks. What more is there to say?"

She was moving again, to the door this time. Damning the moon as she stepped outside, and wishing for the first time in her life that she was someone else. Perhaps a woman who was quick to love and just as quick to forget. Or one who was cynical about love, and men, and saw only the worst in both. Either would be easier than what she was. A woman who still believed.

She looked around as he came through the door. He hadn't bothered to dress and his skin looked soft and smooth in the moonlight. The urge to run to him, to hold him hard, to feel his hands on her again was instant and strong. So she turned and walked to the railing, not wanting him near.

He stood beside her but at a distance. "I'm curious: What do you dream about at night? What do you see when you close your eyes and sleep?"

She almost laughed. "You don't want to know."

He moved a step closer. "Let me ask you this, then. When you think about that sunset wedding, do you see yourself alone afterwards? For weeks at a time, maybe months. Sometimes knowing where your husband is, sometimes not. Is that what you see?"

"Of course not—"

"Then you understand why I can't offer you what you want."

She looked away. "I don't remember asking for a thing."

"You don't have to," he murmured. "I knew the first time I kissed you. You're the type of woman who equates sex with love, and love with marriage. It's old-fashioned as hell, but there it is, and you can't change who you are. Just as I can't change who I am."

She looked down at her hands. "I wouldn't want you to."

He leaned back against the railing. "So where do we go from here?"

"Nowhere," she said, and turned back to the house. "I just want you to leave."

ELEVEN

Mark pulled up in front of the address Sofia Margolies had given him. Roy Winston Elementary, a nondescript, flat-roof public school in an aging neighborhood.

The population at Roy Winston was bolstered with busloads of kids from new developments. Mark arrived at dismissal and stood well back as a laughing, jostling, noisy line of children filed through the door. He tried to see if he could spot Chuck's daughter, Brittany, in the crowd, but the picture in his mind was the same as the one in Chuck's wallet. And none of the children looked to be four years old.

When the line began to thin, he went through the door and immediately reported to the glass window on his left. A woman seated at the desk on the other side glanced up.

"Mark Robison to see Sofia Margolies."

She slid a binder toward him. "Sign in. Third door on the right."

Student artwork adorned the walls along the hall. Smiling suns, stick families—some things were eternal, he thought as he reached the principal's office. Then he saw Sofia Margolies and realized some things would never be the same.

Sofia was no grim-faced principal with white hair and

wire-rimmed glasses. She was sitting on the floor with a little boy, trying to tug the knot out of a sneaker lace with her teeth. Both were laughing and pulling faces. When she finally worked the knot free, she let her tongue hang out of her mouth while she retied the bow, further delighting the little boy.

Shoes fixed, she helped him to his feet and, when he dashed out of the office, grabbed a cup from her desk and took a long drink. She turned when Mark knocked on the door and waved him in while she drained the cup.

"How can I help you?" she asked, shuddering once as she set the cup down.

He held out a hand. "Mark Robison. We spoke on the phone yesterday."

She squared her shoulders and stretched herself up, growing taller before his eyes. But it was the change in her expression that fascinated him. The smile was long gone, and her eyes no longer held light and humor. In a matter of seconds, she'd become the embodiment of every grim-faced principal he'd ever met.

"Sit down," she said, and walked around behind her desk. She lifted the receiver as she sat, dialed a number and swiveled the chair around so her back was to him. "He's here," she said into the phone, then swung around and hung up the phone. "Security is on the way. Just in case you make trouble." She folded her hands on the desk. "Tell me again what my ex-husband wants."

"A tape of the school play," Mark said, refusing to look over his shoulder when he heard footsteps behind him. "Brittany told him over the phone that she's singing—"

"She's the lead," Sofia cut in. "And not because she's my daughter." Her mouth twitched, almost smiling. "The girl is good."

Mark gave a single solemn nod. "That's why Chuck is looking forward to seeing the tape."

This time, Sofia did smile, and it was enough to raise the tiny hairs on the back of Mark's neck.

"Chuck always did have a sense of humor." She rolled the chair back from the desk and stood up. "It was nice to meet you, Mr. Robison. And you can tell Chuck from me that he can go straight to hell. There will be no tape of that performance or anything else heading his way."

Mark held up a hand, confused. "But when you said you'd meet with me—"

"I just wanted to see what the friend of a scumbag looks like. And I must say, I'm disappointed. You actually look like a nice guy." She glanced back at him. "Chuck is lucky to have you on his side. Just be sure he pays you for the gas, or the airline ticket. He can afford it." She looked past him to the door. "Good-bye, Mr. Robison. Security will show you out."

Mark felt the man behind him as he rose. "But he hasn't seen her in so long."

"Exactly," Sofia said, and opened a filing cabinet. "When he's finally interested enough, he'll find a way to get here. In the meantime, Brittany will have to be content with phone calls and presents." Sofia pulled out a file and slammed the drawer shut. "Soon, I'm sure the presents will be enough."

He cast a quick glance at the guard. He wasn't tall, but he was solid and dumb—always a nasty combination. Mark shifted his attention back to Sofia. "Ms. Margolies, be reasonable—"

"I have been reasonable." She sent him another chilling smile. "Otherwise you'd have been thrown out the moment you set foot in the building." She turned her back on him and straightened a stack of paper. "And if you're thinking of sneaking in, or getting someone to pose as a parent, save yourself the trouble. Entry is by ticket only, and they sold out weeks ago." She looked back at him. "Good day, Mr. Robison."

Rachel stepped back from the dressmaker's form and shook her head. "I don't fink it wiw wook."

The bridal party at the table fell silent, the teapot stopped singing, and the bride slowly turned her head. "I beg your pardon?"

Rachel took the pins out of her mouth. "I said it's not going to work."

Melissa Scott-Wilson dabbed at her lips with a napkin. "What are you talking about?"

"The flowers you brought," Rachel said, and stabbed the pins into the cushion on her wrist, taking care to avoid her skin this time. Then she scooped up the little embroidered forget-me-nots scattered on the tray beside her and held them out to Melissa. "I'm sorry, but I just can't find a way to make them work."

The bride made no move to take the flowers. "I thought we decided to scatter them across the bodice."

Rachel gave her dress a sharp tug and squared her shoulders. "You decided, Melissa. I merely said I'd try, which I did, and confirmed what I knew the moment you unwrapped them. They ruin the line, conflict with the lace, and turn the dress into something I won't put my label on." She lifted the woman's hand and placed the flowers in her palm. "They just don't work."

The bride looked down at the flowers, then back at Rachel. "Rachel, let me be blunt. I don't care about your label, your opinion, or anything else for that matter." She thrust the flowers toward her. "These flowers were part of my mother-in-law's gown and I want them to be part of mine. Do I make myself clear?"

"Perfectly," Rachel said, and folded her arms. "And

since they're that important, you can sew them on the garter, pin them in your hair, or staple them to your underwear for all I care. But they are not going on that gown."

Amanda came through the swinging door with another tray of pastries and a big smile. "How we doing in here, folks? I've got more petits fours and the kettle is just about to whistle. . . ."

"I don't have to take this," the bride said and slid her chair back.

Amanda backed up a step. "I could always make coffee—"

"No coffee," Rachel snapped. "Melissa is just leaving."

The bride's mouth tightened; then she stuffed the forget-me-nots into her purse and the rest of the bridal party scraped back their chairs. "I'll have Henderson's in Reddington pick up the gown," she said, and led her party through the door. "I'm finished with the Bridery."

"And the Bridery has never been happier," Rachel said and slammed the door.

"Let me guess," Amanda said, plucking a petit four from the tray as she sat down. "You said no to the forget-me-nots."

"I'm pretty sure I told her to staple them to her underwear." Rachel winced, still staring at the door. "I can't believe I did that. What was I thinking?" She put a hand on the doorknob. "I have to stop them. I have to apologize—"

"Rachel, wait," Amanda called, already on her way to the door. "Ask yourself one question first. Did it feel right?"

Rachel glanced over at the dress. "Absolutely. But it was her dress, her wedding—"

"And if she's smart, she'll listen to you." She put an

arm around Rachel's shoulder and led her back to the table. "At least let it cool down a bit before you do anything." She held out the tray. "Have a petit four."

Rachel shook her head in disgust and stuffed one into her mouth. "Never have I served store-bought pastry at a final fitting." She sighed as she licked her fingers, certain she could still smell burnt scones and scorched linens, and wondering if it was possible to glue the handle back on the sugar bowl.

She tried to remember a worse day, came up empty, and reached for another pastry. "They're very good," she admitted, then shot Amanda a guilty look. "Did I thank you for picking them up?"

She laughed. "You meant to," she said, then plunked herself down at the table and folded her hands in front of her. "Now, if you're finally ready to tell me what's going on, I'd love to hear it."

Rachel flopped into a chair and dropped her head back. "Nothing is going on. I'm just a little jumpy."

"I know jumpy, and this is bigger." Amanda picked up a petit four and waved it in the air. "This is misery or anxiety or . . ." The petit four froze midwave and she stared at Rachel. "Or love."

Rachel rubbed at a knot in her shoulders. "You were closer with anxiety."

"Whatever you say." Amanda dropped the pastry on a plate and sat back. "So, how's it going with that Kevin guy from the wedding?" She shrugged when Rachel looked over at her. "You know what they say, 'Candidness is next to godliness.' "

Rachel sighed and closed her eyes, knowing it would take longer to argue than answer. "It isn't. We're still playing telephone tag."

"Okay, how about the one next door?" She lowered

her voice and leaned closer. "He looked awfully interesting."

"Haven't seen him," Rachel said.

Not since she'd told him to leave. It was as though he'd vanished completely. No Jeep in the driveway, no parties on the porch, no sign of him at all. Yet it didn't seem to matter that he wasn't around. She could still feel his fingers in her hair, taste his kiss on her lips, and no matter how hard she tried, she couldn't shake the feeling that she'd been a fool.

She sat up quickly. "I'll go get some tea."

"He's the one, isn't he?" Amanda laid a hand on her arm, her touch gentle and her eyes knowing. "The man in the dream."

Rachel had to smile. "How would I know? I didn't see a face, remember?" Her shoulders slumped as her gaze was drawn to the window. "But he sure feels like the one."

Amanda's voice grew soft. "Tell me about him."

Rachel got to her feet and started stacking plates. "He's good-looking, charming, has an odd sense of humor." She piled cups into cups and balanced them on top of the plates. "He drives a Jeep, just discovered he likes babies . . ." She squeezed her eyes shut for a moment, then snatched up the stack of dishes. "And when he kisses me, I don't want him to stop."

Amanda made a grab for the cups, catching them just as they started to tip. "And the problem is . . . ?"

Rachel tossed her a quick, wry smile as she headed for the kitchen. "Did I mention that he lives in London, has a bullet wound in his shoulder, and is leaving town in two weeks?"

Amanda followed, cradling the cups in her arms. "Go back to the bullet wound."

"Nothing sinister," Rachel said lightly, then banged the door open with her hip. "Just an occupational hazard."

Amanda caught the door on the back swing and juggled the cups to the counter. "He's a cop?"

"Worse. The man chases terrorists with a video camera. What kind of fool does that for a living?" She set the dishes in the sink, turned on the taps, and leapt as the spray hit the plates. "But he has excellent taste. Ordered the most beautiful dress from me."

Amanda's voice went flat. "Oh, God, he's married." She turned off the taps and handed Rachel a tea towel. "Or is he gay?"

"Neither." Rachel mopped her face while she filled Amanda in on the contest and what had happened at Julie's wedding.

"The confirmation arrived yesterday and the fabrics came this morning. I've got two weeks to make the damn dress. Which isn't long enough." She threw the towel down. "And that's why I'm so jumpy."

"If you don't think you can do it, why did you agree?"

Rachel raised her hands in a gesture of helplessness. "Because of Mark. He made me believe that I can do it. And that I can win, too."

Amanda tilted her head to the side. "Sounds like this Mark could be good for you."

Rachel considered the possibility as she wandered back to the showroom. And smiled to herself when she saw Melissa Scott-Wilson's wedding gown. A week ago she would never have told a client where to put her forget-me-nots. But even now, when the practical side of her was tempted to make that call, to bring Melissa back, she couldn't quite bring herself to pick up the phone. Because it still felt right. Her gaze strayed to the window and the empty beach house next door. Maybe he had been good for her, but it didn't change the fact that he was leaving in two weeks. Or was already gone.

"So, what do you think?" Amanda said. Rachel turned and Amanda grinned at her over the dummy's shoulder. "Any regrets?"

"About Melissa?" Rachel studied the dress again and shook her head. "Not a one."

Amanda gestured to the window. "And when you look out there . . . any regrets?"

Rachel walked over and leaned her elbows on the frame, her heart all but stopping when she saw his Jeep in the driveway for the first time in three days. But still, he was nowhere in sight. She glanced at the clock, wondering if he was inside getting his news fix or out walking the beach; realizing again how little she knew about him and how little it mattered.

She gave Amanda a tiny smile. "Only that he's leaving too soon," she said, then turned and busied herself with clearing the table.

"Two weeks," Amanda acknowledged. "Which rules him out as the man from the dream." She grabbed her purse from the desk and headed for the door. "But the way I see it, those two weeks are going to pass one way or another. You can spend them in here burning scones and thinking about him. Or you can go over there and get what you want." She opened the door and glanced back at Rachel. "And when he's gone, which will you regret more?"

The door swung shut behind her, leaving Rachel alone in the showroom, torn between practicality and what felt right.

The phone rang, and she walked over to the desk. The display read KEVIN GRANT. The one who lived in Tampa and was quite possibly the man of her dreams—with blond hair.

The phone rang again. One more ring and the machine would grab it. Her fingers hovered above the receiver. If she picked it up, everything could change. He'd already suggested they meet for dinner and a movie—a Hollywood blockbuster he'd been dying to see. One she'd thought about seeing herself. But she couldn't help wondering what he'd say if she suggested a life-altering short instead. And which she would regret missing more.

The phone rang again. Rachel curled her fingers into her palm, thinking of cliffs and leaps of faith as she raced for the door, grabbing a cup along the way.

TWELVE

Rachel pressed the doorbell and stepped back, her heart pounding when she heard the sound of footsteps above the chimes.

She moistened lips that were suddenly dry, wiped palms that were oddly damp, and was just about to head for the stairs when the door opened.

He wore jeans. Nothing else. Just jeans that rode low on his hips, looked well-worn and comfortable, and made it difficult for Rachel to think. His mouth was tight and grim, his hair ruffled, as though he'd been pushing his hands through it. The hall was dark behind him and he looked distracted, impatient, as he squinted into the sun, his eyes adjusting.

She knew a moment of fear, thinking she was too late. That there was someone in there with him and he would send her away. Then he smiled, that slow, sexy curve of the lips that she liked so well, and she understood that she was right on time.

But instead of making it easier, he leaned a shoulder against the door and folded his arms, leaving everything up to her.

She smiled, bolder now, and lifted the cup that she'd brought. "I ran out of coffee," she said, finding a voice that was soft and husky, exciting because it was hers. "I wondered where I could borrow some." She paused, watching his smile widen as she took a single step closer. "And I thought of you."

His eyes held hers as he reached out, his fingers gently caressing hers as he took the cup.

"Wait here," he said, and Rachel's heart pounded when he came back with the coffee and closed the door.

She rang the bell again and had to suppress a giggle when he opened the door. "Sugar?" she said, feeling sexy and silly, and wanting him more than she could believe when he handed her a yogurt container and closed the door.

She drew in a breath, hit the bell, and couldn't control a burst of triumphant laughter when he reached out and dragged her inside, coffee tin and yogurt container bouncing down the front steps behind her.

"What now?" he asked, grinning as he backed her against the wall.

"This should be fine," she said, looping her arms around his neck and pulling him down, hungry for the taste, the feel, the smell of him.

But he held back, his gaze level and direct. "Are you sure this is what you want?"

She saw the heat in his eyes, felt it in his hands, and knew she would settle for nothing less. She laid her hands against his chest, her fingers curling into the dusting of hair, feeling the warmth of his skin, the beat of his heart, and knew she wouldn't turn back now. "It's all I want," she whispered. "With no expectations on either side. We don't give it a name, and when it's over, we agree not to write."

"Not even a postcard," he whispered, cupping her face in his hands and kissing her softly, gently, his tongue like velvet, stroking, teasing, dipping between her lips and retreating again and again, leaving her breathless, frustrated. He chuckled when she squirmed and reached and dove her fingers into his hair, drawing him to her; kissing him deeply, thoroughly, taking what she wanted in a way she never had before.

When she finally drew her head back and opened her eyes, he was looking at her as though for the first time, seeing what, she wasn't sure. She felt her face warm and started to pull away. But he shook his head, his gaze fixing on her mouth as he slipped his arms around her waist. She saw the shift in him then, the sudden tension as he turned serious; his hands drawing her close, moving up and down her back, molding her to him.

"We fit together," he whispered, and touched his lips to hers. "Do you feel it?"

She felt nothing else. Nothing but the hard length of his body pressed against the softness of her own, filling every curve and hollow, and making her impatient for the feel of his skin against hers.

As though he had heard, as though he had always heard, he lifted a hand between them, his fingers deft and quick with the buttons of her dress. Pushing it from her shoulders, he bent to kiss the spot at the base of her throat where her pulse beat strong and fast.

He stroked his palms over her breasts, making slow, lazy circles, until her nipples strained against the lace of her bra. He lowered his head, his mouth closing on one round bud, teasing her through the restrictive bonds of lace and silk. Rachel dropped her head back, lost in sensation as she swayed against him, refusing to think beyond this moment. Just when she was sure she would go mad if she didn't feel the full heat of his mouth on her breasts, the lace was gone and his mouth was on her, greedy and searching, and unlike anything she had ever known.

She sighed and arched her back, and Mark felt his control slip another notch. He lifted his head, needing to look at her, to see her eyes closed, her lips parted and moist from his kiss. That she had come to him was wonder enough; that she wanted him so openly left him floundering, unable to believe, yet unwilling to let go.

But for all that she was passionate, sexual, there was a sweet naïveté in her response, an artlessness that touched him deeply. Made him want to bury himself inside her and stay forever, believing that this woman with the ruffled curtains and the trusting eyes could love him, a man without roots, without home, who had seen too much to believe in simple pleasures and homespun values.

She opened her eyes and smiled, and he knew he could slide into a love that had no future, but no way to end. They were too different, too far apart. If not for his sister's wedding, their paths would never have crossed, and maybe that would have been better. But now that he'd held her, kissed her, he couldn't walk away. All he could do was love her, cherish her, and when the time came to leave, know in his heart that it was for the best.

He covered her mouth with his, breathing in her sigh as he ran his hands down the length of her body, pushing the dress before him. The dress fell in a puddle at their feet, and she gasped when his hand moved between her thighs. She stilled, and he thought she might pull away, but then her hands were on his buckle, tugging impatiently as he stroked her through the silk, and there was no turning back.

He slid his jeans and briefs down and off, kicking them to the side as he hooked his thumbs into the elastic of her panties. Slowly he drew them down over her hips, her thighs, and let them slide to the floor. She stood before him, naked, beautiful, but he saw the blush rise into her face as she moved to cover herself.

Her eyes widened as he moved her hands to her sides, accepting no such modesty. "Let me look at you," he murmured, and released her hands.

Rachel watched the hunger build in his eyes as his gaze

drifted slowly over her, lingering on her breasts, the curve of her waist, and lower, making her feel wanted as never before.

Shaken by the strength of her own response, her own need, she opened her eyes and tried to push away. But he bent to her then, touching his lips to hers and whispering words of encouragement as he dipped inside her, undoing her completely. She trembled and gripped his shoulders, her legs grown weak and liquid. Had there ever been a touch so sure, a voice so compelling? The answer drifted inside her head with half-heard words of love as he found what pleased her most, but made her lead him still. She gave herself over completely then, thrusting hard against his hand as she slowly came apart, knowing instinctively that he would keep her safe.

Her knees gave beneath her and he wrapped his arms around her, pressing her back against the wall and lifting her up. Her eyes flew open and her fingers gripped his shoulders. "Here?" she whispered, shocked and thrilled by what he meant to do.

"Anywhere," he murmured, and she felt him, hard and full against her flesh.

She opened to him, taking him deeper and wrapping herself around him. When at last he filled her completely, he stilled, his body trembling with the effort to hold back, to make it last. She lifted a hand and stroked his cheek, his jaw; then she kissed him, and he was lost. He moved within her, and she found the rhythm and built on it, loving the way he looked as he lost control—eyes closed, head thrown back, and her name on his lips when release finally came.

Slowly, he let her down. Her feet touched the ground and she found her footing, but he turned his own back to the wall and pulled her to him, wrapping his arms around her and cradling her against his chest. She curled her fingers into the hair on his chest and listened while the beat of his heart, as fast and urgent as her own, gradually steadied and calmed.

She looked up at him and smiled. "Now what?"

He grinned and pressed a kiss to the top of her head. "Now, we go to your place." He gathered up her dress and held it out to her. "And we start all over again."

They ran across the stretch of beach to her house, laughing and jostling each other, each determined to be first, and mindless of the curious glances from shell gatherers and Frisbee throwers. Aware only that the distance between the houses had never seemed so great.

They burst through the front door and she stood beside him breathless, panting, and momentarily shy. When had she last had a man in her home, her bed? Too long ago, she told herself, and turned, loving the heat in his eyes and the strength in his hands as he swept her dress up and off and carried her through the swinging door.

Her room was exactly as he remembered, the color like morning sun, soft and buttery, and easy on the eyes. Potted palms shared floor space with an odd, eclectic mix of furniture—a rattan table, a pine armoire, a rosy slipper chair that made him look twice. And in the corner, a brass bed with a frothy eyelet cover, a long skirt, and pillows of every description.

He laid her on the bed, pushing pillows and cushions out of the way as he followed her down, and doing his best to ignore the squeaks and moans from the springs.

"That has got to be fixed," he growled, and she laughed, wrapping her legs around him and drawing him into her world, her life, her very soul.

* * *

At last they lay still, skin cooling and hearts slowing while the setting sun cast long shadows on the wall. He sighed, and Rachel propped herself up on one elbow to look at him. He lay on his belly, one arm thrown across her hip, staking his claim, his place, while his legs took up most of the bed.

She smiled and ran a hand across his shoulders, laying her palm gently on the scar, accepting, finally, that it was part of him. A mark of what he did, what he was, and reminding herself not to want or expect anything beyond this moment.

They had nine days, no more. She wouldn't fool herself into believing that he would stay, or convince herself that she could leave. She would let it be what it was and simply enjoy, without trying to put a name to it, or make more rules for it. And when he left, she would regret nothing.

He opened his eyes and she swept his hair back so she could see the depth of blue and the length of his lashes. He grinned, and she traced a fingertip along the fullness of his lips, gasping when he took it into his mouth and laughing when he bit.

"Hungry?" she asked, rolling him over with her foot and crawling on top to hold him there.

He nodded and reached for her, but she slipped through his fingers and out of the bed. She tossed him his jeans and crossed to the armoire. "How are you with a barbecue?"

His first thought had been to go out. To take her to Charley C's and finally find out if their grouper really was to die for. But as he watched her pull on a silky robe and belt it at the waist, he realized he didn't want to see her dressed in anything else. And wasn't ready to share her with anyone else just yet either.

"Pretty good," he said, and tugged on his jeans. "What did you have in mind?"

"I've got steaks and chicken in the freezer. Some shrimp, too, I think." She pulled her hair back and fastened it at her nape with a clip. "Of course, there's always pasta if you prefer."

He wasn't surprised. She was the kind of woman whose freezer would always be full and her pantry well stocked. She would probably be appalled to find nothing more than a good tequila and assorted mustards in his fridge; both of which, he had found, could make even the worst take-out foods palatable.

But he had years of tasteless food ahead of him. And the idea of burning meat over an open fire stirred his inner Texan and brought back a recipe for barbecue sauce that had been known to make grown men weep.

"Steak," he said, following her to the kitchen. "And a sauce you will remember forever."

Rachel topped up their wineglasses while he stacked the last of the dishes into the dishwasher and snapped it closed.

"Now be honest," he said as he accepted a glass. "Was that the best sauce you've ever had, or what?"

"It should be bottled and marketed worldwide," she said, and rose up on her toes, touching her lips to his, lightly, easily, as though it was the most natural thing in the world to have him there in her kitchen, washing dishes and talking about sauce.

Then again, they'd spent the last hour discussing the true meaning of blue rare, the merits of briquettes, and what is meant by the mystery of mesquite, all while flipping steaks, tossing salad, and simmering sauce. As though they'd been doing it forever.

"I love it when you talk business," he whispered, hauling her in and kissing her in a most unbusinesslike manner. Then he lifted his head and grinned. "Speaking of business, how's my dress coming?"

"Fine," she said, reaching her fingers into his hair, not wanting to think about the Bridery or the contest or anything at all right now. "The confirmation came yesterday, and the fabrics arrived this morning. Everything's on track."

He held back. "But?"

"But nothing," she said, avoiding his eyes. "I told you, it's fine."

"Then why is there no sign of it anywhere?" He gestured to the studio on the other side of the kitchen. "When I was in here last, you had sketches of your works in progress tacked to the corkboard. The ice-blue dress isn't up there." He looked around. "In fact, it's not anywhere, and that makes me wonder why."

"I'd forgotten your keen observation skills," she said, and looked into his eyes, knowing there was no way to hide. And finding no need to anymore. "Because I'm a little nervous. And as long as I don't cut the fabric, we can still send it back."

"What are you talking about? You know yourself that those designs are good." He shook his head. "I honestly think you can win."

She smiled, knowing she could get used to having him on her side. And pulled away so she wouldn't.

She picked up her wineglass and walked the length of the kitchen. "I've told you before, I have no credentials. And these contests attract design students from all over. Kids nineteen, twenty years old at the most, all active in some of the finest colleges in the world."

She paused at the door of her studio, her gaze moving over the drafting table, the pencils, the drawings tacked to her board. All the things that usually brought her joy but now felt like a sham.

"And everything I know, I've taught myself," she said, so softly he almost missed it. But there was no pride in her tone, only an apology he couldn't understand.

"It's funny," she continued. "I knew there was no money for college when I was growing up. No money for anything, when you come right down to it, but it never bothered me. I learned to sew for myself, to make patterns and sketch ideas. Eventually, I fell in love with design, with the creative freedom of it, and I knew it was what I wanted to do. I scoured flea markets for ideas, spent hours in the library reading fashion history and magazines, always thinking for some reason that I'd go to art school one day."

She shook her head and looked over at him. "But it never happened. I went to work right after high school. My parents moved to Sarasota, so then I had rent to pay, and bills. I kept telling myself that I'd go next year. Always next year."

"And it never came," Mark offered, and she smiled.

"Funny how that happens, isn't it?"

"And the wedding gowns?" he asked, wanting to understand how the practical little girl grew into a practical woman with a love of fantasy.

"The weddings were always there," she said, her eyes drifting back to the studio. "From the time I was little, and I used to put on my mother's veil and my father would dance me around the kitchen, I was hooked."

"You had a good family," he said.

She nodded. "Believe it or not, there are a number of them out there." She headed across to the swinging door. "When my parents were killed, we all inherited a bit of money. I figured my share would buy me one year for the Bridery, or one year of college. I chose the Bridery, hoping that if the business did well, I'd still go to college and have it all. But it's always one thing after another. The car, the insurance . . ."

Her voice trailed off and she shrugged. "So next week at the contest, the judges will see my name, my age, and a blank space where my college affiliation should be. And before I take a single step on that runway, they'll already have me pegged. A wannabe, a nothing." She downed the rest of her wine, slapped the glass on the counter. "Just another dressmaker who's too stupid to stay home. And if you want to know the truth, I'm afraid it will turn out that they're right."

He couldn't pin the precise moment when it had happened. Perhaps when he mentioned the dress, or when she looked at the calendar. All he knew was that the confidence and spirit that were usually so much a part of her were gone. And he couldn't bear to think of her losing her dream now.

"That's ridiculous." He captured her arm and made her face him. "That's not what you are, and you know it."

"Maybe," she said, and then gave him a small, sad smile. "I just wish there was more time to find out."

"Nine days isn't enough?"

She motioned him to follow her to the showroom. "See this?" She pointed to a schedule tacked to the board above her desk. "Today is Friday. I have a final fitting on Saturday, a consultation with a new bride on Monday, and a second fitting for a mother of the bride on Wednesday. The contest is the following weekend." Her hand dropped from the calendar as she turned to him. "Take away at least a day for traveling, and I don't see how I can do it."

He shook his head in disbelief. "Are you saying you want to back out?"

"No, of course not." She looked back at the schedule. "Not yet, anyway."

"If you had more time, though, you'd feel better."

She glanced back, confused. "Yes, but—"

"All right. We'll fly to Miami. There's an extra day."

She held up a hand. "Now, wait—"

"Second, you need scones and tea for the final fitting, right?" He tapped a finger on his chest. "Leave that part to me."

"Hold on—"

"Just think about it," he said. "You can do the fitting, then go back and sew while I serve."

"You serve?"

He smiled. "I do a mean cup of tea." He laced his fingers with hers and led her back to the kitchen. "Third, you cancel the consultation until you get back—"

"I can't possibly."

"Rachel, do you want this contest or not?"

She nodded, realizing only then exactly how much.

"Then tell her to wait. Now the mother of the bride I can't do much with . . ."

She looked up at him, wondering if he knew that he was doing it again. Running interference, trying to rescue her. And knowing she would miss it when he left.

"And the sewing—"

She raised a hand, keeping it light, keeping it easy. "I do all the sewing."

He gave her a bland look as they reached her bedroom door. "That's understood. I was going to offer to answer the phone."

She raised a brow as he led her to the bed. "You want to be my secretary?"

He looked hurt. "Administrative assistant," he said. "Because one way or another, you are going to enter that contest. And you are going to show them what a dressmaker on the beach can do." He took her in his arms. "Does any of this help?"

It didn't matter whether or not he'd actually made more time; what mattered was that Rachel was no longer afraid. She'd go to the contest. Walk on the runway. And damn anyone who tried to stop her.

"Oh, yes," she said, and went to him, lacing her fingers together behind his head, drawing him down.

Rachel felt his hesitation. "Is something wrong?"

He seemed to be searching for words, at a loss for the first time since she'd met him. "I don't want you to take what I've said the wrong way. I'm not trying to push into your life, or take over, or even assume I'm welcome to stay the night. As much as I want to be with you, I'll leave when you say the word."

This was new ground for Rachel. She had no experience with short-term relationships, no understanding of the etiquette. All she knew was that they'd started something that afternoon, and she wanted to hold on to it as long as possible.

"I only have one thing to say." She saw a flicker of apprehension and looped her arms around him, holding him closer. "You'll need a toothbrush."

He laughed, not in triumph but relief, and held her hard against him. "You can't know how much I wanted to hear you say that." He slipped a hand inside the robe, cupping her breast and smiling against her lips as her nipple grew taut and hard beneath his palm.

She closed her eyes and leaned into his touch, knowing she'd crossed the line and was falling fast. Falling in love with a man who had come in a dream and would be gone by full moon.

THIRTEEN

Rachel woke to sunshine, birdsong, and an empty pillow beside her. She told herself it was fine, no expectations and no guilt. But the sting of disappointment was on her before she could stop it.

She tried to push it aside as she did the sheet, but his scent, his touch were still on her skin, stirring memories of his hands, his mouth, his clever tongue. Kissing, teasing, turning her inside out and taking her to the edge again and again, finding her secrets and making them his own.

"Look at me," he'd said, and she saw again the tender longing in his eyes as he rose above her, filling her vision as he filled her body, until there was nothing in the world but him, and nothing left but to hold on tight as they were both swept over the edge. Clinging. Drowning. Safe. For now.

She shoved the sheets firmly to one side and sat up, but she could still hear his voice inside her head.

"He shoots, he scores."

She screwed up her nose and glanced at the door.

"And the crowd goes wild."

Rachel grinned, shoved her hair out of her face, and snatched her robe from the floor. He wasn't inside her head at all. He was in the showroom. And God help him if he'd touched anything.

Mark and the cutting table were halfway through the front door when she swung around the corner into the showroom. He froze, watching her skid to a stop in front of the desk and making a mental note to sleep in from now on.

Her robe was barely fastened and her hair was all tangled and unruly from having his hands in it so much last night. It framed her angel face with wild curls, making her eyes seem wider, her mouth softer. Mark felt his heart squeeze as she raised a hand to push her hair back from her face. She looked exactly as she had when he'd kissed her earlier and left her sleeping—like a woman who'd been well loved the night before and was having a hard time waking up the next morning.

"Are we bringing this thing in or not?" Brodie called from the porch. Then he poked his curly head through the door and grinned. "You must be Rachel. Nice to meet you."

She blinked and clutched the robe tighter across her breasts. Mark and people. What else had she expected?

"You, too," she said and smiled, wondering absently how many more were out there on her porch, and whether there was any coffee and if she had enough cups. And what in God's name they were doing with her table.

"I can explain," Mark said, setting his end down as Amanda crawled in under the table.

"Hi, sleepyhead," she said, then sat up, blew her bangs out of her eyes, and shook what might have been a scone at her. "Mark has come up with a recipe for the best darn hockey pucks this side of Toronto."

Rachel looked over at him. "You made pucks?"

"Scones." He shrugged as Amanda dropped it into the wastebasket with a thud. "I experimented."

"They also make dandy paperweights." Amanda dusted her hands on her shorts and smiled at Rachel. "So, when do we get started on that dress?"

Rachel shook her head and slowly backed away. "Just give me a few minutes."

"Take your time," Amanda said, and took over Mark's spot at the end of the table. "Brodie and I will finish up here. You won't believe what he's done to it."

"I can only imagine," Rachel muttered, trying not to put her cutting table and hockey puck scones in the same thought. In the kitchen, she glanced around, amazed that there were no signs of baking anywhere. Then she thought of Mrs. Dempster's new white kitchen and hurried into the bedroom.

He was right behind her. "I was sure you were going to lock me out," he said as he closed the bedroom door.

She shot him a bland look as she yanked open a dresser drawer. "There's no lock on the door." She pulled out shorts and a sleeveless blouse, and tossed them on the bed. "You could have warned me about the company."

"Probably, but I didn't have the heart to wake you." He leaned a hip against the dresser. "Besides, I only knew about Brodie. Amanda was a surprise."

"Amanda is always a surprise," she said dryly, then gave the drawer a push and opened another. "So where did you make scones?" She glanced back at him. "And what did you do to my cutting table?"

"Scones were made in the kitchen and the cutting table no longer has a wobble." He pulled the coaster she'd been using to prop the leg from his back pocket and laid it on the dresser. "It was driving me crazy."

She laughed. "Just wait till you open the fridge."

"Fixed that, too," he said, and shrugged when she raised a brow. "I was up early."

She realized then that he wasn't trying to interfere or

take over. He was just doing what needed to be done. What came naturally. And he had no idea how rare that was.

She turned to face him. "The question is, did you sleep?"

He lifted one of the ties on her robe and drew her closer. "A little."

She laid her hands against his chest and leaned into him. "Is there anything else I should know about? Any more company waiting in the wings?"

He touched his lips to hers. "Just me."

"The early riser," she murmured, then pushed him away and turned back to the drawer. "When I woke up, I thought you'd left."

"How could I?" He watched her scrunch a pair of ivory panties and a bra tightly into her hands and had to smile. After last night, there wasn't an inch of her body he didn't know intimately. Nowhere he hadn't touched her, kissed her, yet she was still shy with him. He took hold of her shoulders and turned her to face him. "I have to answer the phone, remember?"

She moistened her lips as he ran his knuckles down the inside of her arm, his fingertips grazing the side of her breast. "You were serious about that, then?"

"I was serious about all of it." His hand closed around her wrist. "The phone, the scones . . ." He slowly opened her fingers. "Everything."

She held his gaze even as a blush warmed her face. "Were there any messages?"

He narrowed his eyes while he thought. "Melissa Scott-Wilson said she's changed her mind. She'd like to come by this evening for the final fitting. I told her I'd let her know. Tammy and Gordon want to book an appointment to talk about their Las Vegas wedding dress." He slowly withdrew the silky underwear from her hand. "And Kevin wants you to call him."

It wasn't the first time he'd been jealous where she was concerned, but it was still foreign to him. Foreign and completely misplaced. The ground rules had been set, the borders drawn. They weren't going to put a name on what they had; they were simply going to enjoy. And he had no right to question her phone calls.

He tossed the bra and panties on to the bed with the rest of her clothes and tried for a suitably casual stance. "Is Kevin someone I should know about?"

"I hardly know him myself," she said, then turned and closed the drawer, an odd smile on her face. "So Melissa has changed her mind." She gathered up her clothes, making no attempt to hide anything from him this time, and dashed around the corner to the bathroom. "If she calls again, tell her she can come at seven. And tell her . . ."

Her instructions were cut off when the phone in the showroom started to ring. Mark was already on his way before she had the bathroom door fully open. "If that's Tammy," she called after him, "I'm not available for at least a week." She stepped into the hall. "And I should warn you, I could get used to having an assistant."

"That makes one of us," Mark called and ducked the shorts she pitched at him. He rounded the corner into the kitchen. "Melissa can come at seven," he repeated as he entered the showroom. "Tammy can wait a week." He made a grab for the phone, read the name on the display, and slowly pulled his hand back. "And Kevin is out of luck."

He waited until the call went to voice mail, then picked up the message he had taken earlier, dialed Melissa Scott-Wilson's number, and left her a message. That done, he strolled over to where Brodie and Amanda were seated on the cutting table. "Okay, this is serious. Who knows anything about making scones?"

Fifteen minutes later, Rachel was tucking her blouse into the shorts, pouring coffee, and wondering why it was so quiet in the showroom. She carried her mug through the door and peered around the screen. Amanda was seated behind the desk with the sketch of the ice-blue wedding gown in her hand, while Mark and Brodie hunched over a laptop computer at the cutting table.

Amanda looked up as Rachel approached. "They're researching scones. Apparently the varieties are limitless."

"He hasn't given up, then." Rachel shook her head and yanked open the top drawer of the filing cabinet beside the desk. "Is that enthusiasm or bullheadedness?"

"Probably a bit of both." Amanda set the drawing down as she got to her feet. "And I have to admit, I'm green."

Rachel rummaged through the patterns in the drawer. "Because of the scones?"

"Because of Mark," Amanda whispered, and peered over Rachel's shoulder as she flipped through the packages. "What are you looking for?"

"I'm hoping I have something on hand that will work for the bodice of that gown." She paused at one pattern, considered, rejected, and moved on to the next. "If not, it's going to take time to come up with a new one."

Amanda pulled out a package, screwed up her nose, and stuffed it back in the drawer. "Forget it. I've got exactly what you need at home." She lifted Rachel's hand from the packages and closed the drawer. "I'll get it and you can have a look." She turned Rachel around and walked her a few steps from the desk. "But right now, I am dying to know." She cast a quick glance around, then leaned in close. "Any regrets?"

Rachel heard Mark laugh and looked over at him. He and Brodie were still at the computer, Mark watching, Brodie tapping keys. The two of them laughed again; then Mark lifted his eyes and caught her staring. She smiled, a little awkwardly, despite her determination to be bold. His smile faded, growing pensive as he held her gaze. She wasn't sure what she saw in his eyes and didn't want to guess or hope. All she knew was that it made her heart pound, and made her glad he was there.

"Regrets?" she said, and turned back to Amanda. "Not one."

"I knew it." Amanda thumped the cabinet with a fist. "He may not be the one from the dream, but there's still a lot to be said for man like that. Good-looking, employed . . ." She lowered her voice and spoke out of the corner of her mouth. "He also has a very interesting friend."

Rachel laughed and reached for her coffee. "What about the stockbroker?"

"He crashed. Apparently, I am too weird for Wall Street." She gave a careless shrug. "So I held a second of silence to honor the end of the relationship and came over here."

Rachel sat on the corner of the desk and studied Amanda's face. The red fringe of bangs over startling green eyes, the slender aquiline nose, and the mouth that was full and given to quick, easy laughter. And she could only assume that the stockbroker was either blind or a fool. "Are you okay?"

Amanda looked truly puzzled. "Why wouldn't I be? The moment I pulled into your driveway, I spotted Mark. And right beside him, the most beautiful curly-haired man I have ever seen." She raised her chin. "It's like the old saying: 'A door opens and so does a window.' "

"Closes," Rachel muttered, then gave her a quick smile. "A door closes."

Amanda nodded. "That's the one. Anyway, I sat down on your porch and discovered a man who not only likes to talk but is good with his hands." She glanced back at Brodie, a tiny smile curving her lips. "He loves movies and books but never reads the reviews because he likes to be surprised." Amanda's expression changed, softened, as though she was the one surprised. "Did you see what he did for your table? No? Watch this."

She strolled over and hoisted herself up beside the laptop. Brodie grinned up at her. While the world may have tilted for Amanda, for the first time since Rachel moved it in, the table didn't budge. She had to smile. Amanda was right; Brodie was indeed good with his hands.

She watched them walk away from the laptop, leaving Mark alone, the two of them already lost in conversation. Amanda gave her a discreet thumbs-up behind Brodie's back. That was what she admired about Amanda; the stockbroker had hurt her, but she didn't let it hold her back, or keep her from jumping in again. And Rachel could only hope that Brodie really did like surprises.

She set her coffee down and let her attention shift to Mark. He was leaning over the laptop still, his fingers light and deft on the keyboard, his eyes never leaving the screen. The easygoing manner was gone. He was intense and focused now, as he'd been at the Carbones'. It was the side of him she knew so little about. The side that would take him away.

Rachel slipped off the desk and wandered closer, fully expecting that scones had given way to stringers or news flashes. And was only mildly surprised to find that it was E-mail on his screen instead.

She stood beside him, resisting the temptation to read over his shoulder. "News from London?"

He shook his head. "Central America. A friend of mine is covering a story there. Something big is going to break very soon, and he's asked me to do a favor for him while I'm here."

He straightened and reached for her, looping his arm around her waist and pulling her close. She found herself moving to him, fitting herself against him as though she could never be close enough.

"But it's not coming together the way I had hoped." He sighed and absently stroked his fingertips across her hip. A simple gesture, innocent really. Yet somehow every touch seemed intimate, a memory of what they'd shared. A promise of what was to come.

"He just sent an E-mail asking how it's going, and I don't have the heart to tell him it's not."

Rachel shook off the strange musings, the odd longings, suddenly anxious to know about his work, his friends. To fill in all the gaps quickly, because they had so little time.

She leaned her head into his shoulder. "What does he want you to do?"

Mark hesitated, staring at the screen and feeling ridiculous all over again. "He wants me to tape his daughter singing in a school play."

Rachel drew her head back and looked at him. "And you can't do it?"

Mark sighed. "It's a long story." Her eyes told him that she would have listened, wanted to listen. But Brodie was approaching, and there was no time. He pulled away and stepped toward Brodie. "You on your way now?"

"They're waiting for me at the shop." Brodie turned his attention to Rachel. "It was nice to meet you, officially."

She offered a hand. "Thanks for fixing the table."

His grip was firm, his smile real. "Anything to help

you win that contest." He nodded to Mark on his way to the door. "I'll call you later." Then he looked to Amanda and hesitated, the former confidence slipping a notch. "You need a lift anywhere?"

"As a matter of fact, I have to go home for a minute." She waved at Rachel. "I'll be back with that pattern and we can start fitting it this afternoon." She looked up at Brodie as they went through the door. "So, tell me—you ever play the stock market?"

"What's the right answer?" Mark asked as the door closed behind them.

"About the stock market?" Rachel laughed. "The answer is no."

"I'll have to tell him," Mark said, capturing her hand and pulling her back to him. "Later."

She moved against him, and he avoided the questions in her eyes, letting his gaze fix instead on her mouth as he wrapped an arm around her neck and settled her head into the crook of his elbow. "I have wanted to do this all morning," he murmured, closing his eyes as he bent to her.

She held herself back from him for a moment, and he knew an instant of panic, of fear that he had lost her already. Then she made a low, sweet sound deep in her throat as he covered her mouth with his, and Mark held on harder; drinking her in and filling himself up with the taste he'd longed for, and would miss for the rest of his life.

When both their hearts were pounding, he lifted his head and looked at her, loving the way her eyes fluttered open and her lips curved slowly, lazily, letting him know she wasn't nearly through yet. And it was only the beeping of his laptop that made them both turn.

"Mail?" Rachel asked as she stepped out of his arms.

"Battery," Mark muttered, making a mental note to keep the damn thing plugged in from then on.

"Just as well," Rachel said, smoothing her hands over her shorts as she headed for the kitchen. "Melissa Scott-Wilson will expect the scones she didn't get the other day, which means I'll have just enough time to get them in the oven before Amanda gets back with that pattern."

Mark had seen the way Brodie looked at Amanda, and if his guess was right, she wouldn't be back any time soon. But he kept it to himself, shut down his computer, and followed her into the kitchen. "Scones are supposed to be my department."

Rachel pulled flour and sugar from the pantry and held them out to him. "I appreciate the effort, but one set of hockey pucks is enough."

"I just need a little coaching." He set the bags on the counter, then leaned a shoulder against the pantry door and wiggled his eyebrows at her. "Believe me, I'm a very quick study."

"Just get me the butter," she said, tossing a tin of baking powder at him as she crossed to the fridge. "What recipe did you use, anyway?"

" 'Scones for Today' or something like that." He set the tin down beside the flour and opened the fridge. "I found it on the Quick and Easy Baking Page."

"No wonder they didn't work out." She walked into the studio and flipped a tape into the stereo. Benny Goodman began the beguine as Rachel came back into the kitchen with a yellowed sheet of paper. "My grandmother's recipe and my grandmother's music." She smiled and laid the page on the counter. "Neither quick nor easy, but guaranteed perfect, every time."

He read over the handwritten recipe. A thimbleful of rising. Two teacups of flour. "If you ask me, this is a recipe for disaster. What kind of thimble are you supposed to use? And what size is the teacup?" He screwed up his nose. "And what the heck is rising?"

"Baking powder," she whispered, then laughed and reached for the sugar bowl next to the coffeemaker. "You have to develop a feel for the recipe. Learn how the batter is supposed to look, how the dough should behave in your hands, that sort of thing."

He slid the page back to her as he pulled out a stool at the counter. "Leaves a lot of room for error."

"Not when you get the hang of it." She took a china teacup from the cupboard, robin's egg blue with a gold rim and a metal thimble inside. She shook the thimble out and set it down beside the flour. "Besides," she said, and tugged a snowy white apron from the drawer, "some things are just better done the old-fashioned way."

Watching her pull that apron over her head while sunshine poured in through the windows and sultry saxophone music drifted all around them, Mark found it easy to believe her. Her world was handstitched beads and thimbles full of rising. A world of wedding gowns and home baking, where love went hand in hand with marriage and kids, and vows were meant to be kept.

While he could see that world, touch it, and even taste it, it was a place he could only visit. His place was in London, Beirut, the Sudan. He didn't have to try hard to picture her in his flat now, turning it from a set of rooms to a home with flowers and ruffles and her poky furniture.

But could she see it? Would she leave if he asked? He didn't even have to ask. The answer was in the smile on her face and the light in her eyes as she clipped her grandmother's recipe to a stand and prepared to make scones the old-fashioned way.

She hauled a heavy ceramic bowl from the cupboard and gave him a thoughtful look. "Would you really like to learn how to do this?"

More than you know, he thought, but merely nodded and rolled up his sleeves as she set the bowl in front of him. They were a good time, not a long time. And as long as he remembered that, they'd both be doing well.

"Measure two heaping cups of flour into the bowl." She slid the bag across the counter and checked the clock on the microwave. "We'll have to hurry. I still have to get Melissa's dress ready for the fitting."

Pushing aside any lingering fantasies, Mark uncurled the top of the bag and moved on to safer ground. "What happened with this Melissa anyway?"

"It's a long story." She gave him a sexy look over the top of the flour bag. "But I'll tell you mine if you tell me yours."

Mark dipped the cup into the bag and watched her turn and flick on the oven, wondering why he'd never noticed the latent sensuality of an apron before.

"Why can't you make a tape for Chuck?" she asked as she cut a three-finger chunk from the pound of butter and wrapped the rest in plastic.

Mark gave his head a shake and dumped the first tea-cupful of flour into the bowl. Then he told her about the divorce, the little girl caught in the middle, and the school play that Chuck would never see.

Rachel popped the lid on the baking powder and reached for the thimble. "Has his ex said definitely not?"

He measured the second cup of flour and poured it into the bowl. "She said that if I step foot inside that school with a camera, she will have me arrested for trespassing."

"That's pretty definite." Rachel measured one heaping thimble of baking powder into the bowl. "Did you speak to the principal?"

"Sofia *is* the principal. I can't see any way around it.

Which is too bad because Chuck hasn't seen his daughter in six years."

Rachel's hands stilled as she turned to him. "Six years is a long time in the life of a child."

"True," he acknowledged. "But in our industry"—he snapped his fingers—"it's gone just like that." Mark sighed as he set the cup down. "Chuck never intended to be gone for so long, but one story has a way of leading into another, and revolutions and hurricanes don't wait for you to get back from holiday. After a while, he figured it would be better if he just stayed away and tried to explain it to her when she was older, when she could understand what happened."

Rachel shook her head. "So he's picturing a tearful reunion at her college graduation."

Mark pulled the bag of flour toward him and rolled down the top. "Something like that, yeah."

Rachel held his gaze a moment longer, then turned her attention back to the bowl. "But his ex-wife isn't making it easy for him."

"Easy?" Mark almost laughed. "She won't even send him a recent snapshot. The last picture he has of Brittany is four years old. If he wants a new one, he has to go to Miami and get it."

Rachel glanced over at him as she sprinkled salt into the mixture. "Then maybe it's time he did just that."

"He can't. Not yet anyway." Mark carried the flour to the pantry and tried to think of some way to explain what was incomprehensible to most people. "This lead in Central America is too hot. His agency needs someone in there right now, to dig around and find out what's going on. If the lead turns out to be solid, this story will be huge, an award winner by all accounts. And Chuck will be the one to break it." He returned to the table and watched her cut the butter into small pieces on a plate.

"It's the kind of assignment field journalists dream about."

She kept her eyes on the butter. "Does it bother you that you weren't the one to go?"

"Not at all," he said, and realized it was true. For the first time since the shooting, he had no desire to be anywhere other than where he was. There was no restlessness, no longing for something beyond his grasp. He was content. And the knowledge hit him hard.

She gave him a tiny smile. "You want me to believe that you'd rather be here measuring flour than out there tracking a story?"

"I know," he said softly, and pressed the lid back on the baking powder. "It's the damndest thing, isn't it?"

FOURTEEN

Rachel watched him carry the tin to the cupboard and take his time about putting it away. He was shaken, she could see that. And she told her heart to slow down, to keep from jumping to conclusions or reading anything into what he'd said.

He was enjoying his time with her, that was all. There would be no declaration of love, or talk of a future. His fiancée had convinced him that he wasn't cut out for long-term relationships. That he made a better memory than reality. So he'd put his heart into his work instead, and had no intention of directing it elsewhere. They shared a bed, a few laughs, and a stake in an ice-blue wedding gown. But beyond that, nothing. He wouldn't tell her details of the ambush, wouldn't let her close enough to find out what it was that haunted him about that day, or trust her to understand.

She only wished there was a way to let him know that he could tell her anything because she loved him exactly as he was, with no changes and no guarantees. That he could stay forever or leave tomorrow, and it wouldn't alter the way she felt. And if he asked her to go with him? There was every possibility that she would.

But she wasn't naive enough to think that one night could change the patterns of a lifetime, no matter how much she would have liked it to be true. So she put a smile on her face and laughter in her voice. "Are you baking or not?" she called, giving him a way to come back, to be with her for as long as possible.

He turned, and a tiny smile curved his lips. "I guess I am."

She held out a spoon as he came toward her, this man who was bold and passionate, tender and caring. And had more love to give than even he knew, if only he'd let himself believe.

"Stir," she said, watching his smile broaden to that grin she loved so much. And wondering how any woman could ever believe he would be better as a memory.

"About your friend, Chuck," she said, changing the subject, determined to keep it light. "Since Sofia only knows you, why don't I go in and tape the show?"

Mark looked at her curiously while he stirred. "Why would you want to do that?"

She shrugged. "To help you out. And Chuck, too, I suppose."

"Well, it's a nice thought, but you'd need a ticket to get past the front door, and the show sold out weeks ago. Sofia made a point of showing me the receipts."

"She's not making this easy, is she?" Rachel glanced into the bowl. "That should do it," she said, taking the spoon and tossing it into the sink. "Now comes the tricky part: rubbing the butter."

He folded his arms and leaned a hip against the cupboard. "And where, exactly, do we rub it?"

"Into the flour," she said blandly, and scraped the slivers of butter into the bowl. "You have to be gentle but quick, and you use only two fingers and your thumb." She held up her hands to demonstrate. "It's the same action as snapping your fingers." She snapped, to show him how easy it was. "But then you soften it, like this."

She rubbed her thumb gently across the pads of her fingers. "See?"

He raised a brow. "Is this a joke?"

Her fingers stilled. "Do I look like I'm joking?" She put her hands into the bowl and blended the slivers of butter with the flour. "Now get your hands in here."

She pressed her lips together to keep from smiling as he dipped his hands in beside hers, glad to have him back again.

"You start by finding the bits of butter," she continued. "That's right. And now you rub. Gently, remember? Much better."

His jaw twitched. "Why do I get the feeling that you want to laugh?"

"I have no idea," she said, and laid a hand over his, slowing the movement, softening his touch. "I can tell that you're going to be very good at this."

He lifted only his eyes. "I'm glad you approve."

She did smile then, and slowly drew her hand back, enjoying the way his mouth tightened and his gaze lowered to her lips, her throat, her breasts. Yet she was the first to turn away, knowing there would be no scones if she didn't. And Amanda would be there soon.

She dipped her chin, focusing on the bowl and the butter—and the fact that he really was getting the hang of it. "Okay, I have an idea," she said, concentrating on the mixture. "If Sofia won't make it easy, how about we turn it into something she can't resist?"

"And how do we do that?"

"Let me ask you this first: If the school wanted to tape the show for their own reasons, they could, right?"

He nodded. "I suppose so. Why?"

"Because every school in the country is looking for ways to raise money. I know, because I'm always the first one my nieces and nephews call when they have something to sell. Raffle tickets, chocolate-covered almonds, you name it, the schools will sell it." She pulled her hands out of the bowl and washed them at the sink. "Keep going. I'll get the milk."

His eyes followed her to the fridge. "What do raffle tickets have to do with Chuck?"

She carried a carton back to the table. "Nothing, but a professional-quality video, produced free of charge and donated to the school, could have everything to do with him getting to see his daughter perform."

"Rachel, I'm a cameraman, not a production company. I can only do basic editing with my camera. Nothing with titles or special effects, and all of that is expensive."

She smiled at him. "Why don't you call Chuck and find out how much he'd be willing to pay?"

He took his hands out of the bowl and turned on the tap. "What for?"

"Because, if Sofia is the principal, I believe she'll be hard put to turn this offer down. Not every family owns a video camera, and if the school can offer them a professional tape of their child's special night at a reasonable cost, I believe it will sell out faster than the tickets." She pointed the carton at him. "And I think she'll be especially fond of the idea if she knows Chuck is footing the bill to produce it."

He grinned as he dried his hands on a tea towel. "You are a devious woman."

"I do my best."

He walked around behind her. "I'll talk to Chuck about it and then give Sofia a call."

He hadn't yet touched her, yet Rachel's skin was already warm, anticipating. She moistened her lips and flipped open the milk. "It might be better if I called her. Since she's not too fond of you."

"Good thinking," he murmured, his breath warm on

her ear. She heard the whisper of a bow being pulled just before the apron fell to the ground. "But I still can't figure out why you're so set on helping."

She swayed against him and closed her eyes. "I don't know, really. I've never met Chuck, but for some reason I feel sorry for him. Maybe seeing his daughter on tape will show him how much he's already missed. And how fast the time is passing."

"I'll call him tonight," he whispered as his lips skimmed the side of her neck. "Tell me again why we're making scones."

"For Melissa's fitting." She reached for her grandmother's teacup. But her fingers closed on nothing when he edged the collar of her blouse aside and kissed her shoulder, making gooseflesh rise on her skin. "It's a tradition."

He looped his arms around her waist. "What if we break tradition?"

"Can't," she whispered, closing her eyes as she swayed against him.

"Give me one good reason," he whispered.

Rachel drew in a long breath as he tugged her blouse out of her shorts. And let it out as a sigh when he started undoing the buttons.

A hundred reasons to stop him ran through her head. Practical, rational reasons that made absolute sense and should have been heeded at once. Then he slipped the blouse from her shoulders, and her mind went blessedly blank, with only one thought remaining.

"Petits four," she whispered, then turned and took hold of his belt. Then she smiled, realizing she was about to start a whole new tradition. One just for herself.

His eyes narrowed as she slowly worked the leather through the buckle. "What are petits four?"

She gave the belt a tug and drew in a shaky breath

when it lay open in her hands. She was on foreign ground, making it up as she went along. And feeling stronger than she could ever remember.

"Trust me." She held his gaze as she undid the snap on his jeans. "You'll love them."

He looked down at the snap, then raised a brow. "Are you trying to take advantage of me?"

She slipped her hands under his T-shirt and lifted it up and over his head. Then she splayed her fingers on his hard, flat belly and pressed her lips to his chest. "That's exactly what I'm doing."

"Thank God," he said, and closed his eyes as she slowly lowered his zipper.

He felt the tremble in her fingers as she pushed his jeans down. Her hands, so soft and gentle, slid over his thighs, making his breath catch as her fingertips only brushed his sex again and again. When he couldn't stand it any longer, he opened his eyes and saw the pleasure and triumph in her eyes. Fixing him with that look, she rose up on her toes, kissing his lips while she closed her hand around him.

Mark heard himself moan and laid his hand over hers, guiding her, teaching her, as he opened his mouth and welcomed the sweet, tentative strokes of her tongue. He raised his head, and despite his best intentions, he couldn't help sinking his fingers into her hair and drawing her closer to deepen the kiss, to show her what she did to him, how much she made him want her. And how very much he needed her.

He drew his head back and studied her face, memorizing the curve of her cheek, the line of her jaw, and the odd tilt of her eyes. There was no danger of his falling in love with her. That point had already been passed. That he loved her was certain. That he couldn't have her forever, only a bad joke on him.

As much as she might look at him now with those wide
eyes and see something he could not for the life of him
understand, he knew that in time she would grow tired of
the pagers and the midnight flights. The stories that went
on for weeks or months, and never really let go.

The best he could do now was to hold her. And when
she took his hand to lead him to the bedroom, there was
nothing he could do but follow.

The sun was just starting to set and afternoon heat was
slowly giving way to a cool gulf breeze as Melissa Scott-
Wilson slid her arms into the dress. "I can't wait to see
this," she said, deftly adjusting the bodice while Rachel
fastened the row of tiny covered buttons at the back.

She was purposely taking her time, checking every detail, giving Melissa the kind of treatment she'd missed
the last time. She looked up as laughter rippled over from
the tea table, hoping Mark could keep Melissa's mother
and the bridesmaids entertained a while longer.

"It's wonderful," Melissa said, her eyes bright and her
smile wide as she twisted from side to side, making Rachel chase the last button. "Absolutely wonderful."

"I'm glad you like it." Rachel laughed as she stepped
back to admire.

This gown was one of her best, no question about it.
Sleek and stylish, yet with a touch of romance in the
details. And best of all, not a forget-me-not in sight.

She slipped the pincushion from her wrist, pleased
again that she'd taken a stand, and knowing who she had
to thank for it. A smile touched her lips. And exactly
how she was going to do it.

"You're looking awfully smug," Melissa said.

Rachel caught her eye in the mirror. "And you're looking utterly beautiful."

"I *feel* beautiful," Melissa said and twirled in a circle, her laughter light and girlish, a refreshing change from the carefully controlled chuckles she usually allowed herself. Then she stopped and looked directly at Rachel. "I haven't said it in so many words, but I want you to know that you were right about the forget-me-nots." She lowered her voice and leaned closer. "I wanted my future mother-in-law to like me so badly, I was willing to do anything." She rolled her eyes and turned back to the mirror. "Thanks for knowing better."

"Just doing my job," Rachel said lightly. "What happened to them, anyway?"

"My mom put them on the garter." Melissa gave her a wry smile. "I thought it would be more comfortable than stapling them to my underwear."

"I still can't believe I said that." Rachel waved her around the side of the screen. "Come on. Everyone is dying to see. Just stay well back from the table, and don't you dare touch anything while you're wearing that gown.

"Here she is," Rachel called as they stepped around the screen, but the rest of the announcement died on her lips. The showroom was deserted. Not a bridesmaid anywhere. Even Melissa's doting mother was gone.

"This is odd," Rachel said, crossing to the table.

The teacups were still half-full, the petits four and sandwiches barely touched. The last thing she remembered was Mark pouring tea and doing background vocals for the teapot. The five women at the table had joined in, including Melissa's mother, which had surprised everyone. Except Rachel.

It had simply been Mark at his finest, just doing what needed to be done. She looked around again. But where were they now?

Amanda came through the front door with a muslin bodice in her hand. "Nice dress," she said to Melissa.

then waved the bodice at Rachel. "This will be ready to fit very soon."

Through the open door came the sound of feminine voices, hooting and cheering. And above them all, Melissa's mother, calling out in a high, clear voice, "Come oooon, seven."

Amanda left the door open and kept going to the cutting table. "In case you're wondering, the party's outside on the driveway."

"The driveway?" Melissa looked at Rachel, who could only shrug.

"I'll see what's going on," she said, heading out the door while Melissa picked up her skirts and hustled over to the window.

Rachel raced down the stairs, around the corner, and drew up short.

"Seven," Mark called.

Melissa's mother punched a fist into the air. "I am hot tonight."

Three of the four bridesmaids did a little dance, and the fourth one merely threw up her hands in disgust.

Melissa's mother snapped her fingers. "Hand mama the dice, boy. 'Cause she is on a roll."

"Place your bets, ladies," Mark called. "Same shooter coming up."

On the driveway at the side of the house, he'd drawn two lines—with dressmaker's chalk, Rachel noted. Both were about six feet long and ran perpendicular to the wall. The one on the right was labeled PASS LINE, the other, DON'T PASS. The bridesmaids laid stacks of pennies on the line and Mrs. Scott-Wilson got down on one knee.

"Shooter is ready," Mark called, and glanced up as Rachel approached.

The man actually had the gall to smile at her.

"You're just in time, babe." He gestured to the lines.

"We have a five-penny maximum, *pass* and *don't pass* bets only. Better hurry, these dice are hot."

"Mark," she said evenly.

Mrs. Scott-Wilson waved a hand. "No time to talk now," she said, then threw back her head and shook the dice furiously. "Come oooonn, seven."

The window above them swung open. "Mother," Melissa called. "What are you doing?"

"Winning big, honey. Winning big." Her arm shot out and the dice skittered across the pavement. Silence descended as all eyes watched them bang against the side of the house and come back, tumbling, tumbling, slower and slower. Finally coming to rest.

"Snake eyes," Mark called. "The lady craps out."

Melissa's mother laughed and slapped him on the arm. "Let me shoot," one of the bridesmaids called, and Mark dropped the dice into her hand.

"New shooter coming in," he called. "Ladies, place your bets."

Rachel waved her hands. "Mark, this has to stop. The tea is cold and the—"

"What's the limit?"

Rachel jerked her head around as Mr. Washington from next door came strolling down the driveway, his wife by his side.

"Whatever you do," Mrs. Washington said, "do not let Bill shoot." She turned to Rachel. "He simply cannot roll straight. It's very embarrassing."

"I'm sure it is," Rachel said, then gave Mark a tight-lipped smile. "We have a fitting going on inside."

"No problem. Let's take the game in there," he said in such an agreeable tone, she wanted to hit him.

"You cannot take—"

"Don't start without me," Melissa called as she rounded the corner, dressed in the pants and jacket she'd been wearing earlier. She looked at Rachel. "Don't worry, I hung the gown up. Actually, Amanda did." She pulled a handful of change from the pocket of her jacket and hunkered down beside Mark. "How do I play?"

He took five pennies from her and jingled them in his palm. "The trick with this game is not to spend too much time trying to make sense of it." He looked up at Rachel, his smile holding a secret warmth. "Because some things in life don't make sense. And this is just one of them."

He focused his attention on the bride again. "First thing you have to know is that your mother can't shoot for beans."

Rachel stood back, listening to the laughter and the good-natured ribbing that went back and forth across the makeshift craps table. Melissa looked happy, her mother flushed and radiant, and the bridesmaid who was about to throw the dice just a little nervous.

Bill and Margaret Washington had taken up positions on either side and were carefully counting out pennies between them while they added their own comments to the instructions being given to the bride.

"*Pass* automatically wins on a seven or eleven. *Don't pass* loses. But if you have to ride it out, *don't pass* wins if the point is rolled before a seven."

Rachel listened, trying too hard to make sense of it, and finally giving up, figuring he was right. Some things in life just had to be accepted and enjoyed. Like spontaneous crap games where there should have been petits four. And men with impossible blue eyes.

She glanced up at the window. Amanda held up the bodice and waved her in. Rachel wavered, caught. It was still the bride's evening, after all.

"Okay, Melissa," Mark said. "You're ready to place your bet." He glanced up at Rachel. "The first of many, I'm sure."

No one seemed to notice as she crept away, but she kept looking back anyway, ready to return at the slightest nod from Melissa. But as the dice skipped across the pavement, Rachel ducked around the corner. And couldn't stop herself from taking the stairs two at a time.

It was well past sunset when Rachel hung the muslin bodice on the rack, satisfied that the fit was right. She slid the bolt of white silk/satin from the shelf, laid it on the table, and slit the top of the plastic. She ran her fingertips over the shimmering fabric and felt herself smile. Tomorrow, the muslin would be taken apart and the pieces used as the pattern. And her drawing would slowly come to life.

"They're calling the game on account of darkness," Amanda said as she came through the front door, the sound of footsteps and laughter following her into the showroom.

"I'll put the kettle on," Rachel said, heading for the kitchen.

"You should probably do a cup count first." Amanda gave her a sheepish grin. "There are a few new faces out there. But don't worry about chairs; most of them have their own."

Rachel looked at her curiously, then crossed to the window. Sure enough, a line of people she didn't recognize were trooping up the stairs. Some with folding chairs, others just finding a spot on the railing, all of them obviously well acquainted with Mark.

"I don't have that many cups," Rachel muttered, then realized that some of her new guests were also carrying bottles of beer or tins of soda.

"Mark brought over a cooler of beer and soft drinks about an hour ago," Amanda explained. "Probably only a few will want tea anyway." She edged toward the door. "You want me to get a count?"

Rachel nodded as Mark came up the stairs. He was part of a group of four men, one of whom was talking animatedly, gesturing expansively with his bottle, obviously in the middle of a story.

Mark sat on the railing, watching and sipping his beer, but for all that he appeared interested, Rachel knew he was distracted, restless. His fingers tapped the neck of the bottle, and his gaze wandered—to the stairs, the beach, and farther to the sea—as though he couldn't wait to leave.

"When does he go?" Amanda asked softly, understanding far more than Rachel realized.

"Eight days." She moved away from the window. "I should put that kettle on."

"Rachel," Amanda called.

But as Rachel turned, Melissa and her mother came through the door, smiling, chatting, calling their hellos. Amanda held Rachel's gaze a moment longer, then sighed, her shoulders slumping as she backed to the door. "You'll need three cups."

Mrs. Scott-Wilson looked from Amanda to Rachel. "There's no need to bother. I don't want you to go to any more trouble than you already have."

Rachel made herself look away from the door, the window. "It's no trouble." She even managed a smile. "Do you take cream or lemon?"

"Mom," Melissa called. "Come and see this."

Melissa stood by the cutting table, examining the drawing of the ice-blue wedding gown that Amanda had taped to the wall.

"This is beautiful," she said, looking back at the sketch. "Whose design is it?"

"Mine." Rachel wandered closer, glad to have something else to think about. "I'll be entering it in the Design Showcase in Miami next week."

It was the first time she'd told anyone other than Amanda. Saying the words somehow made the contest more real, and definitely more frightening.

"If I'd known you did this kind of work," Melissa was saying, "I'd have had you make the bridesmaids' gowns, too. But I had no idea——" She broke off, her face turning red. "That sounded terrible."

Rachel shook her head, her eyes still on the drawing. "How could you know, if I didn't tell you?" She turned back to Melissa's mother. "Have a seat while I put the kettle on."

She pulled out a chair. "I meant to tell you earlier, the table is just lovely. The teapot, the linens, everything is perfect." She reached for a petit four. "And these are delicious."

Rachel bowed her head and put a hand to her chest. "Bought them myself."

The older woman chuckled and bit into the little cake. "And the crap game." She waved a hand. "I haven't had so much fun in a long time." She shook her head as she popped the rest of the petit four into her mouth. "That boyfriend of yours is certainly an interesting fellow."

"Too true," Rachel said, resisting the urge to check out the window, to see if he was there. "But he's not my boyfriend."

Melissa's mother rolled her eyes. "Whatever it is that you girls call them these days, he certainly seems to be a good one." She dusted her fingers on a napkin and took another cake. "Any plans for a wedding gown of your own?"

It was a question Rachel heard all the time, with or without a man around. Over the years she'd stockpiled the answers; Not that I'm aware of. It would be news to me. And the one that went over well at parties—Hey, I only make the things, I don't actually wear them.

She cast a quick glance at the porch. Someone else had taken over his spot on the railing. Mark was gone.

She turned back to Melissa's mother and grinned. "Nothing in the offing. I'll see to the tea," she said, then breezed through to the kitchen. And didn't stop until she reached the sliding door.

He was in the beach house, all the lights off, only the blue glow of the television telling her where he was. She faltered at the front door, the purpose gone from her steps, as recriminations tumbled over themselves inside her head.

How desperate can you be?

Okay, you've found him, now what?

Are you going in or will you just crawl home?

She held on to the door frame for support, her breathing quick and shallow. She'd crept across the back of the houses, like a thief, avoiding her neighbors, her clients, herself.

Her porch was still nicely crowded, the noise level pleasant. Inside, Melissa and her mother would be wondering about the tea.

Her fingers released the door as if burned. What was she thinking?

She was stepping back when he came out of the living room and walked along the hall, past the bedrooms and the bathroom, to the kitchen. She watched him disappear into the darkness, saw the glow of the refrigerator light, and it all came at once. Anger, doubt, and a sudden clarity that pushed her through the door and down the hall to the kitchen.

She smacked the light switch.

He was bent over, his head in the fridge, and he banged it on the shelf as he jerked back. He cursed and rubbed at his head. And looked totally puzzled when he saw her there. "Is something wrong?"

She held up a hand. "Let me say this first. I am under no illusions about what we have here."

He let the fridge door slowly close. "Meaning?"

"Meaning that I know you've been honest from the beginning. Unless I count that first night on the beach, and I try not to." She gave her head a shake, knowing she was rambling and hating it. "I promise you right now that I will not rant or cling or make you feel badly when you leave. But I do want one thing while you're here."

He leaned a shoulder against the fridge. "And what is that?"

She folded her arms, knowing she'd come too far to stop now. "Common courtesy. You come in, you say hello. You're going to be late, you call. And if you come over here to sit in the dark you say, 'Rachel, I'm going next door to sit in the dark.' "

He shook his head. "What are you talking about?"

"The party." She waved a hand in the direction of her cottage. "You just walked away in the middle of it, leaving me to wonder what the hell was wrong and feeling like a fool, while you're over here getting your fix."

He took a step toward her. "My what?"

"Your news fix. Why else is the television still on?" She walked the width of Mrs. Dempster's kitchen, thinking that he'd left it clean at least, and chiding herself for being so mundane, so predictable. She glanced back at him. "I understand. I just wish you'd told me."

"I might have if that was why I left." He leaned a shoulder against the wall and crossed his arms over his chest. "I turned on the television out of habit, Rachel. The way other people turn on lights. And my news fix had nothing to do with my being here. I came back because we ran out of beer over there."

"Beer?" she asked, still holding his gaze, but her face already warming.

He nodded at the table. "I was about to refill the cooler when you came in."

Rachel looked over the counter. The blue-and-white cooler she'd seen on the porch now sat on the floor beside the table, still empty.

She sucked in her cheeks, pursed her lips and looked over at him. "Well, good. And as long as we have that straightened out—"

"Rachel," he said, his voice low enough, gentle enough to slow her steps. But she didn't turn around. "I haven't had to think about anyone else but myself for so long that I'm obviously out of practice. But I promise that the next time I decide to go somewhere and sit in the dark, I'll let you know first." She turned and he came toward her. "Deal?"

"Deal," she said, and he smiled as he drew closer.

She saw something in his eyes. Something sad and lonely, and a little uncertain. And while it was gone as quickly as it had come, she knew they weren't finished yet.

She took the few steps needed to close the gap, to feel the heat of his skin through her dress. And understand what was in those eyes and that smile.

But she was careful not to touch him, not yet. There was too much at stake, and she had too much to say. Touching him would only distract her, and make it impossible to leave when she was through.

"I'll miss you, too," she murmured. "And if you ever decide to come back, just knock on my door and I'll open it." She drew in a deep breath and jumped one last time. "Because I love you."

She didn't give him a chance to answer, simply turned and headed back along the hall, her knees shaking and her heart pounding. "Don't forget the beer," she said and stepped onto the porch. She stopped and looked back. "And just for the record, you're fiancé was an ass."

FIFTEEN

Two days from the full moon, and Rachel knelt in front of the dressmaker's form, positioning the last rosette on the ice-blue gown. She'd originally planned on four, but as the dress took shape, she'd realized one more was needed. When the rose was tacked in place, she sat back on her heels and went over the dress from top to bottom, trying to be objective, critical, to think like a judge. But she'd be damned if she could find anything wrong.

The skirt moved like water, weightless, floating, giving the dress an ethereal look and feel that she hadn't dreamed possible, emphasizing the contrast of the stark white bodice. The dress was at once dreamy and feminine, practical and sensible. Much like a woman, she mused, and got to her feet.

She walked around the form, still not believing that it had come together so quickly or that in three days' time she would be in Miami. She would put on the dress and walk down a runway for the first time in her life; parading her own creation, her design, in front of thousands of people and a panel of judges from all over the world. And there would be nowhere to hide if it fell flat.

She put a hand to her stomach in an effort to quell the butterflies that had taken up residence there two days ago. About the same time she'd made the first cut in the gossamer silk, and known there was no turning back.

She turned as Mark came in from the kitchen, the cell phone pressed to his ear. "That's ridiculous," he was saying. "I've had three quotes and they're all well under that."

He picked up the dinner dishes from the table and carried them back to the kitchen. "You might want to think about that price some more . . ." But the rest of his words were lost as the door swung shut behind him.

Rachel shook her head and went in search of a needle and thread. In the last three days, she had discovered that the man simply could not resist a lost cause. Chuck and Sofia, hockey puck scones, and now her car.

When he'd heard she needed a new engine, it had become his mission to find out more, to be sure the mechanic was right and the price in line. Living with him twenty-four hours a day had given her glimpses of what he must have been like in film school—an obnoxious young man with a dream, a camera, and a need to champion the underdog. Before news agencies, ambushes, and whatever-sells got in the way. And she only wished she'd known him when.

But she contented herself with the knowledge that she'd learned more about him than expected. She now knew that his favorite foods were invariably hot, that he'd read the complete works of Shakespeare, Jane Austen, and Ian Fleming, and that he loved to have company in the shower.

An image of the two of them in her tiny shower stall drifted through her mind. Bumping heads and elbows under the pounding water. Slipping and sliding, laughing and loving until the water went cold, chasing them out to the bedroom, the studio, anywhere at all. She blushed

Lynda Simmons

at the memories, of all the things they'd done, and knew she wouldn't go back and change a single one.

And when they hadn't been loving, when she'd been hunched over the sewing machine and he'd been on the phone, with Chuck or video production firms or yet another service center, they'd talked. About growing up rich and growing up poor. About family and friends and whether one was more important than the other. They'd talked fast and earnest, as though it was important to get everything out at once because time was short, and honesty the only thing they had.

She plucked a needle from the pincushion and sank down in front of the dress again. But for all that they'd shared of themselves, he'd yet to speak of the night at the beach house, or the confession she'd made.

It was as though it had never happened. But every now and then, she would catch him watching her, and the same sadness, the same loneliness she'd seen that night would be there in his eyes, no matter how quick he was to mask it with a smile. She knew it was on his mind, but she would not be the one to bring it up again. It was up to him now.

He strolled into the showroom with a bottle of red wine and two glasses. "We'll have a new price tomorrow," he announced, and sat down behind her on the floor, stretching his legs out on either side of her. "Once it's in, you can decide what you want to do from there."

She nodded and concentrated on threading the needle. "I'm going to miss having an assistant."

"It's an enviable position." He wrapped his arms around her and slid her backward along the floor, settling her against his chest. "With great perks."

"Until you get poked with a needle."

"Then we'll remedy that." He took the needle from her hand, the pincushion from her wrist, and set both aside. "I brought wine to toast the completion of the dress."

"You read my mind." She leaned into him, feeling the beat of his heart and the warmth of his skin through her T-shirt, realizing that this was what she would miss most of all. "Did you settle the details on the video production costs, too?"

He opened the wine and poured two glasses. "Chuck is up for it, whatever the price. He's going to call later to see how it went with Sofia." He handed her one glass and raised the other to the dress. "To the winning entry."

She clinked her glass against his. "To not passing out on the runway."

"You'll be fine," he said, pressing a kiss to the side of her neck. "Are you sure you want to make the call?"

They'd held off on talking to Sofia until Chuck agreed to the price. When Rachel made the call, that's when they'd get the terms. After that, it was anybody's guess.

"I'm sure," she said, closing her eyes and giving herself over to pleasure. "What's the worst that can happen on a phone?"

Mark's ears were still burning from his last phone call to Sofia, but he felt it prudent to keep the details to himself for the moment. Especially when she reached up and pulled him down, seeking his lips.

They both muttered a curse as the bell above the front door tinkled. Julie stood on the doorstep, a tiny bundle in her arms and a weary smile on her face. "Anyone up for a three-ring circus?" She frowned when she spotted Mark. "So there you are. We banged on the door at that beach house for five minutes, positive you were asleep in front of the television." She froze and took a step back. "You two are busy, aren't you?"

"Not anymore," he said, already helping Rachel to her

feet. They crossed to the door together. "Let me see my niece."

Julie pulled back the corner of the receiving blanket, uncovering more of the sleeping face.

Emily slept on, one tiny hand curled beside her cheek, her mouth puckered as if blowing a kiss.

Julie's voice softened. "Did you ever see anything so beautiful?"

"Never," he agreed, meaning it.

"She's already grown so much." Rachel pressed a kiss to Julie's cheek. "Can I hold her?"

"Of course."

Mark watched Julie hover, keeping a close eye as Rachel deftly settled the child on her shoulder, then finally turning back to him, satisfied that her treasure was in good hands. "We stopped in at Harry's mom's and figured we'd drop in here on the way home."

"I'm glad you did," Mark said, wrapping her in a bear hug. "How are you feeling?"

She held on tight and sighed deeply. "Exhausted. Happy." She loosened her hold a little and raised her head. "What are you doing here, anyway?"

Harry came through the door, carrying a baby seat and a diaper bag. And stopped dead when he saw Mark. "So this is where you are."

"Let me help you with that," Mark said, reaching for the diaper bag and an escape.

"Harry, good to see you," Rachel said, accepting a peck on the cheek as Harry came over to see his daughter.

"We won't stay long," he said. "Emily's got us on a very tight schedule." He paused and shot Mark a curious glance. "What are you doing here anyway?"

"Oh, my gawd," Julie gasped, then touched a hand to the baby's cheek and smiled. "Honey, you are about to see why it is so good to be a girl." She breezed through the showroom, heading straight for the dressmaker's form. "The gowns alone make life worth living. Especially ones like this."

"Thanks," Rachel murmured, too busy cooing nonsense into Emily's ear to blow her own horn, so Mark said, "It turned out even better than we'd hoped." And instantly regretted it.

Both Julie and Harry stared at him. *"We?"*

Mark glanced over at Rachel. She just raised a brow and sat down at the table, leaving him to figure it out on his own. And enjoying it, too, by the looks of it. But how could he explain to anyone else what was going on, when he hadn't figured it out for himself?

He turned to Harry, taking the baby seat as well. "How big is Emily now anyway?"

"Five pounds, three ounces," he and Julie said at once.

"And she's so strong," Julie continued.

"See how she holds her head up?" Harry added.

"You missed it," Julie groaned.

"She'll do it again," Harry said, an unmistakable note of pride in his voice. He pulled out a chair at the table and motioned to Julie. "Sit down, babe," he said gently. "You look worn out."

It was true, Mark acknowledged. And Harry didn't look much better. Yet even though they both looked like they could use twenty-four straight hours of sleep, there was an air of deep contentment about them, a peace in Julie that Mark had never seen before. And for the first time in his life, he envied his sister.

Julie touched her daughter's tiny hand and smiled. "That dress is a winner, Rachel. No question about it."

"We'll see," Rachel said, a faraway look in her eyes that had nothing to do with the contest as Emily lifted her head, blinked, and flopped back down again.

Harry jabbed Mark with an elbow. "I told you she'd

do it again. Lifted her head clean up." He turned and dropped his arm. "You never did say what you're doing here."

"Toasting the dress," Mark said, and strolled over to pick up the bottle. "Can I get you two a glass?"

Emily yawned and squeaked, and the wine was forgotten as the three of them huddled around her, agreeing again that she was not only beautiful but talented as well.

"I need to have a picture," Rachel said, and turned to Harry. "There's a camera in the top drawer of the desk. It has a timer. We can get everyone in."

Harry found the camera, Rachel and Julie moved their chairs closer together while he searched for the best place to set it up, and Mark stood back with the wine, watching. The cynic in him, the one that had been quiet for almost a week, was suddenly wide awake and wanting to put a caption to the whole thing. Turn it into a cliché, an ad for long distance, or better yet, insurance. But he couldn't find one that worked.

The scene he was witnessing wasn't unique or earth-shattering, but the excitement, the joy, all of that was real. Julie and Harry were a family now. And it humbled him to know that he would always be on the outside, looking in.

As if she'd heard, Rachel smiled and waved him over. "Emily will be very disappointed if her favorite uncle isn't in the picture."

He set the bottle down. "Only if I get to hold her."

"You have to support her head," Julie said.

"And don't let her know you're nervous," Harry continued.

The list of instructions was long and detailed. And it was finally a group decision that he sit down first, with a cloth on his shoulder, and maybe one on his lap, just in case.

When at last his niece was placed in his arms, Mark expected to feel awkward, foolish even. But when she nestled her head in that spot between his neck and shoulder, he relaxed. And when she sighed, he knew she could stay right there for a long, long time.

Rachel stood behind him, her hands resting lightly on his shoulders. Julie sat on the right and Harry would be on the left eventually.

Harry took one more look through the camera. "Okay, everybody. Smile." He hit the timer and ran to the table, skidding into his spot as the red light blinked a warning.

"It's not working," Mark said through his smile.

"It will," Rachel assured him. "Keep smiling."

The flash went off.

"My eyes were closed," Julie said. "I know my eyes were closed. We'll have to do it again."

Harry was already on his way back to the camera. "Let's get a few shots of the dress first."

Rachel smiled. "I hadn't thought of it."

"Dahling," Julie said, adopting a plummy British accent, "you simply must start thinking portfolio." She got to her feet. "Now where is the best spot?" She pointed. "There, with the screen in the background." She waved a hand at Rachel. "You are going to love this."

Julie went to position the gown, and Mark stayed right where he was. Holding the baby, listening to her breathe, and in no hurry to go anywhere at all. Rachel sat beside him, and while she said nothing, her eyes still had a faraway softness, and her mouth curved in a funny little smile he'd never seen before.

This was what she wanted. Home and family, kids of her own. He could see her as a mother. Indulgent, patient, probably overprotective. Sitting for hours by the water, teaching them how to catch a fish, explaining why they had to let it go, and layering on sunscreen at prescribed intervals.

For a moment, he could almost see the father. The man who would come home every night, bathe the children, read them a story. The same man who would later take Rachel, his wife, to bed, and find that she had plenty of good loving left over for him.

But then the phone rang, Rachel rose, and the notion that it might have been him in that picture faded as quickly as it had come. Leaving in its place an emptiness so cold, so deep that it stole his breath, and made it hard to think.

"Chuck's on the line," Rachel called. Then she put a hand over the receiver and mouthed the words, "Shall I call Sofia?"

"I'll take the baby," Harry said, and before Mark could say anything she was gone, and the real world rushed in to take her place.

Which was just as well. Rachel's dreams were detailed and specific. And he didn't see how he could ever figure into any of them.

He took the phone from her but resisted the urge to take her hand as well. To pull her close and hold on until the cold and loneliness disappeared in the warmth of her smile.

Instead he pressed the phone to his ear. "Chuck, my friend. I have good news and I have bad."

SIXTEEN

While Mark went over the final price of the video, Rachel pulled Sofia's phone number from the corkboard and discovered Kevin Grant's number underneath.

She slowly withdrew the pin and held the card in her hand. Mark would be gone in three days, just about the time Kevin came home. They could have dinner. Go to the show he mentioned. She could pick up her life where she left off, and Mark could slowly fade into the memory he so badly wanted to be.

She glanced over at him. He was lost in his conversation, oblivious to her, to Kevin, to his own heart.

She hesitated, then tossed the card in the wastebasket, knowing she was still caught in a dream and not yet ready for it to end.

She punched Sofia's number into the cell phone, going over in her mind the lines she'd been rehearsing for days. The line picked up on the third ring.

"Sofia Margolies."

The voice was flat, businesslike, and Rachel had called her at home.

Rachel squared her shoulders, any illusions of a quick sell already vanishing.

"Ms. Margolies," Rachel said, her tone equally businesslike, knowing instinctively that anything even re-

motely perky would win no points with Sofia. "You don't
know me, but if you give me a moment, I think you'll
find what I have to say interesting."

Sofia said nothing, but she didn't hang up, which Rachel took as a good sign. She pressed on, introducing
the idea of a video production of the school play, pointing
out the fund-raising potential of such a project, and emphasizing again and again that it was absolutely free.

Sofia grunted. "I've learned that anything that sounds
too good to be true usually is. What's the catch?"

Rachel felt eyes on her back and turned. Harry and
Julie stood a few feet back, listening intently.

"I heard all about it at Brodie's," Harry said in a stage
whisper. "We've been wondering how it turned out ever
since."

Rachel figured they must have heard a juicier version
than she had, because even Emily's eyes were wide open.

"She's talking to Sofia right now," Mark said into the
phone, and gave her a thumbs-up.

Rachel took a deep breath and decided to level with
Sofia. "The catch is that Chuck is the one paying for
the production." She held up a hand. "Sofia, don't hang
up, please. I understand you and Chuck have been divorced for a while—"

"Six years."

Rachel nodded and softened her grip on the phone.
"And in all that time, he hasn't seen much of Brittany—"

"Not even once. He sends presents, money instead.
What do you think a child needs more? Money or a father?"

"A child needs a father," Rachel agreed. "No question."

Mark sucked in a hissing breath. "Not looking good,
Chuck."

"But what did I expect?" Sofia went on. "He was mar-

ried to that camera, never to me. Gone for weeks, sometimes months, then he'd show up out of the blue with
wine and flowers. He told me he'd cut back when we
had a baby, get a regular job, but he lied. When Brittany
was born, I gave him an ultimatum: It's us or the job.
He chose the job. So as far as I'm concerned, if he doesn't
want to come to Miami for the show, he can listen to
the job sing instead. And believe me, it can never sound
as good as his daughter. She has the voice of an angel."

"The voice of an angel," Rachel echoed.

Mark shook his head. "It's getting dicey, Chuck."

Rachel looked over at him, thinking of Chuck holed
up somewhere in Central America, prepared to pay thousands of dollars for a tape of his daughter singing a three-
minute song, because the biggest story of the year was
about to break and he couldn't afford to miss it.

She thought of Julie, the wedding, the baby, everything
that Mark had been part of since coming home. And wondered if he really would have been willing to miss it all
if the lead had been given to him.

"What's your connection to Chuck, anyway?" Sofia
was saying. "Are you a girlfriend or something, because
if you are—"

"I'm not," Rachel assured her. "In fact I've never even
met him."

Sofia's tone was immediately suspicious. "Then why
are you so anxious to help him?"

"Do you remember Mark Robison?"

"How could I forget? So charming, so sincere. So full
of crap." She laughed, but it had a harsh edge. "You
should have seen his face when I told him no. It was the
most fun I've had in years."

"I can imagine," Rachel muttered.

Julie shook her head. "Poor Chuck."

"If you ask me, he's a fool," Harry said.

Mark slapped a hand over the mouthpiece. "When did this become a panel discussion?"

Rachel ignored them all, knowing she had to come up with something quick if she wanted to change Sofia's mind. "Well, if you thought that was fun, then you should really appreciate this plan, because everyone but Chuck comes out a winner."

"How do you figure?" Sofia asked.

Rachel raised hopeful eyebrows at Mark. "Well, a struggling videographer in your area not only makes money but gains some much needed exposure. The school gets a unique fund-raising project with absolutely no costs involved. The students get a keepsake they will remember the rest of their lives, and the parents get a better-quality tape than they could ever produce themselves, at a very reasonable cost."

She drew in a breath, Julie clutched Harry's hand, and Mark told Chuck to hold on a moment longer.

"You get to be the hero with all the kids, of course," Rachel continued, "but especially with your daughter, the star. And Chuck?" She paused for effect. "Why, Chuck gets the bill."

Sofia sniffed. "How big a bill?"

Rachel smiled. "I'll fax you a copy of the quote."

Julie nodded her approval, Harry bowed to the master, and Mark gave her a very impressed two thumbs-up.

"Chuck," he said softly, "I think we may have lift off."

Chuck's voice went cold. "If not, then she can go to hell. I don't care anymore. I'll see the kid when she's older. When I can finally explain my side. Let her know what really happened."

The bitterness was neither sudden nor shocking. Mark had seen how deep-rooted it was in Sofia, as well. What surprised him was the new tack Chuck was taking.

Mark watched the infinite care Harry took with his

daughter, the way he delighted in each tiny gesture, each new discovery. And he wondered what it was that Chuck would say to his own daughter one day.

How he would explain that a guerrilla encampment in Central America had been more important than her school concert. That her third birthday had paled in comparison to a civil war in Somalia. And her first day of school had come in a distant second to the war in Bosnia.

Would she hate him? Try to overlook it? Or simply feel nothing for this man who had taken no part in her life and now had the audacity to ask her to understand? Mark realized then that Chuck simply didn't get it. He'd made his choice. While he'd gained on one side, he could never get back what he'd lost on the other. Mark had accepted a long time ago that you just couldn't have it both ways.

"So what will it be, Sofia?" Rachel asked. "Are we taping or not?"

Sofia clicked a pen, tapped it on a paper, and tossed it aside with a sigh.

"Okay, make your tape. And be sure it's the most expensive one ever produced in this county. No, the whole state, you got that?"

"Absolutely," Rachel said and gave Mark the OK sign. "I'll fax the quote and the agreement to the school today. We'll come by the afternoon of the show to set up."

"One other thing," Sofia said. "Are you involved with this Mark Robison?"

"We're just friends," she said and reached for a pen. "What time is the performance?"

"Seven," Sofia said. "And you listen to me. Make sure that you're careful, that you stay just friends, okay? Men like him, like Chuck, they're not available. Do you know what I'm saying?"

Rachel turned her head. He'd been watching her again,

but this time he made no move to hide it. Instead, his gaze moved over her, intimate and frankly sexual. The effect was immediate and powerful.

They both had phones pressed to their ears, other people on the ends of lines, but the connection between them was stronger, more compelling. She met and held his gaze, making it clear that she loved what was happening, what he was doing to her; only now free enough to be so open with him because she'd left "careful" behind the moment she knocked on his door.

What they had was rare and frightening, and all too easy to walk away from because it made them vulnerable, open to hurt, to pain. But it would last forever if he let it, of that much she was sure. All he had to do was look at her to know.

"Just be certain you know what you're doing," Sofia was saying.

"I do," Rachel said and smiled, pleased that he had been the first to look away. "I'll be fine," she continued and pulled a scrap of paper toward her. "Now, when can we come and set up the camera?"

As she hung up the phone, Julie approached with two glasses of wine. "Well done. I've been rooting for Chuck since Harry told me what Mark was trying to do. The way I look at it, even a fool deserves a little happiness."

Rachel smiled. Rooting for the underdog, she mused. And wondered if Emily had inherited yet another Robison tendency.

Julie handed her a glass. "So, are you going to tell me how it's going with my brother, or shall I just make up something on my own?"

"Just hold on," Rachel said, turning at a knock on the door. "I'll be right back."

The woman on the doorstep smiled and introduced herself as Trudy from the travel agency. "I spoke to Mr.

Robison about some tickets to Miami. He told me to deliver them here." She held out an envelope. "Have a great trip."

"Thank you."

Rachel turned as Julie hoisted her glass. "To the dress."

Rachel waved the envelope as she crossed to the desk. "To Miami." She dropped it in front of Mark, who was still on the phone, ironing out details with Chuck. "Airline tickets," she whispered, and went back to fill Julie in on everything. Almost everything.

Harry strolled over as Mark hung up the phone. "The travel agent obviously knew you'd be here." He rocked from side to side as he gently bounced Emily. "It's just your family you keep in the dark, I suppose."

Mark sat down on the edge of the desk, realizing there was no way out this time, and not sure he'd take it even if he could. "I wasn't keeping anyone in the dark. There just isn't anything to tell." He reached out his hands. "Let me hold her."

Harry didn't hesitate and he didn't hover, for which Mark was grateful. He held Emily in the crook of his arm and she looked him straight in the eye, assessing him as only a baby can. "She's going to break hearts," he said, and touched a fingertip to her cheek.

"It's that Robison side again." Harry folded his arms across his chest. "Happens all too often for my liking."

"Well, it's not happening here."

Emily's forehead bunched, much like her father's.

"Rachel and I are just enjoying some time together," Mark insisted.

"Don't try and snow me," Harry said. "I'm a psychiatrist. I majored in facial expressions." His eyes narrowed as he looked across the room. "And what I see over there is not a woman who is merely having a good time. I see a woman in love." He turned back to Mark. "You do, too, don't you."

It wasn't a question, so Mark didn't feel it necessary to answer as he glanced over at Rachel. Her face was animated, her smile bright. Such a contrast to the other night, when she'd looked him straight in the eye and told him she loved him.

She hadn't intended to, he was certain of it, but she was just too straightforward, too honest to hide anything for long. And even though she hadn't said it since, he felt it every time she touched him, every time she looked at him. And he couldn't for the life of him figure out why.

"I haven't done anything to mislead her," he said, his voice suddenly husky. He cleared his throat and turned away. "She's known from the beginning that I'm only here on vacation. Called me a tourist herself once."

Emily started to fuss and Mark patted her. "We laid out the ground rules before we even started, just so there would be no confusion."

"Ground rules." Harry smiled in spite of himself. "That sounds like Rachel. Always practical." He shoved his hands in his pockets and looked down at the floor. "But she's also a dyed-in-the-wool romantic. I'll lay odds those ground rules went out the window some time ago."

Emily's cry grew louder, and Mark got to his feet. "I can't help that. I never lied to her. Never promised anything I couldn't deliver."

"Did she ever ask for anything?"

Mark walked in a small circle, bouncing the baby the way he had seen Harry do it. "She asked me to tell her before I go out and sit in the dark alone."

"Funny, that's exactly where Julie and I thought you'd be. Do you find that odd?"

Mark turned on him. "Don't start analyzing me, Doctor."

The baby grunted and struggled. Mark whispered in her ear as he walked and bounced. She stopped fussing for a moment to listen.

Harry slapped him on the back. "You're a natural."

"Just observant," Mark said, and shook his head as Emily opened her mouth and wailed. "And obviously it's not enough."

"She senses the tension. Plus she's probably hungry." He took his daughter from Mark, holding her easily as he dug a bottle out of the diaper bag. "I need to warm this."

Mark led him into the kitchen, pointed out the microwave, and stood back while Harry did what was necessary.

"When do you leave?" Harry asked at last, sitting at the counter with Emily while she downed her dinner.

"Right after the contest." He walked the length of the galley kitchen and back, frustrated by the size and the fact that he knew it better than he did his own. He rounded the counter and found the distance to the studio no more satisfying. "The ticket is in with the ones for Miami," he continued. "I asked the travel agent not to say anything when she delivered them."

"Because you're so honest with Rachel."

"That's different and you know it." He pulled out the stool beside Harry and sat down. "You more than anyone should know that the kind of work I do doesn't lend itself to permanent relationships."

Harry nodded. "Just look at Chuck and Sofia."

"Don't patronize me either. I know from personal experience that love doesn't last when the distances are too great."

"True," Harry said, his eyes holding more understanding than Mark expected. "But Rachel is nothing like Joanna."

"You think I don't know that?" He was on his feet again. "She's everything I ever wanted, and I know I'm going to miss her every day of my life."

"Then stay," Harry said, so reasonably that Mark could almost believe it was just that simple.

"And do what?" he demanded. "Local news, perhaps? Spend the rest of my life filming ribbon-cutting ceremonies and dog shows?" He shook his head and wandered back to the studio. "I'd be stark, raving mad in a week."

"Then take her with you."

"She wouldn't go."

Harry set the bottle down, put a cloth on his shoulder, and settled Emily where she could see the world and take her time with a burp. "Have you asked?"

"I don't have to." He sank back down on the stool and smiled at the round blue eyes watching him intently. "She told me what she wants. And it's nothing I can give her."

"Are you sure?"

"Positive." He pushed himself up and wandered around the counter to the sink. "I can't stay; she can't go. That gives us three more days together. And I don't want to think any farther ahead."

SEVENTEEN

"Good evening, ladies and gentlemen, and welcome to Roy Winston Elementary School's Spring Revue." Sofia Margolies waited until the shuffling of feet and the scraping of metal chairs died down. "Tonight's production, while familiar, has been delightfully updated by our music teacher and drama coach, Mr. Hickey."

Rachel zoomed in while Mr. Hickey, a tall man with serious eyebrows, took his bow by the piano.

She and Mark had spent the afternoon setting up two cameras on tripods at the back of the auditorium. The sound would be captured on a direct feed from microphones on the stage, so that no residual noise would find its way onto the tape.

The videographer who rented Mark the equipment had offered to do the taping as well, but Mark had declined, preferring to maintain control over how the tape was shot—just to safeguard Chuck's interest. While Rachel couldn't imagine him handing control of a shoot to anyone for any reason, she was glad he'd held on to this one, especially when he was willing to show her how it was done.

She panned back to Sofia. Going slowly, steadily, the way Mark had shown her. The curtain was still drawn, the stage dark except for the single spotlight on Sofia.

"Our featured performers tonight include . . ."

She wore a gray skirt with a powder-blue sweater set, neat yet approachable, in keeping with the image she projected—a very different image from the one Rachel had expected.

Sofia had been friendly and cooperative during the setup, having the children design posters and chatting about the performance, the costumes, how much the tape was going to cost Chuck. The four-figure estimate from the videographer had made her day, probably her year. Rachel suspected that she had it framed and mounted somewhere in the school, as a reminder of the night she bested Chuck.

But what struck Rachel most about Sofia was the way she cared about the school, the kids, her staff. She wasn't the bitter hoyden Rachel had envisioned, but rather a woman who'd been hurt, yes, but who felt the betrayal of her daughter much more keenly.

When Sofia introduced Brittany, her pride had been evident in her posture, her eyes, the way she spoke to her daughter. Brittany herself was a striking, confident little girl with long dark hair and huge brown eyes like her mother's. It came as no surprise that she was willing to stand up in front of an auditorium full of people and sing solo. Rachel only wished there had been a way to convince Chuck to come for this special night.

"So without further ado . . ." Sofia waved her arm in a broad gesture, and the piano started into a bouncy overture. "Let the show begin."

The chorus marched onto the stage, a neat line of boys and girls sporting Roy Winston school colors—an unfortunate combination of scarlet and gold.

"Zoom out, zoom out," Mark ordered, his hand already going for the button as the children sat down across the front of the stage.

"I'm out," Rachel snapped, and stepped back from the camera. "Maybe you should take over after all."

She saw the flash of irritation. He was working—school play or war games, it was all the same. The images on the tape were all that mattered.

"Stay," he said absently, his attention on the stage. He flashed her a guilty smile. "Please."

Rachel put her eye to the camera again, figuring she had some of it coming. She had, after all, been the one who pestered him into showing her how the camera worked and what to look for in a shot. And it had been her idea to help out with the actual taping. If he'd picked up a pair of scissors in her workroom, she would probably be just as impatient.

The curtain opened. The pianist played the "Sunrise Theme" from *William Tell,* the chorus hummed along, and the lights came up on a pastoral scene. Mountains on the backdrop, pots of flowers here and there, and in the center of the stage, a wooden bridge running over a blue carpet river.

A small boy in a bumblebee costume buzzed out from the wings, obviously the first of Mr. Hickey's delightful updates.

He circled the bridge, flew over to the microphone, and squinted into the lights. "Once upon a time there were three billy goats gruff. . . ."

Mark leaned in close. "Go in tight on the bee, but be ready to back out when the stars make their entrance."

He wasn't focused on the stage now; he was taking in the audience, the squirming toddlers, the teachers standing back by the door.

Rachel held the shot on the bumblebee until the music changed, signaling an entrance. She backed off smoothly, excited by what she saw in the viewfinder, by the way she was handling the camera, and the fact that she was beginning to understand even a small part of his work, his world. Not that it would make much difference now.

The ice-blue wedding gown was finished and hanging in the closet at the hotel. The contest was tomorrow, and he'd be gone soon after. He hadn't mentioned a date or time, but London had called her house looking for him, and she knew it wouldn't be long.

She tried not to think about it as she slowly backed the shot out. Tried not to feel him there beside her and wish that things could be different. But she'd been preparing for this from the beginning. While she wanted nothing more than to make him see how wrong he was about himself, about them, she was also determined to say good-bye with grace, and learn to be content with the memory.

The music changed and Rachel was ready, capturing perfectly the entrance of the first billy goat—a shy and tiny face in a fluffy white costume that made the audience go "Ahhhh."

"Oh, where are my brothers?" she said and looked from side to side.

Mark glanced over at her. "You okay?"

Rachel nodded and zoomed out, preparing for the next entrance. Sure enough, two more goats appeared, each one taller than the last. "Here we are," said the biggest in a deep stage voice.

Mark leaned closer. "When does Brittany sing?"

"When they leave the valley."

"The grass in our meadow is thin and dry," the middle goat said. "What shall we do?"

Rachel put a hand on the camera. "This is it."

Mark nodded. "Keep it tight on Brittany the whole time. Make it a moment to remember for Chuck."

"Or regret," Rachel said softly as Brittany swept in

from stage left, scattering pink and white petals in her wake.

She wore flowers in her hair, green tights, and a yellow tunic—Mr. Hickey's version of a woodland sprite.

"She looks like Peter Pan in drag," Mark muttered.

But the audience laughed with Brittany as she minced and smirked her way to the goats—stealing the show and saving the production.

"Cross over the bridge," she told the goats, dancing to the microphone while the goats worried out loud and the piano played a tinkling introduction.

The spotlight centered on Brittany and so did Rachel.

Brittany put a hand to her heart. "You'll miss the buzz of the bumblebees . . ."

Mark ran a hand over his mouth. "I'd say Mr. Hickey had a hand in the lyrics as well."

"Doubtless," Rachel said. "But it doesn't matter when they're being sung by an angel."

Brittany sang about saying good-bye to flowers and trees and beautiful butterflies, her voice rich and strong, soaring above the senseless words and sending a chill along Rachel's spine.

Could the microphones really capture that voice? she wondered. Do it justice so that Chuck would know how talented his little girl was? Perhaps inspire him enough to come home the next time she performed. Prove Sofia wrong, as she so badly wanted him to do.

She looked over at Mark, but his attention was no longer on the stage. She followed his gaze. He was watching Sofia at the door. She held a tissue clenched in her hand and there were tears in her eyes.

He touched Rachel's shoulder. "You stay with Brittany. I'll get this."

He unscrewed the second camera from the tripod, flipped off the lens cap, and hit RECORD. The red light blinked on and he held the camera on Sofia until the song ended and the applause for Brittany died down.

He glanced back at Rachel. "Go to full stage and hold it there until I get back."

"Trip, trap, trip, trap."

"At least Hickey didn't mess with that," Rachel muttered as she pulled the shot back.

Mark was roaming the aisles now, his face hidden by the camera, the red light on. He was taping the audience, she realized, capturing the reactions. The restlessness of a little boy, the rapt attention of a grandmother, the barely concealed jealousy of a little girl whose brother was occupying center stage.

He was going beyond the obvious, beyond the play itself; turning the tape into something more than a mere record of the events.

"Who's that walking on my bridge?"

Rachel checked the viewfinder, making sure the troll was centered. But she was starting to see the final result differently, to picture it with Mark's footage interspersed, to imagine the reactions of the parents and the students when they saw it.

Brittany would know that her mother had cried. The troll would discover that his sister couldn't help laughing when he said his lines. And the chorus would know just how proud each of their families had been.

"Trip, trap. Trip, trap."

She smiled and knew exactly what he was doing. He was making a life-altering short.

"Everyone is so excited about the tape. The parents, the students, even the staff." Sofia glanced around the parking lot.

Only a few stragglers were left. Parents who had tried

to sneak a moment with a teacher. Children running, chasing each other, too excited to get in the car.

Still Sofia lowered her voice. "Between you and me, the tape has already outsold the almonds in pre-orders alone."

"So the field trips are saved." Mark swung the last camera bag into the backseat of the rental car. "And who knows how much more will sell once word of the finished tape gets around."

He turned as Brittany and Rachel drew up to the car carrying a tripod between them.

"That's the last of it," Rachel said, and turned to Sofia. "We'll drop the tapes off at the videographers tonight. If all goes well, he'll have it back to you within two weeks."

"I'll let you know how it turned out." Sofia smiled and held out a hand. "It really was nice to meet both of you. I just wish her father had been the one holding the camera."

Brittany helped Mark load the tripod into the trunk. "Thanks for everything. And say hi to my dad for me. Tell him my mom hasn't booked anything for the summer holiday yet, so I'm still available any time."

It was the look in her eyes that was hardest for Mark to face. The faith was still there, the hope that her father really meant it when he said he'd send for her. How much longer did Chuck have, before it was gone for good?

"I'll be sure and tell him," he said, signaling to Rachel as he slammed the trunk. "We'd better be going."

In the rearview mirror, Mark saw Brittany and Sofia still waving as he and Rachel pulled away. Sofia had her arm around her daughter's shoulders, protecting her, yet not holding her back. In spite of everything, Sofia was willing to let her go to Chuck, to let him be part of Brittany's life. And he wondered if Chuck even realized how lucky he was.

"She's a good kid," Mark said softly, turning his attention to the road, to the next stop. "I just hope the tape does her justice."

"It won't be for lack of footage," Rachel said. "Judging by the shots you were getting, I'd say Roy Winston is in for a surprise."

"If the videographer edits it properly." Mark stopped the car, waiting for the light to turn. "I have some ideas, some scenes I can see clearly. I only wish I had time to speak to him."

"It's not that late. Why don't we stop, have a drink, and you can write them down?" She looked over at him. "You really seemed to be enjoying yourself tonight. It would be a shame if you didn't have any input into the editing."

He stared ahead at the street. The sun was setting, bringing to life the supper clubs and bars that drew people from all over Miami. Music drifted into the streets, everything from Latin rhythms to swing, inviting them to stop and spend a little time.

But all Mark wanted to do was drop off the tapes and equipment, go back to the hotel, and make love to her.

Tomorrow he'd be leaving, right after the fashion show. He hadn't told her, hadn't shown her the ticket. He wasn't purposely avoiding it; the issue just never came up. They spoke of family, friends, books, politics, but they never spoke of his leaving. It was as though neither of them wanted to face it, when really they were only too aware that it was coming.

But she was right, he had enjoyed himself; more than he'd expected to, if he was honest, but only after he'd started to see it as more than simply a recording of the action. When he'd looked into the faces in the audience and realized that it was more than tiny talent time.

The light turned green and he pulled away from the intersection. "It's probably best if I just leave it with the videographer. He works with these types of productions all the time. He knows what people like to see." He looked over at her. "My view of the final version wouldn't always be flattering or easy to watch."

She smiled. "The best films rarely are."

He knew what she was doing, what she was saying, because it was an echo of what he'd been thinking himself. That maybe he could stay. Just say good-bye to everything he knew and pick up where he'd left off years ago. A man and his camera, tilting at windmills.

The problem, of course, was that the world had turned. The film industry he knew had changed. He had no contacts to draw upon, no favors to call in. Developing scripts and ideas took time and money, and he wasn't an idealist anymore. He wasn't prepared to live in a room and suffer for his art. And he certainly wasn't about to live off Rachel.

The whole notion was crazy, a fantasy. And he hadn't been able to shake it since he turned the camera on Sofia and let the tape run.

He glanced over at her as they stopped for another light. "It won't hurt to jot them down," she said, making him smile. And he started to miss her already.

Traffic where they were now was lighter, the street quieter, almost deserted. He spotted a café on a corner, a parking spot not far away, and wheeled in, suddenly anxious to play out the fantasy, even if only for as long as it took him to drink a cup of coffee. He turned to her as he shut off the engine. "Do you have a pen?"

She threw open the door. "What do you think?"

That she would always have what he needed. And

wouldn't it be a shame if he was making the biggest mistake of his life by walking away.

He slammed the car door and joined her on the sidewalk, loving the way she laced her fingers with his, rose up on her toes, and kissed him full on the mouth. She moved to pull away, but he wasn't ready, not yet. He pulled her to him there on the street, deepening the kiss; feeling her respond, opening to him, wanting him. And knowing for the first time in his life what it was to truly ache for a woman.

The street was quiet, almost deserted, and they held on, neither one caring if a passerby watched or someone stared from a car. Both of them lost and reaching, hoping to find a way to let go, to forget, and still coming up empty.

She stepped back at last, dazed and smiling. "Quick notes," she said. "Very quick."

But as they turned from the car, Mark noticed a taxi pull up right in front of the café. Two men got out and approached the café. They were young, late teens, early twenties. Nothing out of the ordinary in their dress or hair. But the taxi didn't drive away, and Mark was instantly alert, every sense heightened.

Too many years of waiting, watching for signs of trouble, he supposed. But he knew when they reached into their jackets that they weren't going for their wallets.

EIGHTEEN

As the men pulled masks over their heads, Mark drew Rachel back to the car and opened the door, hoping they hadn't been spotted. "Call nine-one-one," he said, motioning to the cell phone.

She stared at him. "Why? What's going on?"

He nodded at the café as the young men entered, guns drawn. "Tell them there's a robbery in progress at the Cake Walk." He reached into the backseat and unzipped the camera bag. "Stay there," he told her, already going through the checklist in his mind. Enough tape left? Battery? Will the light be sufficient?

Rachel's fingers fumbled with the cell phone, punching in numbers, clearing them, punching them in again.

Rachel watched Mark lift the camera from the bag. "Where are you going?" she asked, stumbling from the car when she realized what he was doing. "Are you crazy?"

He shook his head, looking over at her, and she wasn't sure whether she saw sadness or resignation in his eyes. "It's just what I do."

A brisk voice answered the phone. "Police, fire, ambulance."

"You stay there," Mark said.

She watched as he walked away, too numb to do anything but follow his order.

"Ma'am?" the operator said.

"There's a robbery," she said into the phone, and made herself breathe. "Cake Walk Café." She took a few useless steps first to the right, then the left, searching for a street sign. "I don't know the address," she groaned. "Not even the street."

"It's all right, ma'am, we've got it. Stay out of the way, do you understand? Officers are on the way."

Rachel nodded mutely as Mark moved quickly along the line of parked cars toward the taxi. He kept to the driver's side, stayed low to the ground, and focused on the driver. The driver was watching the café through the passenger window, so far unaware that Mark was anywhere near.

She dropped the phone on the ground, afraid to call out, to draw attention, yet terrified to let him go closer.

A car slowed, then sped away. A couple across the road paused. But only Rachel stayed to watch.

Mark ducked behind the taxi, and Rachel could no longer see him. Her throat went dry when the driver shifted in the seat. Had he seen? Did he know? He went back to watching the café, but Rachel found no solace in that.

Mark watched the scene unfold through the lens of his camera. The café was brightly lit, the plateglass window wide, the view unobstructed. While the tape wouldn't be the highest quality, it would clearly show the men lining everyone up in front of the counter, shoving and hollering orders, demanding jewelry, wallets, purses.

In the distance, he heard the sirens. One of the thieves heard it, too. While the first kept at his task, working methodically, efficiently, the second grew nervous, started to rush. He jerked a purse from the hands of a young woman, then pistol-whipped an older man who was having trouble getting a ring off his finger. And when he held the gun to a sobbing waitress's head, screaming at her to shut up, Mark knew the situation was heating up too fast. He'd seen that kind of madness too often to doubt. The girl would be dead before the police arrived.

There was no panic, no sense of right or wrong, or anything else. He simply acted, holding the camera steady as he rose and walked slowly backward.

The driver hit the horn, drawing the attention of the men inside. Half expecting him to go for a gun, Mark ducked behind the next car. But the only threat was still inside the café.

He kept the camera on the door as one of the thieves turned, gun pointed. The other darted past him and fired, once, twice, shattering the plateglass, hitting the side of the taxi. Three times, four.

Mark lost count as he dropped, windows exploding above him and sirens wailing behind him. But it was Rachel's scream that stayed with him as he hit the ground.

Rachel had never stayed on the concierge floor of a hotel. Had never had chocolates on her pillow, or turn-down service, or extra towels without having to ask. She'd planned to enjoy it all. To lie abed with a plate of strawberries, a glass of wine, and Mark beside her. And make sure the DO NOT DISTURB sign was on the door.

Instead, she stood at the window, watching swimmers in the pool and listening to the news, hearing again the story of the robbery. She turned, seeing on the screen what Mark had seen from behind that taxi. Terrified people huddled inside a café, a gunman running toward the door, another shoving past him, lowering a gun, firing— cut to the anchor.

"Lead story on every station." She turned abruptly from the window. "You must be very pleased."

"Right place, right time, nothing more." He pointed the remote. The television went black as he got to his feet. "I'm sorry you had to be there, that's all."

She folded her arms. "Why?"

They hadn't spoken much since leaving the police station. Rachel had stood back from him, even at the scene, and she'd seemed distant, distracted on the ride back. Mark had only had to look at her to know she was still shaken. And he couldn't help thinking that it wasn't only the robbery that terrified her.

He sighed and crossed to the bottle of wine sitting in a bucket of water on the dresser. "Because it's hard to watch when it's real. Television removes you from it, reduces the impact."

"So it's all right for you to put yourself in front of guns, and in the middle of wars, but it's not all right for me to see it?"

He glanced over at her. "Tell me, Rachel, did you enjoy what you saw?"

"Not particularly."

"And what did you see when you come right down to it? Did you see the man's nose break when the kid smashed the side of the gun into his face? Or the way the waitress wet herself when he rubbed the gun across her lips. Did you see any of that?"

She didn't answer and he turned back to the wine. "I didn't think so."

He lifted the bottle out of the water and held it, dripping, over the bucket. He'd ordered it when they checked in, to be delivered at eight-thirty. Half an hour before he figured they'd be back from the performance, and plenty of time to chill. He shoved it back in the water in disgust. So much for seduction.

He walked over and flopped down on the bed. "Believe me, what happened in that café was mild compared to what I see every day."

She came across the room slowly but with purpose in her step. "I didn't like what I saw because I thought you were dead. I heard the gun go off, saw you fall. What else was I to think?"

"That I was doing my job." He linked his fingers behind his head and closed his eyes. "I'm neither careless nor stupid when it comes to my own safety. I couldn't have lasted as long as I have in this business if I was. I calculated the risk and made a decision. Had the situation been different, riskier, I would have stayed where I was."

"I doubt it." He felt the bed dip as she sat on the end. "That's not like you."

He almost smiled. "I never did understand what you were seeing when you looked at me sometimes. But I can tell you now, that you don't know me well enough to say that."

"Only because you won't let me."

He opened his eyes and she continued.

"Your work is a huge part of who you are, yet you won't talk about it, won't even let me try to understand." She looked down at her hands in her lap. "Using the camera, being part of the taping, gave me a glimpse of what it's like, of the detachment that sets in. I started to see the performance only in terms of what I was going to go for next or whether or not I should go in for a close-up." She gave him a tiny, embarrassed smile. "It's not much, but it's a start."

"It's nothing." Mark pushed himself off the bed and grabbed a towel from the bathroom. Seduction be damned. He needed something stronger, but wine would do. "You're thinking of a normal life again. A husband who comes in the door at five, 'Honey, I'm home.' " He dragged the bottle out of the bucket and wrapped it in the towel. "I told you before, my work isn't like that."

"Then tell me what it is like." She took the bottle and laid it on the dresser. "Please."

Mark knew there was no point. That he'd probably regret it later. But looking into her eyes right now, he couldn't find a way to refuse.

"The work is always with you. Everything you see, everything you hear. You know you have to give a cleaned-up version for the news, but the sights, the sounds, especially the smells, they're inside your head forever."

He took her hand and walked out to the balcony. "After all you've witnessed, how can you come home and talk about paint for the kitchen or what kind of flowers would look good along the sidewalk?" He released her and rested his hands on the railing. "You lose the ability to find joy in simple things anymore."

"Especially when you've been shot."

He watched a young woman dive into the pool, skim through the water, and burst through the surface on the other side, triumphant. He turned and headed back inside. "There's that, too."

Rachel closed her eyes a moment, then followed, knowing she was about to cross a line and having no choice. "Mark, tell me what happened in the Sudan."

He was unwrapping the towel from the wine and didn't look up. "You want to know? All right, you've got it." He raised his head and she almost backed away. But she'd seen that look before—the one that was cold and detached, and part of the package.

So she held her ground, to prove to him that she was strong, that she could handle this and him, and anything that life or his job wanted to throw at them. Because only then could she even begin to make him see what else was possible.

He took a corkscrew from the drawer and started to open the wine. "Picture an afternoon so hot you can't breathe. Flies so thick there isn't a surface that's clear of them. And bodies everywhere. By the side of the road, piled on carts; maybe they're covered, maybe they're not, but it doesn't matter because by now you're used to it."

He pulled the cork and poured two glasses of wine. "Now picture an endless line of people walking. Children, women, old folks, all desperate to get out, get away, because the rebels or the terrorists or the army or whoever has done this will be back."

He handed her a glass, a wry smile twisting his lips. "There's not enough food or medication, or even clothes for these people you pass. You're riding in a Jeep or a truck, of course, because you're with the press. You don't have anything they can use, but you do have a camera. So when you stick it in their faces you tell them that this is good, they'll be on the news, it will help. They say nothing, but their eyes tell you what they really think, what you really are."

He lifted the glass to his lips, drained the wine, and filled it again, his knuckles white as he gripped the bottle. "Then a shot is fired. Nothing unusual. People run for cover. You turn, camera ready, and realize it's your driver who's been shot. He slumps over the wheel as the Jeep rolls to a stop. Another shot. And another. Rapid fire now. And all of it aimed at your Jeep, your crew.

"People are watching. One of them sneaks up and takes a camera from the body in the back. You scream for help. He aims the camera at you; the red light comes on. He's taping you. Just as you taped him."

Mark beamed a big smile and held up his glass. " 'I'm helping you,' he says. And there's laughter. Another shot is fired. You're scrambling now, trying to drag your friend in the back, the one who's not quite dead yet, out of the Jeep. You shove him underneath, still screaming for someone to help."

His hand shook as he put the glass down. "Then pain, like fire, in your shoulder. You've been shot. You roll under the Jeep, too. The friend you pushed under ahead of you is dying. You can't save him. You can't save anyone. Not even yourself.

"The man who took the camera is on his knees now, filming you under the Jeep. 'This will be on the news,' he says. 'What more can you want?' In the distance you hear sirens, help on the way. But you also realize that what you're doing isn't noble or good. That's just vanity. You're nothing more than a voyeur, a vulture. But it's what you are, and the only thing you know. And the idea of not doing it anymore scares the hell out of you. More, even, than the idea of dying for it."

He walked to the bed and sat on the edge, drained. "So don't think too highly of me because of that robbery. I was only doing my job. And tomorrow I will get on a plane and go back to it full time."

"Tomorrow," she said softly, and realized she should have known. The moon would be full, the dream over.

But she wasn't ready to believe it. Not while he was there before her, this man who loved so well, yet saved none for himself. Who hated what he was, what he'd become, and couldn't see how anyone else could find him worth loving, worth fighting for.

So she walked to the bed and sat down beside him, putting her faith in love and cake, and grannies with earnest green eyes. And only hoped her heart would understand if she was wrong.

"You have the ticket then," she said.

"In the suitcase. I should have mentioned it sooner—"

"No. It's fine." She laid her palms on his chest. "Just know this when you leave."

She gently pushed him onto his back. "First, I love you."

He opened his eyes wide and she put a finger to his lips, stopping whatever excuse or rationalization he was going to make. She'd heard them all. And now he would hear her.

"Second, I will always think highly of you because you're loving and giving, and you have more courage than anyone I know. And in spite of what you've been told, you would make a wonderful husband and father. And as a lover? You already know the answer to that."

She reached down, grabbed the hem of her dress, lifted it up and off, and tossed it aside. She blushed as he took in the little nothing she'd worn for him. Black, expensive. No more than a quarter yard of fabric to the whole thing, she was sure of it.

He reached for her and she pinned his hands at his sides, holding them there with her knees and delighting in the way his breathing changed and his heart pounded. Then she smiled. He wasn't the only one who could plan a seduction.

She straddled his hips and took her time with the buttons on his shirt. "And if you're honest, I think you'd have to say that you love me, too." She moved her hips in a slow, wicked circle and nodded. "I'll take that as a yes."

She held his gaze as she spread his shirt open, raked her fingernails down his chest, and got busy with his belt. "I told you once that my door will always be open, and that's true. I know it's old-fashioned, but I really do believe that if we love each other enough, anything is possible."

He opened his mouth and she covered it with hers,

making it clear who was doing the talking. When she was sure he could do no more than babble, she raised her head.

"This is all your fault," she said, her fingers tickling in the hair on his belly. "I used to be shy and retiring." She stood up and slid his pants down over his legs, loving the way he was smiling now. "See what you've created?" She lifted his right foot and shook her head. "Socks have got to go."

She pitched them at the dresser and stood back from the bed, running a lazy hand over her body and seeing very clearly what it did to him.

"Rachel . . ." he warned, rising from the bed.

"Something wrong?" Her skin was hot, her heart pounding with anticipation, and she couldn't help but giggle when he lunged.

His arms were strong and sure, wrapping around her and swinging her back onto the bed. They rolled together across the sheets, laughing and tumbling pillows and chocolates. And when he pinned her beneath him, holding her hands above her head and burying his face in her neck, Rachel was sure she heard the moon sigh.

NINETEEN

The owners of the Chateau de Moreau liked to think of it as Belgium on the beach. White geese wandered the grounds, staff addressed the guests as madame and monsieur, and management worked hard to convince the travel and convention world that this was indeed a fabulous concept.

As a result, this year's Designer's Showcase was poised to be the best ever. The luxurious White Salon had been transformed into a dressing room for the contestants, the glittering ballroom was now equipped with special lighting, and a few interesting changes had been made to the runway. According to the organizers enjoying lunch on the terrace, the Chateau could very well become the permanent home of the showcase.

But while the organizers and judges dined amid spring breezes and potted palms, chaos ruled in the White Salon. From the ecowarrior taking loud exception to her neighbor's perfume to the fellow frantically stitching sequins and hollering for someone named Marty, tempers were short, laughter shrill, and tears all too common. Everyone in the room was only too aware that this contest could be the break they needed. The difference between fame and obscurity. And only one would walk away the winner.

Because admittance was restricted to contestants and

models, Rachel wandered the rows alone, trying to remember if she packed any aspirin and searching the hooks for her name. Each contestant had been allotted six feet of wall space, three hooks, a full-length mirror, and a bench. Of course, there were no walls or cubicles, no privacy at all. Just imaginary lines on the carpet that dare not be crossed.

She found herself at last, sandwiched between Tara Banger and Chad Bubar. The run-through in the ballroom had finished half an hour ago, and like most contestants, Tara and Chad had gone straight to the White Salon to prepare for the big moment. Rachel, however, had preferred a quiet anxiety break in the parking lot.

Mark had dutifully paced with her, murmuring assurances and encouragement, and finally resorting to threats when she froze halfway through the lobby.

She smiled at his idea of a threat, still holding on to the hope that he'd still be around that night to carry them out.

She hadn't broached the subject again, or given in to the temptation of listening when he took a call at the hotel that morning. Whatever came next was up to him.

Knowing she couldn't afford to be distracted now, Rachel slid any lingering thoughts of Mark under the bench with her bag and bobbed her head at her neighbors.

Tara was already dressed in her creation, a fetching cocktail gown of gathered Lycra that showed off her lack of curves to perfection. Chad, however, had wisely chosen to bring along a model for his overalls and bra ensemble. The three of them had been chatting over the top of Rachel's hook, making her feel like an intruder as she came between them.

She mumbled apologies, hung up her dress, and knew she was blushing as they openly appraised her work.

"Interesting," Tara said, and offered a hand by way of introduction.

"A class act," Chad agreed, pressing a kiss to her cheek and wishing her luck. Then he stood back. "Honey, I have a lipstick that would be fabulous with that dress." He smiled as he turned back to his model. "Let me know if you're interested."

Across the aisle, a young Chinese woman sent her a shy smile, a tall black man nodded gravely, and a willowy redhead twiddled her fingers.

Rachel smiled, seeing past the affectation and bluster, slowly warming to her neighbors and the fear they all shared.

"Rachel Banks," a voice behind her called. "Is there a Rachel Banks anywhere?"

"Here," she said, raising a hand as she turned.

A security guard grunted and came forward with an envelope. "Mark Robison said this had to get to you right away."

Rachel stared at the envelope as the guard disappeared into the crowd. Then she slid a finger under the flap, peeked inside, and burst out laughing; wondering how he'd known that it would be exactly what she needed right now.

She shook the picture out of the envelope and held it up. Harry, Emily, Julie, Mark, and herself. Mouths open, brows raised, eyes closed—not one of them ready for the flash.

On the back, Mark had written, "We may not be bright, but we're rooting for you. Love, Mark."

A flurry of rapid chatter at the other end of the aisle drew her around. A middle-aged man with thick white hair and a daunting manner rounded the corner, a devoted entourage in tow. She recognized his face; had seen it in fashion magazines for years. Places like Paris and Rome,

New York and Milan flashed through her mind. Just names on a map now, but after the contest, who knew what could happen?

He strolled past like royalty, doling out a nod here, a smile there, creating that most envied of commodities, buzz. He missed Rachel entirely, as his head was turned the other way when he passed. But she still had the runway to come, and her moment in the spotlight, a chance at a dream. She glanced down at the picture in her hand. And her very own cheering section. She propped the picture on the bench and tapped Chad on the shoulder. All she needed now was a fabulous lipstick.

Mark cast another glance over his shoulder as the line moved forward. Only three people stood between him and the ballroom door. He tapped the tickets against his palm, checked his watch, and let out a sigh of relief when he spotted Amanda and Brodie hurrying across the lobby.

They were good together, he admitted. Comfortable, happy. Yet there was something more, something deeper in the way Brodie looked at her, that told Mark that this could be serious. And he couldn't help but envy the time they had to find out.

"The flight was late," Amanda said by way of apology to the people behind Mark. She reached for Brodie's hand as she edged into the line and smiled at Mark. "Has she figured out that we'll be here?"

Mark handed Brodie two tickets. "Not as far as I know."

Brodie gave them a quick once-over. "How close will we be?"

The line moved again. "Five rows back," Mark said, presenting his ticket to the woman at the door. "Right at the end of the runway."

"I still can't believe she's really here," Amanda said as they settled into their seats. She glanced over at Mark, the expression on her face unreadable. "What are you going to do with the dress when the show's over?"

The chandeliers dimmed as the runway lights sprang to life. He turned away, grateful, when a drumroll and a disembodied voice put an end to conversation, and questions he wasn't ready to answer.

"Ladies and gentlemen, the New Designer's Showcase proudly presents—The Best and the Brightest: A Tribute to Talent."

Rachel stood between Tara and Chad's model, smacking her number card against her leg and listening to the applause as numbers One, Two, and Three took to the stage.

They would enter together, then two would hang back while the other took that walk down the runway alone.

Numbers Four, Five, and Six went through the door.

Each contestant had fifteen seconds. The announcer read the name, a line of background, and it was over.

Seven, Eight, and Nine got the nod.

Rachel glanced down at her card as she shuffled forward. Number Eleven. She had to smile. If she was shooting crap, she'd be a winner already.

"Here we go," Tara said, holding her Number Ten in front of her.

"Oh, mama," Chad whispered.

Rachel squeezed both their hands once, raised her number, and followed the applause to the stage.

The lights made it hard to see anything beyond the runway, but she heard her name clearly enough as Tara walked back toward her.

Her legs shook and her feet were already numb, but

she put a smile on her face, making up her mind to do this right.

"Rachel Banks, wearing an ice-blue wedding gown she created in her own shop in Madeira Beach, Florida."

One third of the way. Her eyes had adjusted and she focused on the judges, showing her number, hoping they didn't notice how her hand shook.

Two-thirds of the way, and she still hadn't tripped—a good sign. She made eye contact with the photographers, as they'd been told to do in the run-through. Cameras lifted, flashed—a very good sign.

Almost at the end of the runway. Then she spotted Amanda and nearly did trip. There she was, waving, grinning, clapping so hard, Rachel knew her hands were going to hurt afterward. And she wondered how she had been so lucky to find such a friend.

She found her rhythm again, keeping her strides long, her head up. And feeling that silly tug around her heart when she saw Brodie as well. Maybe this time, she thought, her feet still taking her forward as her gaze fell on Mark.

He watched her smile change, and knew that she'd found him.

She was lovely, vibrant, beyond beautiful in her gown of gossamer silk and cool white satin.

She reached the end of the runway and he was on his feet, couldn't have stopped himself if he tried. Oh, he was proud of her, this woman of courage and strength, who put her heart and soul into everything she did and wasn't afraid to try, to risk.

She stood for her moment, basking in the applause, the nods of approval, the flash of the cameras. But he knew that smile was only for him.

Because she loved him.

Because he loved her, too.

And that was all that mattered.

It sounded so simple when she said it. And he wanted to believe her, to be as sure as she was that it would all work out. That he could blend his life with hers, and together they would create something new and wonderful, something neither of them had ever known before. And she would never regret asking him to stay.

The airline ticket was suddenly a weight in his pocket, reminding him of all the reasons why he should leave. And that there was only one to stay.

She turned, her time over, making her last pass by the judges. Another model was warming up, already dancing, flirting, drawing the attention. No longer interested, Mark took his seat and unclipped the pager at his belt; reading at last the message that had been demanding his attention since the moment Rachel stepped onto the stage.

In front of the judges, Rachel paused, made her final turn, the last chance to make an impression. From the corner of her eye, she caught a movement in the aisle that made her slow down, look back.

He was leaving. The flight was booked; London was waiting. And she was alone with her dream once again.

She held on to her smile, kept her footing. He'd been honest, promised nothing, and she would not falter now. She owed him that, at least. If not for Mark, she wouldn't have had this chance, this moment. She would see it through, with or without him, and only hoped that no one could hear a heart break.

"It's not whether you win or lose, it's how good you look when you play," Amanda said, holding the ice-blue gown against her sundress and frowning into the mirror. "And this definitely looked a lot better on you."

Rachel glanced over as she pulled her bag out from

under the bench. "You have to have the right lipstick." She smiled when Amanda looked skeptical. "Chad taught me that."

She watched Amanda hang the dress back on the hook, not sure that she'd get through this without her. When the other contestants had gone straight from the announcement of the winners to the reception on the terrace, Rachel had sought out Amanda instead.

Brodie was keeping a couple of seats warm for them in the bar while Amanda chatted endlessly; filling up the space, the silence, just as Rachel had hoped she would. And never once mentioning Mark's name.

Amanda picked up Rachel's certificate and waved it at her. "I don't know about lipstick, but I do know that honorable mention is nothing to sneeze at."

"I'm not sneezing at it," Rachel said. "In fact, I'm happy with it."

She set the bag down and took a handful of business cards from her purse and fanned them for Amanda. "These are buyers from New York, Los Angeles, and Chicago who want to come down and see my shop, talk about getting some of my designs into their stores." She held out the cards. "They approached me while I was looking for you."

Amanda flipped through them. "Very impressive."

"And it's exactly what I want." Rachel tucked them back into her purse, knowing it was the truth. Those cards proved that she was more than just a dressmaker on the beach. She had talent and ability, and with enough push, enough fight, she might even make it in New York or Paris or even Milan. But it wasn't what she wanted.

She simply wasn't cut out for the frantic pace of a major design firm. She loved the sound of the waves while she worked, taking tea with a bride, and seeing her smile when the dress was done. She didn't need her picture in a magazine, or her name on anyone's underwear. And her cottage was just too small for a decent entourage.

She reached for the picture Mark had given her, smiling at the faces, the message. When she came right down to it, she had everything she needed. Good friends, family, and a chance to see her designs in some quality stores. The only thing missing was Mark.

She slipped the picture into her purse with the cards, determined not to think about it. Because if she did, she'd cry. And if she cried, her makeup would run. Then she'd have to stop and wash her face, and wait until her nose wasn't so red before she went out into the lobby, which would take some time. And right now the only thing she wanted to do was get out of there, to go home. And start getting used to life without him.

So she crouched in front of the bench and busied herself with packing up shoes, cosmetics, hairpins. "Seems things are good between you and Brodie."

"I try not to think about it."

Rachel snapped her head up. "Why would you say that?"

"Because it is good. Better than anything I've ever known. It feels like the real thing, and I'm scared to death." She brushed a hand over the dress, her smile tiny and dazed, completely unlike her usual confident grin. "You know what they say about putting all your chickens in one basket."

"Eggs," Rachel murmured, and stared at her, unable to take it all in at once. She knew that look, had seen it hundreds of times on the faces of the brides who came to her showroom, but never once on the face of Amanda Goodman. There was no question about it: This time Amanda was truly in love.

"He's asked me to move in," Amanda continued, then

stopped abruptly, her shoulders slumping. "I'm sorry. I shouldn't be talking about this now."

"Because of Mark? Don't be silly." Rachel rose and wrapped her arms around her friend, closing her eyes on the false brightness in her voice and trying not be jealous. "I always knew he was leaving, and we had a good time."

"We had a great time."

Rachel opened her eyes as Amanda stepped away.

He stood in front of Chad's spot, weight on one hip, his hands in his pockets. Yet there was a tension around his mouth that belied the casual pose.

"A great time," Rachel said, hating herself for echoing him, but unable to think, to move; feeling fragile all of a sudden, as though she might break at any moment.

"We'll be in the bar," Amanda said, ducking her head as she slipped past.

Rachel almost called out for her to come back, to stay. But Mark was moving toward her, saying something about honorable mention and congratulations. Making small talk when the only thing she could think about was how much she wanted him to touch her, hold her, keep her from falling apart. And it was all she could do to keep from throwing her bag at him.

"Yes, I was pleased," she said, reaching for the plastic cover, dragging it over the gown. "I don't imagine you'll want to carry the dress on the plane, so I'll need an address where I can ship it."

"Rachel—"

She turned on him. "Don't you dare argue with me. This is your dress, always was. If you don't want to give me your address, I'll ship it to the news agency, but one way or another, it goes with you." She snatched a pen from her purse, a card from her pocket, and thrust them at him. "Just write it down and leave it on the bench."

She didn't watch while he scribbled on the card. Kept

herself occupied with knotting the plastic, gathering up the last of her things, trying not to cry.

"That should do it," he said softly, and placed the card on the bench as she'd asked.

She glanced at it, making sure it was legible. Mark Robison, c/o The Bridery, Madeira Beach. She stopped, looked at it more closely. He'd given her address. She raised her head. "What is this?"

"My address?" He tried to smile but couldn't hold it. "At least I hope it will be, since my lease with Mrs. Dempster runs out tomorrow."

She watched him shift from one foot to the other, uncertain and vulnerable, melting the last of her reserve.

He stood back, his heart pounding hard. Wanting to take her in his arms, to know she wasn't regretting already.

She held out the card. "But you left the show——"

"My pager went off when you stepped onto the runway. I checked it when you turned to leave."

She looked away. "London," she said matter-of-factly, without the rancor, the bitterness he had expected.

"Not London," he said and waited until she turned back. "It was Sofia. The message said it was urgent."

"Urgent?" She took a step toward him. "Sofia didn't seem the type to make up emergencies."

"That's what I thought. So I went to make the call."

"And?"

He ran a hand over his mouth. "Rachel, Chuck is dead."

She came to him, put her arms around him, laid her head on his chest. "What happened?"

He dragged her closer, buried his face in her hair. "They found his body this morning. He'd been murdered in his room. Apparently the lead was solid. He was getting too close."

"He never saw the tape," she whispered.

"And Sofia's beating herself up with guilt." He nodded, sighed. "But it wasn't her fault. It was Chuck's." He pulled away and held Rachel at arm's length. "That's when I knew I couldn't go back."

He watched her reach for him again, still believing they could make it work. But he had to be sure, had to know she understood what she was getting into.

"Rachel, it won't be easy. I've been chasing death for so long, I've almost forgotten what it is to chase life, to hope, to dream. But when I'm with you, I start to remember again."

"You don't have to do this," she said, her voice soft and husky with tears.

He crushed her to him, wondering what he'd done to deserve that kind of faith and trust. And knowing he'd do whatever was necessary to hold on to it.

"You need to know that I don't have all the answers. That I haven't even figured out what I'm going to do with myself. All I know for sure is that I love you, and I always will. But I can't promise I'll be the kind of husband you want."

She raised her head. "Husband?"

He took her face in his hands, needing to see her face, to look into her eyes. "Even if I don't work for the agency, I won't be a nine-to-five kind of guy."

She rose up on her toes, pulling his mouth down to hers. "That's fine."

She couldn't reach, so she kissed his chin instead, making him smile. "You should know that I made some calls, found out about grants and development funds for independent film."

She moved lower, pressing her lips to his throat. "Life-altering shorts," she whispered, nuzzling his shirt collar aside with her nose.

"Yes, but I'll have to travel. To meetings, locations—"

"I'll pack you a lunch," she murmured.

He drew his head back. "Rachel, I'm trying to ask you to marry me."

She smiled up at him. "And I'm trying to say yes."

Then the smile faded and she pulled away, suddenly serious. "I know it won't be the kind of marriage I've always imagined. But then, you're not the kind of man I imagined either." She paused and smiled. "You're more, and I wouldn't change a thing. So, if your work takes you away, that's fine. Just make sure you come back to me."

"Always," he promised and raised his head, hearing voices, footsteps. Contestants returning, models changing. "Let's go home," he said, reaching for the dress and swinging it over his shoulder.

"Not so fast."

Mark looked over at her; she wasn't smiling.

"What about children?"

He picked up her bag. "As many as you want."

"And a wedding on the beach?"

He looped an arm over her shoulder. "At sunset, as planned."

Still she didn't budge. "Beef Wellington for dinner?"

He nodded. "And no cake."

"Don't be ridiculous," she said, wrapping an arm around his waist as they walked. "I know a place that makes a great hazelnut torte."

BOOK YOUR PLACE ON OUR WEBSITE AND MAKE THE READING CONNECTION!

We've created a customized website just for our very special readers, where you can get the inside scoop on everything that's going on with Zebra, Pinnacle and Kensington books.

When you come online, you'll have the exciting opportunity to:

- View covers of upcoming books

- Read sample chapters

- Learn about our future publishing schedule (listed by publication month *and author*)

- Find out when your favorite authors will be visiting a city near you

- Search for and order backlist books from our online catalog

- Check out author bios and background information

- Send e-mail to your favorite authors

- Meet the Kensington staff online

- Join us in weekly chats with authors, readers and other guests

- Get writing guidelines

- AND MUCH MORE!

**Visit our website at
http://www.zebrabooks.com**

COMING IN NOVEMBER
FROM BOUQUET ROMANCES